LS₅

ຯຨຯ ຯຨຯ

Trudy Behymer Sheets

LS$_5$

ឭឈឭ ឭឈឭ

Trudy Behymer Sheets

Flecks of Gold Publishing

Vancouver, WA   98668

Thank you, Todd, for all your dreams—
the inspiration for this book
and for the inspiration in our lives.

One

The cry of a child is like no other sound.

Darkness called at Jake Morgan's kitchen window and he peered outside. Moisture-laden wind whipped his palm tree. Pointed leaves made screeches on his house. Stepping back from the quivering windows, he cringed when the lights flickered and harassed him before they went out, completely.

"Damn." Jake growled and wrung his knotted hands together, and again, scrutinized the nasty world outside his window. Now, with blackness in his house, street lamps and business signs blinked at him. A quick appraisal told Jake that half the houses of Dareing had lost power but that his office at the cemetery stood in the half with lights.

Fumbling in the dark, he unplugged the coffeemaker and picked up his boots from underneath the table only to knock the cat from her dish. He snatched up his jacket, wrestled it over his shoulders and dived outside, seconds before the rain hit him.

"Son-of-a–" Jake slammed the old truck's door and started the engine. He pulled on the headlight switch. The radio blasted to life but his curse that any idiot could predict this weather drowned out the next caution.

He sped on his way. If one caught the signal lights right, the drive through Dareing took ten minutes. Not this morning. Wind gusts hit the road broadside to bounce the Chevy over centerline.

The radio blared. Jake switched it off. "This ain't no storm. This is…this is a damn mud spill." Jake stomped on the brake, halted beside the bermed wall along the narrow road, and strained to see up the crotch between the two knolls that made up Oakwood Cemetery.

He rubbed the back of his neck and the hair that stood on end. His shoulders sank. Out the spattered windshield, a river of mud and grass cast eerie shadows in the headlights. He inched the truck into the strange fog, the mist thick at the crest of the hill.

The old man stared outside. His head jerked in rhythm with the snapping wiper blades. The Oakwood sign stood askew, the posts wrenched to one side and twisted so that he could no longer read the glossy blue print.

When he reached the far end of the acreage, he climbed out of the truck and fought the wind for one more look. But he couldn't face what he saw.

2

Inside the caretaker's shack, Jake prompted the bare light bulb on with a few taps from his shaking finger. He turned on the electric heater and hotplate, set an extra-strong pot of coffee to perk, and sat at the desk to wait. He rubbed his hands together in front of the orange glow.

By the time he gulped the last swallow of caffeine, a trace of morning light grayed the hovering clouds and he headed outside for a quick survey across the top of the hills toward the mud river. He didn't use the well-driven lane, instead, trotted along the graves, one long step, two short. He knew the cadence well. But then his legs buckled and he groped for balance. His knees slapped the wet grass.

"Quake."

When Jake pulled himself up, supported by a tombstone at his side, the marker lurched and jumped ahead and carried him along only to flatten him onto the greens in a face-forward sprawl. The hillside groaned from deep within. Trees and tombstones twisted.

The sounds of raging water shot him to his feet. Cold sweat broke out on his face. He stumbled. Spinning around, he expected the graveyard to disappear under a flood of water.

Fog engulfed him, the earth dead silent, so that the water flow became the only sound.

Jake turned toward the noise. The broken water main bellowed in a geyser above him and cleansed the mangled hillside and rubble to expose streaks of silver caskets and chunks of concrete pads. Jake's jaw clenched tight.

The smell hit him. A sulfur-like stench rose up with the fog and his throat closed fast. Jake ran for the metal pipe used to turn off the main valve and under his weary tug, the faucet squealed so that it shook his whole insides.

And then all sound disappeared. No water gushed. No groaning earth. No wind. Jake strained to hear a squirrel or a bird out to feed. Nothing. He rubbed the rain-mist into his face to cool him and closed his eyes. Jake didn't look at his acreage anymore. From that one glimpse, he knew the cemetery no longer graced the gentle slope of two hills but now lie as a third hill in itself, made from the sod and roots and caskets.

The fog, a breeze, carried up the odor and just for a second Jake paused to identify it. Musty. Rancid. Death. He jogged. He ran. The shed stood thirty yards away but a tree root grabbed his boot and Jake flew head first into the slime, mire that his imagination changed into decomposed bodies.

"Shee-it." Jake shook himself up and when he took a deep breath to clear his mind, his stomach churned. "Dear God in heaven." He tried to remind himself how these hills used to be but for some reason the picture wouldn't come. This graveyard was no longer a quiet place for an old retired man.

Jake cocked his head, his ear heavy with a faint noise, the first one he'd heard in several minutes. He couldn't see any…anyone, just caskets piled up in the crotch of the hills. He could distinguish a gold color casket, a bronze one, all dented at the sides from the jumbled concrete slabs. And that one, that one lid hung wide open.

He heard the murmur again, a cry of sorts, weak and muffled. Human. Jake's big eyes closed.

"No. No–" He spun away. His boots sucked lace-deep into the grime. He tried to fly in retreat, far from the odd whimper, but his shoes held tight. Jake went down in the mud again.

"Ahhh . . . ."

Sweat blistered his back. Ice shuddered his shoulders. He forced himself to listen. "Siamese," he said. "Damn cat sometimes sounds like a baby."

At county headquarters, the officer shook the rain from his overcoat and hung it up on the rack with all the other policeman's gear. The torrent outside seemed unusual. He watched a puddle gather on the cement floor and then join all the other puddles, creating a steady stream to the floor drain. Unusual for the month of July? He didn't know for sure, but after fifteen years of living near San Francisco Bay, he should be used to these Pacific fits. No. Something else made the outdoors feel different. The earthquakes and aftershocks. He never got used to those. "Combination." He couldn't remember a time when the earth shook and the heavens poured all the same night.

Pausing, he took some time to listen to the phones from the other room, the printers and the voices and to breathe. The night had already been inundated with crazy calls. Crazy people.

Once the word, baby, left Jake Morgan's lips, he knew he couldn't ignore the sound. Crazy? Had to be. Anyone going into that stinking mess had to be an idiot.

"Je-sus." Ignoring his stomach, Jake jumped up. He could scarcely move a foot at a time, his boots, caked with mud, slid and squashed in the sod between coffins.

He still couldn't see much. The sun, if there at all, hid behind the gray fog, vapor that generated from the geothermal earth.

When Jake reached a huge bulge of ground he stopped, covered his nose with his woolen jacket, and inhaled through his mouth. Whether he could see any corpses or not he knew they were there, the smell powerful. Then he heard the noise, rustling and scratching and, "ahh…maa."

To the left and down, Jake leaped onto a cement pad, one used to keep the grass ground-level after a burial, and paused. The cry was right below him now and to the side. Jake jumped and landed in a black pool of tepid water and something else, something crunchy and brittle. He screamed but his old throat just burned, and again, he closed his eyes to push away the morbid thoughts. Jake wanted to leave. He wanted to cry, not for the smell or the dead but the overwhelming chaos. His heart didn't quite feel up to what lay ahead.

Near his knee, he grabbed the side handle of a casket and jerked with all his strength to free it from a wedge. The box broke loose. He flew backward up against a marble stone. The handle twisted and the casket dived downward as the lid popped open wide.

He wanted to let it go. He wanted to scream again but a new sound pierced the morning, the cry of a baby.

The baby inside the casket.

Jake's heart pounded in his ears and his neck. The fog and the rain and the sweat poured off his face. He rubbed his temples hard. Jake didn't touch the baby, didn't try to analyze how it got there, just searched in the half-light for a quick way back up.

The tiny casket weighed a ton. All his strength

shook out of his knees. The shock slowed him down and the impatient cry that grew higher and more frightened with his every stumble.

The sky, somewhat lighter now, glowed with mauve hues from the hanging mist and he could see the infant better, thrown to one end of the burial box. The baby shivered from the moisture and wind, the lacy gown spattered with mud. Even in the poor light he could see that one of the child's fingers oozed with brilliant red blood from a cut at the tip.

Ripping open his shirt, Jake reached for the baby and put his hand underneath to support the fragile neck and spine, the infant cold against his chest. "Hush ... Hush," he said and wrapped his jacket around himself and the tiny child. He climbed again. He spread one hand wide to press on its back and used the other hand to grope for holds in the mass of torn earth and tombs.

With the pathway mined with slippery grass and mud, he could only stagger and sway and stumble through; the faster he could get them out of this stinking graveyard the better. But Jake inched along, his load just as cumbersome as dragging the casket. Only now he felt more patient, more composed. The infant no longer screamed but whimpered and hiccupped; Jake's nearness soothed it somehow. And he had spotted the cemetery road, just in sight at the top of one last mound of heaved-up earth.

Jake leaned on a concrete slab, covered his mouth and nose with his collar, and took a moment to catch his breath. His heart sped fast inside his ribs, baby fingers scratched outside. Before him stood the top of a marble tombstone, a once-white angel now mud-sprayed with the body cracked and the wings broken. Pulling himself over it, he held the child tight. "Hush. Hush."

A blanket of warm air embraced them when he stepped into the tool shed. Jake slammed the door shut with his foot to block out the world –the world and the stench.

Stepping inside the noisy inner sanctum, the officer glanced around and then stopped, full-halt. Becky stared at him with the phone at her ear and a pen in her hand. He considered disappearing back into the anteroom.

He didn't budge. The strained expression on Becky's face held his attention far too long. Something in her eyes made him stare. Something…not good. He took a step back.

"David Straus." She pointed her finger at him and crinkled her nose. "Don't you dare."

Grinning, he wondered what his face looked like to have given himself away. "What'd you have, Becky?" he asked and walked over to the desk. "You know I'm about ready to go home. It's 4:30."

"You have an hour-and-a-half. Besides," she said, "this has your name written all over it."

"Because you put it there." He tapped the ink on the printout. "You always give me the–"

"Strange, creepy, weird," she said.

David studied her face again, her raised up eyebrows and how her lips pressed together to make a single dark line. He could tell she felt rattled. She'd worked here too damned long to be rattled and his apprehension slowed his hand to take the paper from her fingers.

Two

David Straus found himself back outside in the drizzle and he turned on the flashing lights for the ten minute drive, not because of the traffic, but to be more visible. Fog had settled in. Stopping the patrol car, he paused along the familiar berm that marked the beginning of Oakwood Cemetery.

"Good God," he said, "half the damn graveyard's down here." Struggling to see through the odd haze and the rain, he remembered Oakwood's geothermal history filled with scientists and engineers and bickering. "Shit." Parking his patrol car at the top of Oakwood, he studied the old Chevy pickup and the ancient ten-by-ten shed. Warm dense fog hung purple on the rumpled mass of trees and distorted earth. He'd yet to find a clear view of the scene.

David reread Becky's printout. He decided that the man staring at him from inside the shed was Mr. Jake Morgan. The old fellow hadn't exaggerated over the telephone, after all. The cemetery, indeed, looked hideous.

The expression on Becky's face popped back into David's mind. A chill crawled along his spine. What would be worse, he'd asked her, finding live babies or dead ones at 4:30 in the morning after two solid hours of tremors and downpour? And why in the hell was the old fart out tromping around the goddamn cemetery to begin with? "Gonna be a long one."

When he opened the car door, the rancid graveyard air flooded into his lungs and he bolted from the car. His slender six-foot frame easily cleared the shed's little doorway. David burst in, holding his gut.

"I, uh, didn't tell ya." Jake backed away from the door and the smell.

David nodded, his usual, formal introduction now far from his mind. He sat down in the swivel chair and wiped the sweat from his face with the palm of his hand and his arm. Reaching into his jacket, he grasped his pad and pen. Jake's name already appeared at the top of the third page. David stared at it. "I've got to get this area sealed off," he said, "the contamination."

He took care of the task in minutes, his goodbye to the disaster crew an impatient groan as he closed the top of his cell phone. He turned to Jake and flipped the coat back so he could see the infant in the old man's arms. The baby sucked on its gray fingers, whimpered and sucked and whimpered.

"I see from your initial call that you tampered

with the evidence."

"Yeah, I touched it," Jake said. "Tried to pack the casket up the hill but left it on top a cement slab about halfway down." He pointed toward the door. "Those caskets are heavy buggers."

"Casket?"

"Sure as hell a casket, one of those real little bronze ones."

"Not a dark colored crate or a metal box, sir, a–"

Jake nodded. "A genuine mortuary casket. Ya know, with shiny lining like they have. Don't recall the color. This here's a girl." Jake bounced the babe for a single silent moment. "But I didn't look for sure."

David held up his hands to stop Jake. The sex of the infant didn't matter right now. The mess outside mattered. The evidence. He inched up from the chair to look out the window and his knees went weak, his stomach tightened into a knot. "Where the hell is that ambulance?" He picked up his tablet and scribbled the time, 5:15, and below it what Morgan had said.

David believed himself to be a strong man. He lived through the Gulf Wars and the grim sights encountered on freeway patrol. Time had numbed his senses to such pictures outside. But seeing an infant in the midst of it all changed everything. What kind of sick monster would bury a baby alive?

The red heat in his face and along the back of his neck didn't come from nausea.

"I'm going down there."

"What? Why for? It's a damn stinkin' mess. I'd never went if I hadn't, hadn't heard it. What's the use now?"

"Evidence, Mr. Morgan." David buttoned his

raincoat up to his neck and pulled the collar high to protect his nose. He planned to shoot the bastard who did it but he had to find him first.

David stepped outside and shut the door. He spun back around. A good strong tremor buckled his legs and he scrambled for balance, dropping straight down into the mud.

"You okay in there?" He could see Jake on the floor, the baby still in the old man's arms. No reply.

Another punch from deep in the earth riveted the door back shut with a crash. David groped for a holly bush. The leave's sharp points stabbed his fingers but he held on tight. The worst of the day's earthquakes hit in a deafening thunder and twisted the foliage right out of his hand. He kept sight of the shed. He watched it writhe and he watched the window shatter to the ground.

Silence followed.

David dashed to the shed. Jake lie on the floor, spread over the child, with a storage cabinet on top of them both. David hefted it away with one arm. "Don't get up, Jake. Wait a minute and see."

"I ain't hurt," he said but took some time to rise, even with David's help. They both stared at the baby.

"Oh Lord." Dropping to his knees, David searched for a pulse or a warm trace of her breath.

"Is she dead? Did I smother it?"

"No." David looked up. Amazement filled his chest. "She's breathing. By God I…I think she's asleep."

"Give 'er up to me," Jake said. "Look at her skin. It's pinkin' up. She's gettin' warm."

Inching his fingers underneath the child; she did feel warm against his cold hands and he helped snuggle the baby back against Jake's chest to where they each tucked a corner of the shirt around a tiny pink cheek. "Now you said you found her about in the middle?"

"Right where everything's all piled up. It all kinda ran to the crotch."

David headed out. Like tempered steel, his stomach hardened against the chaos and the intense heat from inside flexed his muscles. He stared down the hill. The graveyard's slope now lie in a conglomeration of metal and concrete, roots and earth. Perspiration and the last drops of rain gathered at David's brow as he worked his way down through the mushy sod and decay. Pausing a second, he watched a metallic-blue coffin near the edge of the acreage shift and fall from its precarious perch. The lid flopped away, bracing it to balance like a book tossed onto the floor. He pulled the collar higher up over his nose. So long as he knew what made the creaky sound, he could handle the situation all right.

All right, until he ascended a pregnant bulge of earth. A body lay below him, right at his feet, sprawled face down with the legs still in a casket. His stomach headed up to his mouth and he clamped his eyes shut tight. It's whole, not a bit decomposed....

Just in time to see a movement in the body, David opened his eyes, a warning, and he spun around to grab a piece of marble near his shoulder, ready, when the earth shook, again.

No tremor.

Sweat dripped from his face and his shoulders grew heavy as he clung to the tombstone. The smell over-powered his senses. He didn't look toward the body just rubbed his face again in a vain attempt to clear the fog from his mind.

"The baby's casket. The baby's casket." He

chanted the words to keep focused and looked in every other direction to try to spot it.

When he jumped down, his feet landed an inch away from long brown hair woven into the mud. Long shiny hair. Long healthy hair.

David froze.

The earth doesn't just move fingers.

Bending, he touched her hand. The rubbery feel, the odd cool temperature locked deep in his mind. When four bony fingers curled around his thumb, his insides curled, too. Noise rose up from behind him, sirens. Flashing red ambulance lights reflected off the mist but he didn't look up, just stared at the girl on the ground.

Through all the commotion, David's own voice seemed disjointed, deadened by the throb of blood through his temples. Jake Morgan's gruff voice filtered down the hill and shot David back up to his feet.

"Don't go. God. There's another one. Another little girl. Alive."

Heads jerked. Mouths dropped.

"I'm bringing her up."

David rolled the child over and scooped her into his arms. When he lifted, her head fell back. Skinny arms flowed in the air like graceful angel wings. A pair of eyelids, heavy and quivering, forced themselves to open but lacked the energy.

Lungs pumping deep with the rancid air, David plotted an easy path up the hill. His lips were coated with sweat and fog and he told himself the salty moisture made his stomach rumble, not his present position, not because he was stuck in the trench with no easy way out except across the coffin in front of him and into the mangled graves.

"Get some oxygen ready." The little girl's chest jerked with her labored breath. Resting her on the lid of the casket first, he hopped upon it himself so that his boot banged the side.

The bang made an echo.

David frowned. The girl lay still. Her eyelids and fingers were the only things that twitched and when he bent to one knee to bring her against him, another thump sounded, like before, followed by a low mournful whine. David swore the girl had made the noise and he studied her leathery lips.

No, this child didn't utter the lament.

"Son-of-a-bitch." Another bump resounded and the vibration fired up through his knee so that his whole insides shuddered. David staggered from the casket, from the idea that a human being buried three of their own kind, alive. Children.

A well-aimed blow with his boot snapped the coffin lid wide open. His shout rang high, his words unintelligible. He found a boy, somewhat older than the girl, maybe five or six years and gray, like the baby.

"What's going on?" Someone gagged from behind him.

"Another kid," he said. "You take this one." When David faced the paramedic a thought struck him like thunder. "Who the hell perverted enough to do this would go to the bother of caskets?"

"I–" The young man tried to speak. David shoved the girl into his arms.

"Guess you can't out-figure the distorted bastards. Guess that's what a pervert is."

"I'm going to be sick."

"No shit," David said. "Me too. Get her up there

15

and you can puke all you want."

Swiveling around, the young man obeyed and began the climb back up the hill, no words, just a muffled choke through an attempt to keep down breakfast. David reached into the cotton-lined coffin. Vibrant green eyes stared straight at him.

"Sal…ly." The boy screamed and he sprang upright. "Come on, Sal." Three words exhausted the lad. His eyelids fell shut. David gathered him into his arms.

They crested the hill the same time as the county's disaster van. David laid the boy on the stretcher and waited to watch the paramedic wrap the oxygen mask around the small round head, waited as the boy's chest rose in full deep breaths, again and again. Reaching into the brown tweed suit-jacket, David felt eager to see what rattled between them during the hike up.

"A comic book?"

David turned to face the officer who'd spoken, Sgt. Gable in charge of the disaster crew. David felt good that Gable answered the call.

"Three kids," David said, "all different ages. All buried in expensive caskets. I think these two…" He pointed. "These two may be brother and sister."

"Sorta look alike," Gable said.

David nodded. He hadn't noticed that so much. "I found them next to each other. He called the name Sally. Come on, Sal."

"Come on?"

"Yeah." David cringed so that he felt his eyebrows collide in the middle of his forehead. He groaned. "I suppose the baby is related, too. God, I hate to think there's a whole damn bunch in on this."

"One person couldn't possibly do it." Sgt. Gable's

lip curled. "Could they?"

David didn't answer, just reminded himself that anything was possible. "Well, I'll be damned," he said. "Look at this comic."

"Marvel." Gable pulled out an evidence bag from his uniform vest. "Spider Man," he said. "My boy used to read them all the time."

"But look at the date."

"December ninety-one. Looks brand new."

David did a rough mental calculation. July 2007 minus December 1991. "This book is what . . . fifteen, sixteen years old. Someone must collect them. Someone actually took the time—"

"We're ready to go, officer."

Glancing up toward the ambulance, David stuffed the plastic-wrapped comic into Gable's gear. "Evidence," he said with a smile. But then he frowned with a flash of a memory. Evidence. He darted away so that his long strides took him back across the mangled graveyard in seconds. "Head out," he said from behind the hanging mist, "but don't go until I wave you on."

He jogged past the two plots where he'd found the children, past the main area of rubble, to the farthest end where another patch of earth had heaved a pile of cement, wood and remains. He remembered how another casket turned over like a book, how it tumbled from a movement when everything else stood still.

One good kick flipped the coffin up and over, and for a wild second David thought he'd be sick. The geothermal stench from inside nearly strangled him. He spun away, bent at the waist to pinch his churning gut off from his mouth only to stumble sideways into a coffin with all his weight. The lid, half-cocked, busted wide open. "Jesus good God Almighty."

His arms shook so bad he could barely reach for the body inside, the living human being that groped for him and gasped for air.

"Help. Drowning. Help."

David pressed the lad to his sweat-soaked chest. His heart pounded. They both needed air, but the fear and horror chiseled into the young freckled face meant something far deeper.

The ambulance met them at the top of the hill. "Take 'em to Brigham," he said, and the ambulance sped away. Flashing red beams reflected off the morning. Sirens wailed. David ran to his patrol car, shouting to Gable. "You know that every single casket has to be checked."

"I'll pack up the kid's caskets. Jake spotted the baby's. Fingerprints are going to be near impossible–"

"I know." David slammed the squad car door. He knew, as well, that any vehicle tracks from the night's hideous crime escaped beneath the rain and the mud and the slime.

"Shit," he said, and drove away.

Three

David brushed off his pants and shirt. The mud cakes came away but the stink of Oakwood Cemetery had burrowed into his clothes and his nose. His mind.

The white strobe light at Brigham Hospital's emergency entrance burned in his eyes, a reminder of the time he'd ridden in an ambulance –thirty years ago. He doubted these children felt the same as he had. He'd only broken his leg. Six feet of earth covered these young ones.

"God." David still couldn't accept the calamity. His gut still gnawed at his ribcage.

"They're all responding to the oxygen, sir," the paramedic told him.

David nodded, the paramedic a much better color

now after packing the girl up the hill. David checked his own skin color, sure that at one point he'd turned as white as the stretcher blanket, too.

Pushing on his stomach, he entered Brigham's emergency wing behind a trail of technicians. Several nurses rushed through the hall. He spoke to the eldest one.

"They aren't victims of a flood or anything," he said, and stepped very near the woman to grasp her arm. "We found them in a graveyard."

Grace Smith's head jerked up and when she gripped the boy's gray hand, her eyes grew wide.

"They have to be isolated," David said. "Now. Contamination. I want the least people around them as possible. Save their clothes. Everything. I'm going to need every thread for evidence."

Maybe like himself, the nurse didn't know what to say. But Grace Smith knew of police procedure involving crime victims, her change in orders to the others around them came without delay. All the children were directed to an isolation ward several doors away and at the far end of another long wide corridor.

"Dr. King, our head pediatrician, has been assigned to this case," Grace said, and pointed to the elevator. "That's the doctor. She's the one who needs to know the facts."

King. David repeated the name, surprised by his regard of the woman doctor. He studied her eyes. Electric blue. Whoa.

Out of habit, he found his sheriff's badge and held it in his dirt-stained palm. Dr. King looked him over.

"I get the feeling this batch isn't the usual storm victims we've been treating," she said.

"Three kids and a baby," he told her, "all have been buried alive. The earthquakes brought them back up about an hour ago." David checked his watch, the time just past six a.m. "Sorry about the smell."

"What's it from?"

He pinched his lips together. He tasted salt. "Geothermal sulfur nastiness," he said, "and let's just say. . . not everyone unearthed was alive."

"Are they alert?" Never faltering, the doctor quickened her pace toward the isolation chambers.

"Fading in and out." David took her arm to stop her in the middle of the busy hallway. He whispered. "I'm going to be blunt with you. This has made me sick and I'm going to do everything in my power to put the pervert who did it in prison. There is little hope of getting much evidence from the muddy mess they came from –that's why I'm here. Any information I'm going to get will have to come from the children." Still holding her arm, David led the way to the closed doors at the end of the hall. "If you can pull the older ones through, they can tell me what I need to know."

Dr. King nodded. She hurried her steps. "How long have they been without sufficient oxygen? Any guesses?"

"Six hours? They're all the same odd gray color. The baby's come out of it some but, you know, being underground for any amount of time would restrict their air supply."

"I wonder if they've been drugged."

"They'd have to be," David said, "how the hell else would you get a kid into a coffin?"

Dr. King's pretty eyes narrowed as her mouth drew into a tight pink line. "Through my experiences,

Officer, I've seen parents convince their offspring to do some very bizarre things and somehow, for some God forsaken reason, the children protect them. I imagine when abused youngsters come to your bureau they're ready to speak up –or have no choice."

"Well…do all you can, please." David ran his dirty fingers through a clump of wet hair that had stuck to his forehead. Smiling, he extended his hand. "By the way," he said, "my name is David Straus."

"Call me Jessica."

She declined the handshake, but her darling little grimace and arched up eyebrows seemed to sooth his angry heart in an instant and David knew she would be on his side. At the sink, right next to her, he washed as best he could and followed her into Isolation, the room crowded despite the large size. Four beds had been pulled to a rough semi-circle with nurses and technicians hovered everywhere. A mass of information blasted at them from all directions and David picked out the blood pressure data and respiration. He watched in silence while nurses hooked up the children to brain and heart monitors.

"He's no longer cyanotic," Grace said.

David and Jessica turned in unison toward the oldest boy.

"His responses are quick and lungs seem to be functioning normally."

"Excellent."

David watched on as Jessica smiled at the boy and studied the boy's bright red hair and bony freckled wrist. She held his hand, very lightly, in her fingers and his huge brown eyes followed her every motion. She adjusted the synthetic airway.

"Can you talk to me?" she asked and the boy nodded.

His eyebrows knitted into a single rusty strand. "I was saved," he said. "Who saved me?"

"This nice sheriff saved you," she said. "His name is David. Do you think you can tell him your name and maybe where you live?"

With one step forward, David watched, again, the way Jessica stroked the boy's rubbery skin. Did her touch come solely from affection or strictly for the investigation? Did it matter? For some reason, today, it did matter. He inhaled.

Leaning on one elbow, the boy tried to sit up.

"Don't do that, honey," she said. "Just please lie still, we've got a few wires—"

"I feel real weird."

"Weird?" she asked. "How? Nauseous, dizzy, sleepy, fuzzy?"

"Fuzzy. Tired," he said. "I feel like I mowed the lawn all day." When the young man rubbed his palms into his eyes, his cheeks puffed out with a long labored sigh.

Jessica patted him again and then backed away to talk to Grace Smith. David tried to listen. He wanted to know, just as surely as he wanted to conduct his own investigation.

"We're you at the picnic?"

The high strained voice spun David back around or was it the question? David didn't touch the lad, just allowed the words to filter through his mind. "Picnic?" he said. "No. You did say picnic."

"Are Ma and Dad here?"

"No, they're—"

"Why aren't they here?" The boy tried to sit up again but changed his mind. "Did you find me down the river?" he asked. "My mother and father are looking for me. I remember a big red rock that someone painted a nasty word on. Ma and Dad are before that, on the other side. Please go back and get them."

"Son, uh…." No brain damage here, at least David didn't think so. Perhaps a little shock. "I'm sorry," he said. "I didn't find you by a river, where–"

"Today's my birthday." The boy popped up with a jerk and a buzzer sounded off from the machine. "I wanna go home."

"We can't let you go home now, dear, not until we know more about you." Jessica spoke the words as she began to reattach the machine. David squinted into her big eyes of blue. The river? A picnic? The lad could be disoriented but somehow, that didn't fit the current picture.

"You've played cops and robbers haven't you?" David asked. "Let's play like you're the–"

"We don't need to play no dumb games."

Stepping back, David didn't want to play a dumb game either and he reached into his jacket for his notepad and pen. "Okay, son," he said, "what is your name?"

"Steven Robert Adams, Junior. I'm nine years old today, June eighth."

Four

David Straus scribbled to keep up with the information Steven Adams threw his way –add 157 NW 47 dar − ph 548-64

"Whoa there," David said, "slow down. You said the eighth?"

"No." Steven's face turned bright red. "I said northwest forty-seventh." He repeated the address while he stared at the stark hospital walls. His bony fingers twitched.

"I didn't misunderstand your address, son," David said, "but your birthday. Did you say June eighth? Do you know what year you were born?"

"Nineteen eighty-two."

"You were born in eighty-two and you're nine

years old?" When the boy agreed, David looked up at Jessica. A quick calculation told him that Steven Robert Adams, Junior, was sixteen years behind. David's eyes narrowed as he watched the doctor's lips form a soft oval, her request that he keep silent about the boy's mistake. But David already planned to keep quiet. Something told him that young Steven would argue the year discrepancy.

For a moment, David envied Steven. David's mind didn't feel so confident this early morning. Stress can disorient a person. But in this case, who felt stressed out, Steven or himself? David reached up to his shirt where the new <u>Spider Man</u> comic book had rubbed his skin when he'd packed the other child up the hill. He recalled that date, 1991, sixteen years ago.

"How about your father and mother's names?" David asked.

"Steven Robert Adams, Senior. And Sheila Lorrain Adams. My sister is Connie Ann, seven years old, and the twins are David Lee and Daniel Linn. They're five and Kristy is nine months old."

Amazed, David again, shook his head. "Then it looks like you're the oldest in the family. Is that kid over there one of your brothers?" Careful of the wires, David helped Steven lean toward the center of the room. He pointed at the dark-haired boy.

"No. That's not my brother."

"Can you see them clearly? That little girl? Do you know them?"

"No. I don't know any of them."

"How about the tiny baby over there." David pointed. "Is she your nine month old sister?"

"No." Steven's eyes lit up. "Kristy has short, red curly hair just like mine."

"You're a real smart kid, Steve, real alert, considering–"

"Steve–n. And I almost drown."

"Drown? Yes…the river."

"Well, it's not really a river, just a big canal, you know, the one that goes through the city park. Only we were farther down where the brown tables are and I got in that current." Steven's voice cracked. His chest rose in a full heavy breath. "Dad's gonna be real mad. He told me not to go that far 'cause the river was high, ya know, from the flood last weekend."

"And the current pulled you under," David said.

"Under and away." With no help, Steven sat up straight. The monitor wires went with him. "I can swim good," he said. "Honest. I kept trying for air, getting my breath, but I couldn't fight the water. It really pulled me. I couldn't move my legs. I tried to get to that rock."

"With the nasty word."

"Yeah. But I didn't make it." Steven grew silent. He rubbed his chest and forehead. "Is that where you found me, by that rock?"

David gave the boy a half-smile. He didn't want to lie, point blank. But he couldn't tell the truth, either. The truth would add clutter. David did know one thing, though, no floods of any degree occurred in the county last weekend. In fact, he couldn't remember–

"Are you Sgt. Straus?"

He spun around, shaken from his cogitation, and showed his badge. "I'm Straus."

"Sgt. Gable asked me to notify you, they're bringing another victim."

"Another victim? Are you sure?"

"I'm sure, sir, that that's the exact message, yes."

David did an about–face as the silver and white stretcher banged through door. His stomach hit the floor. Beneath strands of wet stringy hair showed a cheek and temple of that now familiar gray.

"I don't know him either," Steven said. "Who are these guys, and why am I with them? I wish you'd go get my mom and dad."

As David stared at the fifth unearthed child a jumble of questions, of raw nerves, collected in his brain and halted right behind his eyeballs so they ached. He patted Steven's shoulder and walked away. Dark complexion peeked from the wet limp suit jacket of this new arrival− a boy with hair that looked tar-black from the rain and . . . whatever. David rubbed his temples and eyes and the back of his neck. Could be Latino, a great contrast to the others. Had a new cult erupted? One that stole children and then buried them alive? If so, why didn't Steven remember being abducted...unless , he was unconscious from the near drowning.

"These two are coming around, Doctor."

As if invited, David stood behind Jessica near the little girl and boy, the two he'd found beside one another in matching caskets. Like Steven, their clothes drooped on scrawny arms. Their faces were spotted with dirt. David didn't know if he felt good or bad after he realized that all the outfits looked brand new. The boys wore white shirts and suits, the little girl had on a ruffled dress, trimmed with ivory buttons at the collar, just like she'd been laid to rest at a funeral.

Good holy God. David stifled the groan, the sick hot disgust that rose up from his gut as bile.

"Sally." Arms waved. A wail pierced the room. "Sally."

"Kut?" Adrenaline shot the girl upwards. Monitor wires snapped and she screamed for the boy. He struggled to reach her.

"Get them together." Jessica's voice sounded high above all the others and stretchers rolled. The noise in the room, the energy, amplified and startled the infant into a high-pitched scream. "Give the baby some water, just a few ounces."

"I'm thirsty, too."

"Mommy. Kut. I want Mommy and Daddy."

Jumping to the bedside, David gathered the children into his arms and he hugged them tight to his chest. He squeezed them and they burrowed their faces into his neck, their tears, their perspiration like a hot damp rag. His arms trembled. His stomach shook. His heart pounded hard in his ears.

"Move your arm, please, just a touch." Jessica said. "We need the monitors hooked back up here, David."

"It's all right. It's okay," he said. "It's okay. You'll be all right."

Jessica worked around him, she worked around the nurses and wires and beeping machines all the while that David stood fast. If they'd have sent him away, he wouldn't have gone.

"Mommy. Where's my mommy?"

"You're safe now, baby, I promise. Nothing's going to hurt you." With tenderness hardly recognized as his own, David kissed their fiery cheeks, their wet-stained eyes, and his chest rose with a breath that stuck right in his throat. He cuddled them. He rocked them. He pet their hair, for the huge white room and blaring lights even made him uneasy. He didn't step back from the children, not until their little bodies quit shaking –not until his own body stopped the earthquake inside his chest.

When the boy glanced up, David smiled. He guessed now, as he ran his fingers through the tawny tangled hair, that the boy looked seven or eight, the young face gaunt, skin tight and drawn. "You'll have to help me find your mommy."

"They're dead, aren't they?"

David's smile vanished. "I...I don't know son, that's something you'll have to tell me. I want to help. Do you know your name?"

"Kurt."

"And my name is David. This is Sally, right?"

"She's my little sister."

Kurt cinched his arm around the sniffing girl at his side, his eyes wider than any David had ever seen. And what in God's name should he ask this kid? What clicked through that brain, filled up those huge green eyes and turned the sunken cheeks to bright red? David stroked their hands.

"How old are you, Sally?"

"She's three-and-a-half," Kurt said. "I'm seven."

David winked at the girl but his mouth could only suggest another smile as he jotted down the information. He wanted Sally to speak for herself. Her eyes said she could. Staring at the paper, he sketched a tiny angel– a box for the body, triangles for wings. He inhaled. He looked up. "What about your mom and dad?" he said. "What are their names?"

"Neal Johnson is Daddy, Sara Ellen–"

"Mommy. They'a on fia. Go get them. Kut, Mommy's down they'a."

"Stop it. They're dead Sally, or they'd be here,

30

too. Don't you see? We were saved."

Crumbling into her brother's arms, Sally's sobs nearly echoed through the room. Kurt tightened his grip. Was he convinced that his painful acceptance of their situation worked best? David wondered if that kind of truth spelled mental torture for ones so young.

"Can you tell me about your parents and the fire, Kurt?" he asked. David's insides ached to even look at the kid, let alone pressure him for answers. But this new information gnawed at him…it absolutely confused him. He hadn't heard of any fire in the county, just accidents and injuries from the earthquakes. "And please tell me where you live, the address, if you know it."

Kurt wiped the moisture from his sister's nose and eyes onto the lapel of his suit. "We live on Tenth Street. It's the big brown two story house that's right across from Ericksen School."

David's mouth dropped open. He rubbed the sweat away that sprang to his brow. No fires occurred in Dareing last night and certainly none that claimed the lives of two adults. "Kurt, uh, what day is this, do you know?"

"Sure, I guess, at least yesterday was June seventh. We got out of school."

"Jess? Jessica, did you hear that?" David darted over but had to wait while she checked the youngest boy's eyes. He watched the pupils sparkle and contract when she flashed the luminous signal into them.

"No, I'm sorry David. What did you ask?"

"Steven and Kurt both say it's June eighth. Steven says nineteen ninety-one."

"Yes, I remember."

"Could someone have brainwashed these kids

31

with drugs?"

"Most definitely."

David glanced around, unable to get past the extreme differences between the children's ages and looks. Why such an odd array? "If a cult is involved," he said, "it doesn't add up. Usually they have one thing in common, all one sex, all one age, one race."

"I've not much experience with cults."

"Yeah, well, neither do I, no expert anyway." David inhaled. He studied the children, again. "The kids speak so well of their folks," he said, "I don't think this is a family thing. I think they've all been separated somehow and abducted. Steven nearly drowned in the canal. The Johnsons were in a fire."

David chewed on his bottom lip. A fire that happened some time ago, if ever. He walked back to Kurt. "Tell me, son, what's the last thing you remember?"

Wrapping both arms around his sister, Kurt looked straight into David's eyes. "I was in bed and when I woke up something was funny. Daddy let me stay up late and watch *The Simpsons* but I don't know what time. I remember I was asleep. I think Sally woke me up 'cause she was crying, making funny noises in her room. She does that sometimes. Mommie doesn't hear her downstairs so I go get her and we sleep in my bed. She's a'scared of the dark."

"My thwoat hut," Sally said. "I couldn't bweath."

Kurt stiffened. "It was the fire. When I went to get Sally it was all hot and red downstairs. There was fire all over. Sally was just standing at the hall coughing and crying for Mommie but I know the fire was at them. It was reddest right by the kitchen and their bedroom. I grabbed her but she wouldn't come. I started screaming and coughing, too. I remember the smoke. It was yucky and burned my mouth and nose and I jerked her arm and she fell down but I dragged her to my room."

Kurt choked again, on his words. Sally's clutch on his arm turned her fingers white. "We hid in my bedroom and closed the door but we still couldn't breathe. Smoke was all over and, and then Sally quit crying. She quit coughing and making those funny noises. I thought she was dead. I shook her like I shook my cat. My cat died once when the garbage man ran over it. Sally did just like Tiger and her head just limped and her arms but . . . I guess she's okay. The fireman must have come. I don't remember seeing him," Kurt said, "but I heard the siren. I wanted to call them out the window but I couldn't get Sally to go with me. I couldn't leave her. I…I didn't feel very good."

Kurt rubbed his chest. A strained, lost expression changed his face until it etched deep haggard lines that David knew no child should ever bear.

"But I feel okay now." Kurt looked over at his sister, as if he tried to figure out what did feel right, if anything.

David jerked when Jessica's soft fingers curled around his wrist to pull him away from the children. He stood back and watched the nurses settle the distressed brother and sister onto the beds, together, and cover them with flannel blankets. David didn't walk away, he remained, still, until he saw that they would stay quiet.

"I won't." His whisper answered the doctor's blue eyes. He didn't intend to quiz them anymore and send them on another emotional rocket ride. Besides, their answers got him nowhere.

This fire Kurt and Sally experienced took place. Undisputedly. No child their age would understand how smoke could strangle them. But when did the fire happen? June 8, yes. David nodded to himself, desperate for an answer to clear up the matter, a clue to clean up his own bewilderment.

"Jessica…." He found the physician beside the infant girl. "Jessica," he said, "the kids have this date in common but I'm not aware of any street drug that could blank a memory, erase it to exactly a month ago. That's outrageous. None remember the recent past. Could the trauma do it?"

"They could have been drugged continually," she said.

"But would they come out of a situation like that so quickly? Like this?" David waved toward the children. "I bet you can't find a single thing wrong with these guys. They act healthy and normal, well taken care of."

Jessica's frown cut his sentence.

"I know," she said. "But I need to take tests, lung scans, especially on Kurt and Sally. If they were inhaling smoke, there's no doubt internal damage."

"Even after this length of time?"

"Depends on the extent."

"But Jessica…." David saved his arguments for himself, the same contradictions that had hounded him before. Dareing had no large fires last month, or the past three months, and then only in a warehouse. And why the hell was it so hot in here?

He mopped his brow and rubbed his watery eyes as if to rewind an internal energy clock. He started again. What about June 8, a year ago? A possibility.

34

David pulled the tie from around his neck and then stuffed the tie in his back pocket.

"Has the new little guy come around yet?" David ran his fingers through his hair and took a step forward to stand at Jessica's elbow.

"He woke up when Kurt started talking," she said.

"Said anything yet?"

"Not yet, but he's acting just like the others."

Jessica brushed her thumb over the baby's rose colored cheek and ran the fine, matted hair through her fingers. "He was drowsy at first," she said, "but I'm sure he'll become lucid, too." She looked up. "I'm going to call in an internist, Gordon Bishop. He is an expert, David. He's seen a lot, and remembers it all."

David nodded, glad that someone had a definite avenue to follow. But Gordon Bishop would not locate the families, that job still fell on David's shoulders and right now, the weight felt pretty heavy.

He left her and headed toward the youngest, dark skinned boy with no choice but to wait until the child perked up and could speak. Something told him this kid would throw a curve ball, just like the rest of them. At least now he expected one. David did know what to do with the confusing information −missing person files. Steven Adams may even be listed as a drowning victim. His parents may believe his body still lay at the bottom of the city waterway.

Again, David scanned his memory. No way could he recall a dredging in Dareing. "Shit," he said under his breath, and stood beside bed number five.

David touched the young boy's arm and watched

the wide eyes open even further, dark wary eyes that scrutinized every motion in the room. He squeezed the warm arm to reassure the boy and plunged ahead. "How are you?"

The boy never closed his eyes nor did he blink, only continued his survey of the large strange room.

"Can you tell me your name?"

"Tony."

"Is that all?" David asked. "Just Tony?"

"Anthony Llamas Rey."

"Oh, so Tony's your nickname. And how old are you, Mr. Rey?"

Tony held up a widespread hand.

Okay. David nodded. Five. He rubbed his chin, hard. He rubbed his ear, along the top where it felt like a hot glowing coal. How much information he received from this little one may very well depend upon how he asked the questions. "Now I know this might seem like a dumb thing," he said, "but do you know what day this is?"

The boy shook his head, eyes heedful upon David's face.

"Little kids don't know that sort of thing."

Glancing to his side, David noted the high voice, a child's voice yet spoken very adult-like. "Are you supposed to be up Steven?" he asked. "Where are your sensors? Did you unhook yourself?"

"Have you forgotten about my parents?" Steven said. "I wish you'd call 'em, or let me."

For a second Steven reminded David of a boy he knew in school, always had the answers, always got A's in class. "I bet your teachers like you."

"Sure they do."

"What school do you go to?"

"Ericksen," Steven said. "I'm an upperclassman. Fifth grade."

David smiled. "Do you go to school, Tony?"

Tony's small round head went from side to side.

"I guess you'll go next year, then."

"Yes," Steven said. "Kids go to first grade when they're six."

David's crooked his mouth to the side."Ericksen?" When he repeated the word he looked at Kurt, Kurt and his brown, two-story home. "Hey, Steve…Steven, have you heard about any big fire around Ericksen School, a big house?"

Steven pulled David near and whispered, just like David had done to Jessica earlier. "That kid doesn't know what he's talking about. There wasn't any fire in the brown house by my school." Steven's shoulders straightened as he tried to stand taller. "My dad's a volunteer fireman. He goes to all the calls."

Frowning, David licked his dry lips. For some unknown reason, he trusted Steven, believed he would know about any fires. Yet, he didn't doubt Kurt's story any less.

"Steven," he said, "how about sitting back over there and let me talk with Tony alone. I think he's shy." Steven hesitated a moment before he obeyed, no argument, he just turned to leave. "Then I'll get right down to the station afterward," David said, "call your folks."

Stopping, Steven turned back and for a moment −a second, David thought sure the boy would start to cry. Indeed, time and fear had swallowed up the intellectual facade. David knew just how that felt and all at once he wished that he could console the young lad like he had the brother and sister, but Grace must have noticed the very same thing. She walked over and drew Steven into her arms.

David inhaled, if only to console his own bit of jangled nerves. "Do you know your mom or dad's name?" he asked and took hold of Tony's hand.

"I don't have a daddy."

"But do you remember him at all?"

Again, the shaking head. This time, Tony added a shrug. The action drew David's attention to attire. Tony wore a suit but of much cheaper quality than Kurt's and Steven's, and the sleeves fell short around the dark bony wrists.

"How about your mother?" David asked. "You see, if you can tell me her name and where you live, I can find her for you."

"Some people call her Marie."

"Does your mom go to work?"

Tony's eyes closed down tight, a gesture, David soon learned, that helped the boy think. "She goes somewhere at night a lot."

"And you go to a babysitter's?"

"Yeah."

"Do you know her name?"

"Lori. She lives in the apmentments with us." Tony tried to sit up. "Levi's whole house is upstairs."

"Levi?"

"He's my very bestest friend in the whole world. We play trucks outside by the dirt pile. His momma comes over and talks to mine."

David wrote down the facts. Dirt pile. Upstairs apartment. There must be a hundred places fitting Tony's description. A thousand?   He looked at his watch, shocked of the time, 8:30, no longer night. His late shift ended over two hours ago. He should call in.

"Do you know a street name, or the color of your apartment? A grocery store nearby?" David's questions trailed on. Tony picked at the cuff of his white shirt.

"Our house is green. We have new blue towels in the bathroom now. They have flowers on 'em."

"Tony, son, what's the last thing you remember?"

Tony's ruddy lips tightened and he answered without opening his eyes. "Momma and I went to the show. We went to see the space show, ya know, with Astro."

"The Jetson's?" David smiled, and then Tony did too, but it faded from his face. "I don't think I remember it."

"The show, you mean?"

"I watched one, just some dumb bears. It wasn't very fun though.   Momma came back and spanked me 'cause I played with the lights. She said the car'd go and I'd get hurt if I touched things. She said she'd get some popcorn and a orange." Tony sighed.

"Your mom went to get popcorn? She didn't stay in the car with you?"

"No." Tony stared back at David.

"Do you go to the drive-in a lot?" David asked. He changed their reference to the show on purpose and watched for any reaction. And where in the hell had Tony been to even know about such a thing as a drive-in movie?

Tony squinted his eyes. "We go there a lot but Levi gets to come. I don't like to be all by myself."

David expected a rush of tears from Tony, his

voice wobbled and his chin quavered. But no tears fell.

"I know I'm not s'pose to touch the buttons but Momma comes sometimes if I do."

"Where is your mom when you watch the show?"

"She gets me popcorn?"

"Did anyone else bring you anything or take you from the car?"

"No. Woodypecker came on. It was kinda cold and I told Momma. She turned on that one button, the flipper one. I play with it sometimes," he said, "but she doesn't come when I play with that one. It just makes the hot come in the car."

"The heater? The car was running? Son, did someone drive the car away while you were waiting?"

"No."

David's shoulders sank. Tony wasn't taken from the movies in a stolen car. "What happened when you got home?"

"I dunno. I guess Momma carried me to bed. She does sometimes when I play possum." A slight smile steadied Tony's trembling chin. "She thinks I'm asleep."

"Sure." David grinned, too. He used to play possum –decades ago. "But you were asleep, no playing that night?"

"I sleeped in the car," Tony said. "I got tired of waiting for my popcorn and Woodypecker is dumb so I laid down. I didn't touch no buttons though."

"Good boy." David rubbed Tony's flat tummy and decided that Marie Rey used the drive-in for a cheap babysitter and spent her time in another car. Tony could have been snatched while sleeping and never known it. Nor his mother. David bit his lip.

"Any clues from this end?" Jessica asked. She

appeared at David's side to check Tony's blood pressure after the long conversation. She patted Tony's hand and brushed the hair from his forehead.

"Not really," David said, "but I have a hunch all these kids were away from their parents and taken somewhere."

"And well cared for," Jessica said.

She seemed bewildered from the fact and David knew perfectly well that he had the very same look in his own eyes. He understood her confusion, firsthand. "Why would someone save the kids," he said, "nurse them back to health and–" He stopped. Steven Adams's stare bore a hole right through their conversation. "Have, uh, you called this Dr. Bishop in yet?" David asked.

"Bishop's in surgery. I wanted to get a scanner on them first, anyway."

"Jessica," David said, "this is a wild shot, and may have no connection, but get a lung scan on Tony, too. He sat in a car with the engine running. Said he got sleepy."

"Carbon monoxide?"

David shrugged so that his arms moved out from his sides. Sometimes ideas popped into his head with no clues of their origin, or destination. "A wild shot," he said.

Dr. King added Tony's name to the testing chart and they both stared at the paper. Then as if she'd read his mind, Jessica jotted infant girl below.

"These kids are no doubt listed as missing," David said. "I'm going to the bureau now and notify the parents, but under no circumstances can they be released, not until I get my follow-up finished and I hear from the clean-up crew. You run as many tests as you can for contamination. I'll call you as soon as I get things rolling."

David wrote his full name and cell phone number on a small piece of paper and tucked it in Jessica's jacket pocket. He left the antiseptic smell of the huge medical center behind, with a young inquisitive face in his mind. Steven Adams, the oldest boy, the bravest, somehow understanding. All of the children seemed calm, all bright and attentive. For a moment, David decided that they'd accepted their situation without question, as if a sixth sense had developed inside them.

"No. That's silly." He rubbed his eyes and scratched the back of his head, fully aware that his brain had jumped way beyond the facts.

But he had no hard facts, and that's when he always paid attention to the simmering unguarded volcano in his gut.

Five

"Have you heard from Gable?" David yelled the question from just inside county headquarters. He wanted a million things done and he wanted them finished an hour ago, before he'd even left Brigham Hospital.

A young sheriff's deputy jogged along side him down the hall. "Gable says it's a hell of a stinking disaster. Unofficially."

"Unofficially." David halted. "There isn't any other way to describe Oakwood. Have they found anyone else?"

"No one alive," the deputy said, "just cadavers all over the place. Gable says to tell you most every body lay intact, either all or partially in their casket, near enough to put them back into the right one." The officer's already fair complexion paled. "Said that valley where most of them ended up is the worst and will take at least three weeks to clean up, that is, organize. Sergeant, what's going on there?"

"Go see." David sat down at his desk. "I'm sure Gable would love the help."

"No. Uh, no thanks. I'm getting things squared away on this end. I have orders from Gable to contact the funeral homes involved with the burials at Oakwood so they can somehow match records and corpses, plant them again." The tall blond deputy snickered at his pun. "You wouldn't happen to know which mortuaries, would you, sir?"

David's fingers hovered over the keyboard of his computer then he swiveled his chair to face the wall. Christ…where to begin. Connecting onto missing persons, he stared at the pad he'd placed on the desk. Behind Kurt and Sally's names, he rewrote their last name, spelled a different way –Johnston, just in case. And how the hell did Tony spell his last name? R-a-y or R-e-y? And the baby…he would have to check from birth to what…eighteen months? That might be a stretch. Steven Robert Adams, Junior. The address and phone number stared back at him. David had all he needed for Steven, right on the page. "Why wait for a goddamn print-out?" For some reason, he wanted to see these people in person.

"What's that, sir?"

"You still here?" David spun around. "Get me a hot tea, would ya? Strong as it'll get. Use two tea bags if you have to and load it with sugar. In the yellow dispenser," he said before the deputy disappeared.

Flipping open his cell phone, David punched in the number for Steven's parents. As the call rang through, and while he glanced at the monitor for the correct screen, he scanned the regular, old fashioned Dareing phone book for a Neal Johnson, Kurt and Sally's father. After seven rings for the Adams's, he got nowhere. "Shit," he said, and Dareing's directory listed no Neal Johnson, nor were there any in the neighboring towns. "Shit a pot full."

"Your tea, sergeant."

"Thanks." David took the flimsy cup and tipped it to his lips. The hot liquid burned his tongue and his throat but he kept pouring it in to appease the raw knotted ball in his stomach. When he tossed the cup into the trash, the deputy appeared in his peripheral vision. "What are you waiting for, kid?"

"Need anything else?"

David smiled. "I need an unlisted phone number for Neal or Sara Johnson, from Dareing, or a town very near. I'm going there now." David jumped to his feet and gathered up his pad and pen. "And I'd like the missing person records for an Anthony Llamas Rey, don't know the spelling and any infant girls from the county." He halted and frowned –just the county, didn't want to overwhelm himself anymore than he felt right now. "Yeah…that's it," he said, "gotta check out some leads." He resumed his aim toward the door. "And I'd very much like the info on my desk when I get back."

David drove his own car, a newer Toyota that didn't reek from his clothes worn earlier that day. To say the least, his usual squad needed a major detail and would be a good twelve hours in the shop. Still, he wanted to drive. He needed to drive and no interruptions badgered him while he covered the short distance to Dareing, only his far-reaching thoughts. Dates and times just didn't fall logically. Steven's birth date, June 1982, puzzled him, and the clue from the comic book in Kurt's pocket, 1991. Again, he blamed the discrepancies on drugs. But why would their abductors go the bother of brainwashing so thoroughly? "Guinea pigs." He moaned out loud just as he turned his pewter-gray sedan down Tenth Street. David planned to check out Kurt and Sally's two-story home on his way to talk to Steven's parents.

Old Ericksen School sat seven blocks off Dareing's main street, and nearing the area, David spotted several people in their yards to clean up after the storm. He could see no major damage, no heaved-up earth like at the graveyard. Garbage cans rolled on their sides. Severed tree limbs lay scattered and broken. A fence or two teetered in the leftover breeze.

David saw more telephone repair trucks than usual. No wonder the Adams's didn't answer the call. He felt better thinking that when he located their home, someone might be there after all. When he'd left the station, he'd warned himself this might be a wasted trip and he shifted in his seat. He'd much rather drive than pace at headquarters. He'd much rather talk to these people, face to face.

Stopping at the corner of the large elementary building, he glanced down each side street —no two-story houses. The school, playground and adjoining park covered three city blocks so he drove around but still, he spotted only single stories. He swore, the way Kurt described it, the house would be right across the street.

Even Steven Adams hadn't disputed the location and acted as if he saw the home everyday.

David drove around the blocks again, this time to study each place individually. Maybe Kurt's two-story was an attic of some kind, but David couldn't even see anything that resembled that type of structure. All the places looked older, built around the same time as the schoolhouse, all track homes. A few remodeled houses stood out, but even those appeared to be at least ten or fifteen years old.

Another trip around the school seemed useless but David went anyway, then turned up and down each side street and across to widen his area of search.

"God," he said, "there isn't a damn two-story anywhere." Driving back to the building, David parked the car under the green city sign ERICKSEN PRIMARY GRADE EDUCATION. "I'm sure they agreed on this."

Across the street, an older man and his wife worked in their yard and David sat and stared at them while they gathered up pieces of a metal storage shed blown apart by the storm. With no idea of what he might ask, he pulled into their driveway. They looked settled in their modest home; retired people always seemed to know the news in the neighborhood.

"Hello Officer," the man said. "You look like you're lost."

An understatement. David introduced himself. "Not much of your shed left," he said.

"No." The couple answered in unison and brushed the dirt from their hands.

"We're lucky though, Officer," the woman said, "Wilson's across the way got a tree limb through the window and the rain almost ruined the carpet."

Frowning, David glanced behind him. He'd noticed nothing like that and had been around the block several times.

"The dining room glass in the back," she said.

"Oh." David nodded. The backyard. Yes, these folks knew the scoop. "I'm trying to locate a family," he said. "Are you familiar with a Neal Johnson? My information says he lives next to Ericksen School in a brown two-story house." The man and wife looked at one another and David sensed a jackpot in their expressions of pure surprise. "Do you know the Johnson's?" he asked. "They've had some family troubles." Waiting for an answer, his comment exaggerated the couples already wrinkled brows. His shoulders sank.

"Sgt. Straus," the man said, "I don't think we can help you much." He smiled and chuckled as if his own thoughts cleared his bewilderment. "You see, the Neal Johnson's we knew died in a fire."

"Yes. I know about the fire. You say they died, for sure?"

"It was a huge fire, Officer," the woman said, "had the whole neighborhood up all night."

Again, David surveyed the nearby homes. None of them looked recently remodeled. "Which one was it?" he asked.

"Right there." They pointed across the play-ground. "That newest white house. It used to be a two story."

"But it burned clear to the foundation," the woman said, "and the next owners just built a whole new place."

David stiffened. He felt like his ribs caved onto

his heart. "You say they built a new one?" he said. The home didn't look new, not one single board. "Or did they move one in?"

"No, all new." The man chuckled again. "Of course that's been about fifteen years ago."

David stared at them. He thought his jaw might drop clear off his face. "Are you saying the big fire that killed Neal and Sara Ellen Johnson happened fifteen years ago?"

"At least that, yes sir."

All words escaped David, all thoughts, like a cocoon had wrapped him up so tight that he couldn't hear or speak. The world grew dark around the edges of his eyes and he had to tell himself to breathe. "I, uh, I guess maybe you're right," he said. "I think we must be talking about different Johnson's." But even after he heard his own voice, David couldn't convince himself that they *were* different. "The family I need had a couple kids."

"Kurt and Sally," the woman said.

"K-Kurt and Sally?" Stumbling backward, he pinched the top of his nose to make sure he hadn't fainted. "And what happened to them?" He rubbed his eyes with the palms of his hands. "Where'd the kids go?"

"Well, by some miracle, the fireman rescued the children's bodies from the upstairs but it was so engulfed downstairs that the parents couldn't be found, until later, of course. It seems to me," she said, "that the state took over everything –no relatives. The Johnson's were rather poor at the time; Neal had been unemployed for quite a few months. Sally and Kurt were buried at Oakwood Cemetery. A few neighbors brought nice clothes for the little ones and I believe a young friend sent a book of some sort. Do you remember, dear?"

49

Without waiting for a reply, the woman went on to tell the tumultuous history of Oakwood Cemetery but David never heard it. He just stared at them, stunned. They both stared back.

"That's really all we know, Officer," the man said. "Our memories aren't what they used to be."

David wanted to agree. He wanted to disagree. He wanted to disregard the entire conversation. He could say he'd been hallucinating, felt damn weary enough to hallucinate. But he couldn't forget anything. Not when they'd named the children.

And the cemetery.

And the book. He could have told her what kind.

"Damn." David shut his eyes and rubbed his temples hard, an attempt to stop the throb of pain inside his head. He wanted to go home and sleep…for a year.

"Are you all right, Sergeant? Maybe you should come in and sit down, have some coffee."

"No." He shook his head. "I mean…I'm fine." He looked up. His attention locked upon the old white house. "Thanks anyway." He wanted to blurt the whole strange tale to them, but his thoughts –he couldn't seem to keep hold of any of them.

Shaking their hands, he thanked them for the help, at least he thought he did. He couldn't remember. Nor did he recall climbing into the car and starting the engine.

But he didn't drive, not now. He knew better. He picked up the pen and pad at his side and did a quick calculation, one he'd done before. "Two thousand seven minus fifteen years. Nineteen-ninety-two." Heat flared into his face. He wiped it away with the sweat. "There's got to be a logical reason. To hell with this weirdo garbage."

David punched the car into reverse and lurched from the driveway. He headed to Steven Adams's home, positive all would be cleared up by them. He forced a picture to stay in his mind, one of ecstatic jubilant parents, grateful that he had found their son.

David arrived at 47th Street in fifteen minutes. Broken branches cluttered the narrow road, severed wild mustard blooms and telephone repair trucks added color. David felt better seeing the odd conglomeration. The telephone trucks told him that he'd guessed right when he decide not to redial Steven Adams's home. He rolled down his window.

Most of the houses on 47th set off the street on an acre or more of land with the addresses displayed on green county fire signs. David came upon the number, 1157, but double-checked his notebook before he headed his car down the lane. He stopped beside the graveled walkway that led to the door and sat very still.

Looking over, he decided the Adams's home was built at least thirty years ago in a rustic ranch style. Trimmed grass edged the picket fence. Shrubs and flowers encompassed a porch that stretched out along two sides of the house. David wondered how they kept up the place so well with five kids about. He paused to check for tricycles and toys. He saw none. "Backyard," he said and ventured to the door.

A tall, slim woman near age fifty answered. She, too, looked nothing like the Sheila Adams in David's imagination —no red hair.

"I'm Sgt. Straus from the sheriff's bureau," he said and had his badge already in his hand. "Are you Mrs.

Steven Adams?"

"No sir. I'm Donita Roman."

She wore an odd expression and David studied her. He couldn't figure why she might hide anything. "Is this the Adams's residence?" he asked.

"No," she said. "My husband and I own this home."

Clenching his hand tight around the badge, David chewed on the inside of his cheek. "Do you have any neighbors named Adams, Ma'am?"

"Not that I know of."

"How long have you lived at this address?" He read his notes. "One One five seven northwest forty-seventh?"

"Almost   fourteen   years   now."

That damn time span again. Jesus.   David stiffened with the inward complaint and bit his lower lip to hold his words a little tighter. He tried to leave but his shoes had turned into lead.   He didn't want to leave; Donita Roman's eyes controlled him.

"Sergeant," she said, "I think maybe we bought this house from a man name Steve Adams. It's been a long time. I'm not real sure."

Grabbing the porch railing for a bit of support, David stumbled forward. "Would you have mortgage papers anywhere handy, or a bill of sale, that you could check?" He held his breath. "It would be very helpful to me, Mrs. Roman."

She invited him in and David stood alone in the living room. He noticed a three-tiered shelf against the wall with one ceramic rabbit placed in the middle rack. A brown paper bag and vacuum stood below it. David related to the rabbit —one caught on a freeway. So what if they bought this house from Steve Adams? What in the hell difference could that information make? Maybe Steve Adams did live here, long before young Steven was born.

"This is the sale contract."

Mrs. Roman re-entered the room as she removed the thick batch of papers from the envelope. She stopped near the coffee table and flipped through them to the last one. Four signatures appeared at the bottom of the page, the Roman's on one side, Steven Robert Adams Sr. and Sheila Lorrain Adams across the page. The notarized date glared at him. April 30. "Nineteen ninety-four?" Holy shit.

"Is this what you needed Sergeant?"

Goddamnit. He pressed both hands, hard on his temples. "I can't believe…" David thought he might need a brown paper bag –to breathe into. But the light-headed fog soon passed. After all, he expected this. Didn't he? "Yes Ma'am, I . . . I thank you very much." David forced some logic to his brain. "You wouldn't happen to remember anything . . . anything at all about why the Adams's sold out or about the children?"

"I don't remember much at all." Donita Roman shook her head that same slow way. "I think Mr. Adams got a promotion, or maybe transferred, something, and that they moved to Orange County. All I knew about their family was that they had some darling twins." She smiled. "And they all had red hair."

David didn't smile. He just nodded as Steven's red curls jumped in his mind. When David turned to leave, he knew he'd found the correct house. Young Steven's family once lived here all right, four years before Steven was even born. Any person nine years old today

53

would have arrived the year 1998. Wouldn't they?

Did he wake up a damned idiot this morning?

Speeding back down the street, David grew more irritated than frustrated and when he returned to headquarters, no new telephone numbers or print-outs awaited on his desk. He erupted on the first person he saw, the blond deputy.

"Didn't any of my stuff get done? What the hell does it take to get things accomplished around here during the day?"

"I left you a note right here, sir."

"A what? A note? Shit. I didn't want a note."

"And that unlisted number you ask me to find, Sergeant, I've checked all over the district—"

"They're dead." David caught his breath. "Thanks, kid." Collapsing in his old cushioned chair, he rubbed his face with both hands. "Do you have time to chase another tail?"

"Yes sir."

"I need a file from nineteen ninety-two. No... ninety-one," David said with a frown, "on the same people, Neal and Sara Johnson." David swallowed hard. "And Kurt and Sally Johnson."

"A file? Yes, but what kind?"

David looked up from the note in his hand. "Did I say file? I meant death certificate, filed with this county through Dareing. Bring me the hard copy so I can keep it here."

The younger officer turned but didn't leave. David knew the request seemed strange, one doesn't ask for an unlisted phone number, then death certificates on the same people without it sounding odd.

"As soon as you can, kid," David said, and

proceeded to actually read what had been done. Nothing. The deputy found nothing to print out. Nothing on Rey and not one single infant girl had been abducted in the county. Shit. He slumped back into his chair. In a way that was good, wasn't it? No one wanted babies abducted but Christ. When the day began, he stood in corpses up to his ass. Why should the printouts be easy?

Flipping through his notebook, Tony Rey's name appeared, and his mother, Marie. David's gut said he'd not get very far along that road; he had the very least clues concerning the Rey's. No. He needed to locate the Adams's. He had to speak to them face to face. He had to see the color of their hair. Orange County didn't fall anywhere near his jurisdiction. Unofficial as hell. They might even haul him off in a straight jacket.

For a second, his mind flashed to Kurt and Sally. If they died in the fire, and the state buried them at Oakwood like the old couple said....

"No. No." He spoke out loud. He shook his head. Dayshift considered him nuts anyway, crazy, with all his seniority, to keep signing up for the shittiest duty available. Well, after this day ended, he might just start to agree with them.

David rang up the central computer clerk for a tracer on Steve Adams. "And run one on Marie Rey," he said. "Don't know the spelling, and I've no clues, whatsoever, on any priors except that it might be in Dareing."

While he waited for the familiar hum to come over his printer, David grabbed a doughnut from the nearby counter and tossed fifty cents next to the plate. The cadence of the paper spun him around. "Got it already?" David petted the gray console and read the information. S.R. Adams–C.R. "Current residence," he said, and underlined the address. Anaheim, CA.

David checked his watch. Thirteen-twenty-four. He could catch a commuter flight and be in Anaheim in two hours. If all went well, if the Adams's didn't turn him into the state mental hospital, he could be back in time for his shift tonight.

Six

David didn't sleep during the short flight to Anaheim, his mind hell-bent to dredge through the same strange details over and over, inside and out. Kurt and Sally dominated his thoughts, the trail to their door mined with eerie coincidences. Were his Kurt and Sally and the Kurt and Sally the old folks referred to the same?

No way. No way in hell. He scratched his chin and rubbed his neck. He aimed the fresh air vent straight into his face.

A rental car and the Adams's street number took little effort to find and David sat, parked for a minute to gather his mental bearings, in front of a large stucco house with a metal roof. A sweet-smelling Oleander hedge framed the yard and decking stretched the length of the home's west side. A new camper and freewheeler sat in the driveway to await the weekend. Steve Adams must have gotten that promotion.

David brushed the lint from his slacks and tucked in his shirt; he should at least look presentable, not look like he felt, and his persistent knock brought a beautiful red-haired teenage girl to the door. She looked about eighteen years old but this day and age, he didn't assume anything. "I'm Sgt. David Straus from the San Francisco County Sheriff's Bureau," he said. "Is your mother or father home?"

With a grin and a nod and the door ajar, the girl left him to stand on the porch steps alone.

"I don't know," David overheard her say, "but he's tall and absolutely handsome. A sheriff of some kind."

When the door opened again, his smile faded. Mother looked serious. He re-introduced himself and showed the badge.

"How can I help you?" she asked.

Without a glance downward, David could see her breasts rise with apprehension. He could see trepidation etch into her brow. "I'm hoping that are you Sheila Lorrain Adams, married to a Steven Robert Adams?"

"Oh Lord. Something's happened to Steve–"

"No." David held up his palms to stop her. "No, Mrs. Adams," he said, "there hasn't been an accident." David stumbled on the word and wondered why she'd named her husband instead of her son. He frowned. Hadn't he told her he came from San Francisco? With a missing son there, they would have connections. David looked at the deck and his shoes with unfocused eyes. "I take it your husband isn't home right now."

While Sheila Adams shook her head, David noticed her clothes and slender shape. She kept herself well for having five kids and her long fingers, as they ran through the loose curls of her brown hair, shook like autumn leaves.

"Did you need to speak to him directly?" she asked. "If there is a message, I'll guarantee he gets it."

"I would prefer talking to both of you." Another pause. David shuffled his feet. He hadn't considered the fact that Steve Adams wouldn't be home. He hadn't considered anything or prepared himself with anything to say. Or maybe, he just couldn't think that far ahead today. "Is he at work, Mrs. Adams?"

"Yes, but I'm sure he'll be home within the hour."

David nodded with a firm grasp on the familiar –his notebook. "You must be Connie," he said with a wink at the teenager.

"Oh no. Wow. I'm Kristy. Do I look twenty-three?"

"Twenty-three." David choked on the words and the page blurred before him. By young Steven's account, Kristy was nine months old. Connie was seven. "I . . . I definitely need to speak to you and your husband, Ma'am, as soon as I can." When she agreed, David felt worse. Strain and confusion hollowed out every line of her face. He had no idea what to say to make her feel at ease. They just needed to talk. "Could I come back, say around six? Do you think he'd be home then?"

David could tell he'd picked a bad time. Dinner. He reconsidered, but if they delayed, he wouldn't be able to catch the return flight for his next shift.

"Mrs. Adams, I am very sorry. I wish I could tell you more but I don't have a lot of hours to spare."

59

"Six is fine," she said. "Could I have your name again, please?"

He told her and wrote it down, along with his department number and phone. "Thank you," he said, and with no goodbye turned down the walkway, met by two, speeding young men on matching racers. They darted around him and into the open garage.

"David, damn you."

At the sound of his name, David swiveled around, only to hear the other lad laugh at some private joke. Again, he stared at the notebook in his hand –David Lee, Daniel Linn. Spinning back, he took a step forward and caught one last glimpse of the young men as they jogged to the front door. One had longer hair, the other a bit heavier, but he'd bet this life –twins.

A dinner of mixed nuts and vending-machine double espresso passed the next fifty minutes for David. At six o'clock sharp he stepped back on the Adams's front porch. Steven Sr. answered the door this time, a thin man with broad shoulders. A silent man with questions that probed David's brain. A calm man with wild red curly hair. David swallowed the lump that crept up in his throat, amazed at the resemblance, the link between father and son.

After brief introductions, Steve opened the door wide and David stepped into a pleasant friendly atmosphere. The twins, and he could tell that they were twins, sat in front of the living room entertainment center watching baseball. The teenage girl stood in the kitchen and peeked around the corner at him with a cell phone pressed to her ear. He smiled again, just as Sheila came through the doorway beside her daughter.

"Mrs. Adams," he said, "I'm sorry to screw up your dinnertime this way."

"No problem." Steve Adams answered for his wife but his stare upon David grew more intense with each moment. "Would you please tell us what this is all about?"

"Yes, of course, as soon as we can find some place quiet...private." David glanced at the twins. "Where would you prefer?"

Sheila picked at the hem of her blouse. "Rather than disturb the game, is our bedroom all right?"

"Yes." David didn't care if they talked in the bathtub. He was just as eager to get their story as they were to get his.

Sheila led the small group down the lighted hallway. "We have no family room or den," she said, just as David halted before an array of pictures on the wall.

His feet stuck to the floor. "When was this photo taken?"

"Oh heavens." Sheila took a few steps back toward him. "Let's see...Kristy was just born so around nineteen ninety. Thanksgiving, I think."

The enlarged view of the Adams's tipped David's gut clear over. He pushed on his stomach. He swallowed his heart. He dared not look at the picture more, not until he spoke to Steve and Sheila. The group was an exact match to the family Steven Jr. had described. Steven was there, too, and looked just like he did today, healthy, alert, and nine.

Managing a smile, David held out his hand and Sheila moved ahead. He could feel his throat tighten with every step. He could feel Steve's vision, hot, on the back

of his neck. What in God's name was he going to say?
When Steve Adams shut the bedroom door the air darted
with unspoken questions, a third of which were David's.
Questions for them. Questions of himself.

"I've got to sit down." He pulled out a chair from
the nearby vanity and faced the bed. Steve and Sheila sat
upon the stiff mattress. David took a deep breath, but this
time when he spoke his words sounded so coarse and low
that he had to clear his throat and begin again. "Could
you please tell me about the last time you saw your son,
Steven Jr."

David watched two faces turn red, two faces turn
white, and for a wild second he thought the couple might
throw him through the window. They both leaned
forward. They grasped their knees instead of his throat.

"Not until you tell us a few things, Sergeant."

Steve Adams remained perched on the edge of the
bed, his muscles tense and ready. But the quiver in his
words told David the demand erupted more from
frustration than anger.

"The only reason you've got this far," Steve said,
"is because I've called your bureau. They said you're
legit, but had no answers for me."

"I apologize, Mr. Adams, and I want you to know,
at the moment, I am off duty. This can only be
considered unofficial. You don't have to talk to me at all
but please, sir." David stood up, and for support,
clenched both hands on the back of the chair. He studied
their faces, their eyes that told him they had nothing to
hide. He knew they would help if he'd just explain.

So explain. Say it. He licked his lips. He wiped
the sweat from his temples.

"At five this morning, I was called out to

Oakwood Cemetery in Dareing. The quakes unearthed almost all of the caskets and there was a living infant girl amid the mess." David sat down again, his story had wet their eyes. "You are familiar with Dareing and Oakwood, aren't you?"

This time, David pushed on his temples, hard. Okay. Stupid-ass question. He was full of them today. He couldn't blame them for not answering.

"I, uh, went down the hill for evidence and to make a long story short, found others, alive. Mrs. Adams . . ." He looked directly at her. She had a pasty film of perspiration all over her face. "Mrs. Adams, one of the children, a boy age nine, said his name was Steven Robert Adams Jr. He gave his mother's name as Sheila Lorrain. He told me of a Connie, and twins named David and Daniel. A baby sister named Kristy."

David glanced at the bedroom door and wiped the river from his own brow. His final explanation hit them head-on, about the date, the picnic, the boy's old address in Dareing and the visit David had made there. He'd hoped his ending would erase the pain from Steve and Sheila's faces. But not so.

"I have no logic for any of this," he said. "I had to trace down my leads, any leads at all. Do you understand? I had to come to you folks. I had no choice. Now if you can say you've never had a son that fits this description we will chalk all this up to coincidence and you'll never–"

"You've got to believe me." Sheila gripped the mattress. "We buried Steven sixteen years ago, and he was dead. I swear to God he was dead."

"I'm not saying he wasn't dead, Sheila." David jumped to her side. "I'm no way saying anything of the sort."

She slumped against her husband's chest. "It was his birthday, just like you said. We told him time and again not to go across to the deep side. We were going to take him out when the next second he was pulled under. He vanished, right before our eyes. Steve jumped in and dived a hundred times. I called nine-one-one. The fire department came in minutes and they searched too, all along the reeds and rocks hoping to find him caught, hoping th-that he was still alive." Sheila wept in her husband's arms, as if the accident happened just yesterday. "We found him the next morning near a big rock."

The rock with the nasty word. David let his shoulders sag. "Steven is still nine years old," he said. "I don't understand what happened. All I know is the clues that brought me here, and . . . and that we're talking about a boy who looks exactly like the one in your family photo."

"I want to see him."

A man of few words, Steve Adams stood up, his fists white, his face red. The look in his eyes eliminated any argument from David. Steve banged open the closet door to grab an overnight case.

"I'm coming too."

"No." Steve spun around. "You're not coming just to go through hell all over again."

"And you don't think it will be hell here," she said, "knowing Steven is alive and not be able to hold him and kiss him?"

"But we don't know that." He grasped his wife's shoulders in a frantic grip. "We don't know it's him."

"Yes we do." She jerked from his clutch and

stumbled to the dresser. "Or you wouldn't be going."

Watching the couple stuff clothes of every sort into the case that Steve had just pulled down, David breathed in their moment of anguish and of wonder and he questioned himself again. Should he have come to these people, face to face, with his dilemma?

"The boy is in the best of care," he said to their backs. "I . . . I wish I could tell you how, why this happened." David knew his words barely penetrated the vibrant air. "You were the first ones Steven asked about." Somehow the statement made him feel better about what he'd done. For what other action could he have taken? All the clues, his only clues, led him here, to this man and to this woman.

Seven

Back in Dareing Wednesday night, David gathered everyone together. Technically, the day was early Thursday morning, 2 a.m., but it still felt like Wednesday to him, the same long day when all of Oakwood, his life, turned inside out.

David hadn't combed his hair for thirty-three hours. His crumpled suit had spots of coffee on the lapel. He could feel the lines of fatigue etched into his frown and the vibrations in the small, very silent hospital conference room, made the lines dry and then moist, hot and then cold. Everyone stared at him. They waited for an explanation. His superior, Sheriff Williamson, sat across the table. The beautiful Dr. Jessica King, the most patient, waited two seats away, next to her impatient

Internist, Gordon Bishop, a wrinkled, gray-haired man with eyes that seemed to bore a hole right through David. The Adams's sat right next to him. Steve and Sheila had yet to see their son.

So David, weary, and looking very much like he'd not slept in days, stared straight back, ready to tell his preposterous story to the group. He now had proof to back his first gut feelings. He had Mr. and Mrs. Adams. He had death certificates on the entire Johnson family, all dated June 8, 1991. Neal and Sara Ellen Johnson's few charred remains were taken to the community mausoleum. Their children, Kurt and Sally, were buried at Oakwood Cemetery.

David had found other new information on his desk, the penal record of Marie Margaret Rey, imprisoned late in 1991 for negligent homicide —the careless killing of her five year old son, Anthony Llamas Rey. She'd left him alone in an automobile at the drive-in where he died from carbon monoxide poisoning. Date, June 8.

As for the fifth child, the infant girl, he had no clues. Yet. If David's hunch proved right, the baby's obituary would be found in the dusty files of Dareing's weekly newspaper for that same time in June.

Yes, David Straus, veteran, Sheriff Sergeant, God loving, felt he held proof strong enough to back his theory about the five graveyard children. He stood up, secure enough to say his first, outrageous statement.

"I believe that the children now in this isolation ward were dead on June eighth, nineteen ninety-one and buried, and for some unknown, miraculous reason, have come back to life."

Thunder shook the room. Voices roared like a hundred crazy people instead of just three, Sheriff

Williamson, Doctors King and Bishop. The Adams's remained silent. They turned pale. During the flight back to San Francisco no one had said those words aloud. Even now, David wondered whether he should have.

He shouted over the din. "If you can find a different, more logical explanation than this one, believe me, I'll be more than happy to accept it." David slammed his fist on the table and turned to Jessica King. "You heard young Steven's conversation, Doctor, you were there with me." David pointed to the boy's parents. "Through Steven's clues, I found this family. These are the people he described, and they, in turn, have described him, along with a very similar account of the incident. They told me a different ending. One with a drowning. The death of their son. Steven believes he's been saved. He's waiting in isolation for his mom and dad to take him home to a family who's aged sixteen years. His baby sister, nine-month-old Kristy, is a pretty, red-haired teenager. His five-year-old twin brothers are in college." David's words flowed unobstructed from his mouth, observations and frightening concepts that he'd sensed in his heart but had kept guarded until now. "What are we suppose to tell him? What are we going to tell anyone? Do you realize what this all means, the medical, psychological aspects? And what about the people out there, the media?" He waved toward the curtained window. "If the public hears about this in the wrong way they could label these beautiful children as…."

David couldn't say it. He couldn't say freaks. Or Gods? He grasped a breath. "If we don't handle this thing right these kids will wish they were dead. We've got to guide their second life now from its beginning so it's a good, purposeful one. We can learn from them."

"Sergeant Straus." Dr. Bishop stood up and bellowed. "We're letting you babble on here like what you've said is the truth. There is no way we are going to believe this absurd story. For god sakes, get hold of yourself."

David sucked in his breath, like he'd just been punched, and his words lodged painfully in his throat. Dazed from Dr. Bishop's sharp voice, he watched Jessica's hand cover his own as she removed the stack of discs and certificates from his clutch. He felt her soft skin and her warmth. He shut his dry eyes to relish a moment of darkness and even the hard metal chair when he sat down. Williamson's voice rang like a reveille in his ears.

"David, you told me you went home, slept off your shift. You're taking crazy."

"I just changed my clothes, sir –the cemetery smell." Williamson had asked him and he'd hedged the answers, knew he'd get caught. "I know it's crazy…" David started to argue but heard another voice and as if in slow motion, he watched Jessica's rose-colored lips as she spoke to Dr. Bishop and Williamson. He listened while she accredited the children's conversation that she'd overheard.

"You said yourself, Dr. Bishop, their blood was neutral."

"And I called for new tests."

"All coming through the same," she said almost to herself, "all neutral. There is no typing or class, or all type. Total pureness. No antigens."

"Which backs my drug hypothesis," Dr. Bishop said.

"Your theory, yes, but you can't name any specific drug or drug form. You admitted that. Oh, I believe there is a restorative, a powerful one we've never heard of and may never again." Jessica paused to look at David. "If indeed, sixteen years have passed since their deaths, a drug could change; factors alter over the years, and in a certain controlled environment…the perfect conditions." Her final whisper lifted Bishop's head so it tilted somewhat, as if the suggestion lay heavy with substance. But then he frowned and rubbed his eyes. "What about the lung and brain scans?" Jessica said.

"What about them?" Bishop asked. "I've never seen more faultless, healthy−"

"But these kids were buried," she said. "That is fact. Their skin was cyanotic, gray to be exact. Stale?"

She looked at David. He could only stare back and shake his head.

"Drugs would do it," Bishop said, "narcotics used to reprogram minds."

"Yes…" Jessica inhaled and nodded and sat up straight in her chair. "Drugs would keep them…alive underground," she said, "by slowing their respiratory system, but where is it in their blood? Where is anything in their blood? Or their tissues? I put a particle of the baby's skin, from where it had been cut, under the magnetic field. I've never seen anything graph out more internally pure and free of bacillus, germs, Dr. Bishop, that we all carry with us just because we live in our polluted world."

The two doctors stared at one another so that giant thought waves cultivated between them. No one else said a word, at least not until Bishop reached for the stack of certificates and discs, now crinkled from David and Jessica's outbursts. Dr. Bishop must consider all the data at hand, consider the most unbelievable, insane theory of all –David's.

"When can we see Steven?" Sheila Adams broke the long silence and Bishop turned to face her. He didn't speak for the moment, just held her in his steady observation.

"We are all forgetting something," he said, "something that could sufficiently dispel this..." Glancing over, he regarded his colleague and David. "I want this meeting with Mr. and Mrs. Adams and Steven, the youngster, to be a controlled experimental situation."

"What in the hell are you saying, Doctor?" Steve Adams's chair hit the wall with a crack. "Experiment?"

Dr. Bishop's hands shot upward to stop Steve from coming after him. "I emphasize only, that the boy may not be the son you buried sixteen years ago."

"So what's a stupid experiment going to prove? All I have to do is look at the kid. I may not have seen Steven for a *hundred* years but by God I'll not ever forget him."

Sheila took her husband's hand and coaxed him back down to the chair. She wiped her eyes. Silence followed, and as David watched the couple, his heart lurched up to his throat all over again. His veins thumped, wild, in his neck until the doctor reworded the proposal.

"I mean, Mr. Adams, Mrs. Adams, that the nature of the meeting should be controlled. There should be no hints to Steven before he sees you that you are..." Bishop paused. "That you are his parents. The boy should give that information himself. I'm assuming his greeting will be either one of two, the reunion of family, or a casual reception of strangers. No one seems to be considering the fact that these children could have been reprogrammed to believe they are someone else."

Only Sheila nodded; she entwined her fingers into her husband's.

"Dr. Bishop," David said, "Steven Jr. has been asking for his parents. He wanted to call them himself. The little guy was anxious. He knows they're worried." David swallowed the words as they came into his throat. "Any nine year old could have been reprogrammed, I'll give you that, but how could any drug transfer those specific memories?"

Bishop pursed his lips, as if to hold his breath…his irritation? "What did you tell him?"

David glanced at Williamson. "I was confused by our conversation but didn't let on, acted as if the situation was routine. I told him that I'd find his folks, first thing."

"Have you seen him since?"

"No, I haven't."

Bishop nodded as he contemplated, David could tell by the way the doctor's thick grayed eyebrows touched over his nose and the way he stood up to look over everyone. "To keep the meeting controlled," Bishop said, "I believe it should be handled as such. In the morning, after breakfast…" Bishop frowned at Dr. King, as if they'd both forgotten something very basic. "They did eat the meal I ordered?"

"Yes." When Jessica King smiled, her blue eyes brightened. "Everything we served. And doctor," she said, "you do remember, that abdominal scan showed no sign of bowel or bladder activity, no normal generation of urine and feces."

Bishop nodded again, his smile stingy when David compared it to Jessica's. Obviously, Bishop's logic had added the facts up to drugs, the only real, substantial explanation he could put to all the odd data they had accumulated, that is...before this meeting. Bishop shifted his shoulders.

"As I was saying," Bishop said, "after breakfast, Dr. King and I should go into Isolation, talk with Steven and the others and get them to relax. The Adams's can come in, and we'll see what happens. I'm sorry to leave you out, Sergeant, but if he sees you with them, or any time before, he may subconsciously connect you, assume anyone to be his parents."

David groaned inside. No way in hell. Not that kid. But he agreed, regardless. He'd go along with Bishop's experiment even though suspicious. And then David smiled at Sheila. Steven would either know these people or not, in any situation. Sometimes this psychological garbage gave him a royal pain. But who would question what may or may not happen under certain circumstances? No one in this room. Not anymore. Folding his arms at his chest, David looked at Dr. Bishop as the more confident voice filtered to his ears.

" . . . believe there is one more important matter we must discuss and agree upon. That this meeting and proposed theory be kept in the strict confidence of only those present. By no event should the conversation we've had tonight be leaked out." Eyebrows raised. Bishop looked at Sheriff Williamson and then faced Jessica King. "The nurses involved in caring for the children will assume, as we have, that they're victims of a live burial. The children, of course, must be kept in the chambers. They can play together but until we learn more and know exactly what we're up against...and the press," he said in a breath, "always seems to get down wind."

Bishop didn't explain further, the piquant air defined what others did not say. They'd all toyed with the concept, and yet nothing felt real.

"It's agreed then?" Bishop asked.

"Agreed."

As the reply of mixed voices sounded inside the room, the doctor vanish through the short narrow side-door of the adjoining area. The tension in David vanished, too. He rested his head in his palms. They felt moist.

"You're on duty, Officer."

Stiffening, David pressed his back straight up against the chair and he looked directly into Sheriff Williamson's narrowed mindful eyes. David knew he'd broken a ton of rules today, which one would his superior call him on first?

"On duty," Williamson said, "until you walk outside with me. I'm driving."

David's slow strained stance got him to his feet, but his body, his brain was doubtful that the exhausting days were over. There remained nothing for him to do at the hospital. He'd hear about the Adams's reunion secondhand, sometime later this morning. Walking to Sheila and Steve, he grasped their shoulders with a squeeze of his fingers. "I'd be more than glad to put you folks up for a few nights."

The way they often stared at one another made David wonder if they shared some kind of telepathy. They did it now. "I live alone," he said, "not much noise or activity but beats the hell out of a motel."

"Thank you," Sheila said, "that would be nice. But...."

"Not tonight," Steve finished. "We'll stay here the

few hours and wait."

"Sure." David would have agreed to anything they wanted. "Wherever, whatever you feel the most comfortable with," he said. He still felt guilty for them being here so distressed, and for some strange reason he wanted to hug them both.

David put his hands in his pockets. This odd situation, whether true or not, made him feel strange, in his throat and in his gut, it made him look closer at people, made him think about everyday folks like the Adams's and how their lives entwine and interlock. And twist up. David ran his fingers through his rumpled hair. "If we don't connect before you want to go to my apartment, call the Sheriff's Bureau," he said, "they'll send a squad for you." He gave them a house key and stood a moment longer to fumble with his change, his badge. His emotions.

"David?"

Jessica's voice fell around him like a soft warm blanket.

"David," she said when he looked over, "they'll be fine. We'll watch out for them."

Don't worry, her blue eyes told him.

"Call my office as soon as you wake up," she said. "If I can't speak to you personally, I promise, I'll leave a message."

He nodded. He touched Jessica's hand, just for a second if that long, and walked away with the Sheriff.

When the conference room door clicked shut, David's mind clicked too, and started to work the details again so he could plan his next moves. He relied, heavily, on his mental calculations, this kind of response he could deal with. He wondered, though, how Jessica ever made it this far. She cared about people, no denying that, she had to or her eyes wouldn't turn so blue. But how did she keep from getting dragged down into a sorrowful pit in her line of work and still remain sensitive and emotional?

"Damnit, I care," he said, and teetered on the curb. He turned around and looked behind him, past the Sheriff and through the tall glass hospital doors.

Eight

Thursday morning came, just as every other morning of David's life, yet when he stood at his unoccupied spare bedroom, a tingle crept up the back of his arms. He rubbed the sleep out of his eyes. He rubbed his unshaven chin. He shivered. The Adams's hadn't shown up. If Steven was not their son, they would have come here to sleep before they returned to Anaheim.

They would have come here to kick his ass.

He slipped a clean tee-shirt over his head and remembered that Jessica had said to call her as soon as he woke up. But he didn't call. He told himself his eagerness looked silly. He felt foolish for being excited. But he didn't know why or try to understand.

David forced himself to eat a decent breakfast. Still, he didn't enjoy his eggs and bacon; he wanted Jessica to call him but the telephone remained silent. He told himself to be patient and with every dry swallow, pushed back those unfamiliar feelings from last night. The electric air. The torn emotions. His emotions. He kept seeing Kurt and Sally, their green eyes and dirty trembling chins. At the hospital his caress upon their frail bodies had come from someone. Yes, he'd hugged them, but not as the same man who sank thigh deep in grime and decay to bring them up the hill. The David he knew could remain neutral and insulated. Sure, he felt concerned, he liked Steve and Sheila, and yet he'd been able to push their faces to the correct place in his brain. Hadn't he?

David's eyelids pulled at the edges when he shut them, so dry. He prayed the phone would ring but in the next instant, his laughter cut the stillness.

If Jessica called, would the news be good or bad? Did he want her to say this miracle had happened? David did understand Gordon Bishop's skepticism. David prided himself on being a great skeptic; he was always the first one to check the underside. Somehow though, after yesterday, his point of awareness shifted, he now dwelled upon both sides. He had touched the miracle.

"God…" He exhaled.

At the kitchen sink, he splashed cold water on his face and the drops trickled down his skin in slow motion. His mind moved in slow motion, and as he tried to focus his attention on the four families involved, he truly, irrefutably, allowed his mind to accept his own theory.

Steven, he knew, would be welcomed back into a loving home with no second thought. The Adams's would not consider the dramatic changes or psychology involved.

Kurt and Sally. He dumped the toast he forgot to butter into the garbage and recalled his conversation with the old neighbors. No relatives, they'd told him. With no family, Kurt and Sally wouldn't have to understand the fact that everyone had aged sixteen years. They could begin their lives where they'd left off, watched over by two carefully chosen people. David believed that Kurt had already accepted his parent's death; Kurt knew they were gone when he pulled Sally into the closet. But was that knowledge instinctive? Had the idea taken root during the time of hibernation? The boy talked so straightforward about his folks. Sally…maybe she knew it too, deep down.

David pondered over the dirty breakfast dishes. He thought of the baby. He couldn't do anything about her until he located the parents. "So why am I here washing this damn plate?"

Talking out loud made David jerk. He grabbed his keys and stuffed his wallet into the front pocket of his jeans. The suds from his hands left his thighs damp but he didn't care, just headed out to county headquarters. Even if he couldn't approach the parents about the baby now, he'd soon know who they were and where they lived.

David's mind now turned faster than the wheels of his car. Marie Rey. He held the most reservations about Marie. He even admitted that he held some prejudices from what she'd done sixteen years ago. Yes, she'd paid her dues in prison, released just six months ago. But was she reformed? Did she feel remorse for her lack of responsibility? David fidgeted in the seat at the red light.

The state pen warden would know the answers. He forced his foot to stay on the brake. He would not speak to Marie, cold turkey, like he had the Adams's, even if he could.

Upon reaching his office at headquarters, David checked his desk for a memo. Nothing. The second passed like every other. Picking up the phone, he paused and all at once wondered if Jessica King and Brigham hadn't been some kind of outrageous marathon dream. But Sheriff Williamson stood in the office hallway near the door, Williamson's face with an expression that no other could read, only David, and perhaps a handful of others.

He pressed the numbers. "Heard from Gable?" he asked while the call rang through.

"He's been in and out," Williamson said. "Says to tell you to check in Clark and Talbot's records."

"The funeral home?" Odd information.

"Yeah, and Bradley left first thing this morning to go through the old issues of Dareing Times."

David nodded, he understood that, but, "Bradley?"

"The new deputy." Williamson grinned. "The kid's adopted you, at least all the orders you've been throwing around here lately. Pretty damn brave to even show your face here after lying to me yesterday."

Laughter felt good and David allowed himself the moment. Bradley…he'd have to remember that. "Dr. Jessica King's office please, Sgt. Straus on the line."

He didn't hear the sweet voice he wanted to but just a trace of the disappointment registered in his brain. He sat on his desk. "She may have left a message for me…Straus," he said and accepted the music in his ear without a grumble. He even smiled when the secretary returned.

"Are you David?"

"I most certainly am, did you find something?"

"Yes. David, it looks like you're right. Bishop and I shall proceed accordingly. We will meet in conference room A at eight p.m. Need you there."

Letting the chill run down his body and out his arms, David gripped the edge of his desk just to feel something solid. He thought he'd already accepted his hunch as being true but now...now Bishop agreed.

"Thanks very much," he said, and he dropped the phone to its cradle. His throat relaxed. The goose flesh disappeared.

"What is it?" Williamson asked.

"Nothing. Just thinking. Have you heard?"

"No." The sheriff shook his head. "I figured you'd be hot to find out. I waited so you could tell me."

David nodded, he appreciated that. Williamson knew he'd want to talk. "My memo said −it looks like you're right."

"Really?" Williamson straightened tall. "I would have lost a month's salary by your face."

"You never could beat me in poker." David walked over to grasp his friend's arm and they stared at one another for a good long time. A good long time to allow the unbelievable to seat itself inside their bodies. "Besides," David said and he inhaled, "aren't you the one always telling me never to judge too quickly?" He stiffened. His smile vanished.

"What David?"

"Rey. Marie," he said, "you know, Tony's mother they sent up. I need to talk to the warden about her. I need to slow down. I owe her that."

David wasted no time to call the women's prison, his introduction brief.

"Marie Rey?" the warden said. "Marie was a model prisoner. What in the world has she done?"

"Nothing, Warden. No. No, Marie came in... she's asked about a job, and–"

"By all means, hire the girl if you can. She put herself through hell the past fifteen years. Personally, Sergeant, I don't think she should have been sent here. Marie was genuinely sorry for her son. Do you know the details?"

"Yes, I do."

"I tried to get her paroled the first several years."

"Paroled? What was the problem?"

"Marie. She wouldn't go for it and honestly, now that I can look back over the entire episode, I can see it wouldn't have worked. She felt such remorse, so regretful and guilty. Staying here fifteen years was her way of punishing herself. Mentally, she wouldn't have accepted freedom."

"How about now?" David asked. "In your own gut opinion, how is she mentally?" David purposely emphasized *gut* so the warden would take a moment for deliberation, to really think her answer through –the warden didn't seem to need the time.

"Marie's a mature woman now, Sergeant. She's stable. I have every bet placed that she will lead a normal, balanced life from here out. I have no reason not to believe that. You know we have psychologists, she's seen them and they feel the same as I do."

David released his breath, in some kind of slow

focused sigh, so that the warden couldn't detect his relief. "I am glad to hear that," he said. Damned glad.

"I don't know what you've been told, Sergeant, or what she's said to you, but Marie was an unwed mother, just barely old enough to be tried in adult court. She was too young to be raising a child of her own. Underprivileged family. Well…" The warden paused, as if she'd shifted in her chair. "It's all behind her. You say you're with the county. Where is she living? I don't recall her speaking of having family nearby."

"I think she's living alone in San Francisco." David scanned the update before him. "She's an aide at Grafton Senior Center."

"And she's looking for another job?"

Liars left a bad taste in David's mouth, bitter or worse when he lied. "Part time." He swallowed.

"Sure. I suppose extra money would come in handy right now."

David stared at the phone after hanging it up. The picture just improved for Marie and her son. They may get another run.

"Sgt. Straus. The Dareing Times."

David spun his chair around. "Bradley, your timing is beautiful. I hope your news is, too."

"News sir." The young officer chuckled and held the paper near his chin. "I think that's a pun," Bradley said. "News…newspaper. Get it?"

"I get it. Only one paper, one baby?"

Bradley handed over the Times. "I double-checked for five months prior and past June ninety-one. This is all I found."

"Five months." David nodded. "That's great, Deputy. I'm impressed."

"Dareing lost a lot of older kids, though." Bradley leaned over David's shoulder and thumbed through the pages to find the obituary. "All died the same weekend. Weird, huh?"

"That *is* weird." David rubbed the back of his neck, an effort to ignore the crawly skin there and at the same time, not appear as though he already knew. Weird...good word.

"I've circled the baby's."

When Bradley edged away from the desk, his hands dropped into the loose back pockets of his uniform. His retreat went unnoticed; David's eyes and attention had focused on the print inside the small red circle.

He studied the obituary then scratched the information in his notepad. Tammy Lynor Alexander, six months. John K Alexander–F," he said, "father. Lynor W...mom." He wrote down the grandparent's names, too. The paper showed a Dareing address but no cause of death.

One out of two ain't bad. He rang for central computer. David ordered the file that would hold the infant girl's death certificate and prints. He gave the parent's names and the old residence for an address update but he didn't feel like waiting the half hour for data. Something urged him to go to Brigham.

Lucky day. David met the Adams's right at the hospital entrance doors. Steve's clothes were wrinkled and Sheila's hair was disheveled. Her eyes were loaded with red strain. Both of them looked something like David felt the day before.

"It's yesterday to him," Steve said, "acts the same, with that kind of intellectual way he had. Says the same dumb phrases –awesome. I forgot things could be awesome. Asked if we'd bring his rap tapes, too."

With eyes half closed, David pictured the reunion of Steve and Sheila with their son. He didn't need a minute by minute account, just heart. "That's where I'm heading."

"Good," Sheila said. "Steven kept asking about you. And David, thanks." She wiped her eyes one more time and grasped David's arm to squeeze it tight. "We just can't say…."

David shook his head to stop her words. Then he smiled. He didn't want thanks; he had nothing to do with the situation but follow leads, something done most every day. But he did understand. "Is there anything I should know? Anything I'm not supposed to say?"

"We're all back in ninety-one for now. Bishop says no television or radio."

"I can handle that," David said. "But what about Kurt and Sally? They think their parents are dead. They are dead." He felt his throat cinch up. "Do we go along?"

When the tears welled in Sheila's eyes again, David knew the answer. What else could they do? Swallowing, the lump inched down his throat. "Were you, uh, heading to my place?"

"Yes." Steve looked down the street. "We talked to Sheriff Williamson a few minutes ago. He's sent someone."

"Bradley." David spotted the squad car and hailed the deputy over. Waving goodbye, he walked through the silent corridors and into Isolation. The air chilled the back of his arms. Or was it the smell? He wondered if the antiseptic odor had permeated itself clear through the walls. He wrote toys in his notebook and entered the room.

"You're surrounded, copper."

David jerked to a halt. "No gun." He reached for the ceiling. "I swear," he said. "Wouldn't shoot an unarmed man, would you?"

The ring of children's laughter filled his head and they moved in closer. The kids had surrounded him alright. David had never been more outnumbered than now.

"Ya just missed Ma and Dad," Steven said, "and thanks for the job well done."

Yes. Steven had caught him, indeed, caught David's tongue and he patted the young man's head. "Looks like you guys have some new beds." He glanced about. New beds. New equipment. The place looked like a jungle. Hopefully, it didn't turn into a zoo. "May I sit on one of them?" Without waiting for an answer he sat on the middle cot. The stiff furniture didn't even move beneath his butt.

"This is my bed," Sally told him with a chest full of pride. "That one's Kut's. Steven gets the big one."

"He's the biggest," David said, "right?"

"Hey, d'ya notice my dad's gray hair?"

Gasping, David shook his head. "I didn't."

"Said I scared him so bad he aged ten years."

Steven thought the comment still quite funny and David snickered, too. He must compliment Steve Sr. on the quick thinking.

"Are you still a cop?"

"Well, sure Tony." David lifted the youngest boy onto his lap and edged a piece of black hair out of Tony's eyes. "I work during the night when you're asleep. That's when I wear my uniform."

"And badge?"

"Yes, Sally, and badge," David said, but Tony's wide eyes kept his attention. They looked like two polished obsidian stones.

"Steven said you'd find my momma, too."

The air hardened. David could feel it in his shoulders, like steel. And if it weren't for the constant tick of monitors there would have been no sound in the room at all. Every eye rounded, every ear cocked, they awaited David's reply. He wondered how one simple question could make him feel so strange? Damn. These weren't just kids to him anymore. Damn it to hell. Sometime in the night, in his head, they had transformed into emotion and guts and heart, born of far greater courage than David had ever known in himself. Shit.

"Tony, I'm...uh, already looking for her. I'm working—"

"Tonight? When I'm sleepin'. Oh boy." Tony leaped from David's knee to jump up and down with the other kids eager to copy him. How innocent they all were. The steel in his shoulders flexed and he shifted to ease the weight. Too innocent. Too trusting. Why didn't they ask him to look for Momma right now, instead of sit on his ass and wait for his shift? They didn't ask that.

They should have.

"You see," he said over the commotion, "it's going to take a little longer to find her because I don't know exactly where you live?"

The kids stopped. "Put an APB out for her," Steven said. "Call in the SWAT team."

"Yeah, the swats."

When Tony's eyes lit up, David didn't know whether to laugh or choke. "Sorry," he said, "that isn't their job."

"Oh." Tony's shoulders sank. "I guess that's okay. But I miss her a lot. Like at night."

"I know Tony and I understand. I do. I promise, I'm doing the best I can."

Heat filled David's face, his whole body, as if he'd been touched by fire...his feet, his fingers. His head. Kurt cuddled very near him and Steven sat on the other side. Sally and Tony each settled on his knees. These children depended on him. They banked on his help. They had reached out to him today with all they owned and he could do nothing but grasp hold and hang tight, pray his inadequacies, by the grace of God, somehow, would allow him to do what he promised to do.

"Can you guys do something for me?" David licked the dryness from his lips so he could finish the sentence. "It might not be easy sometimes, but I'd feel better knowing you were doing it." He closed his eyes. "You're going to be here, together, for a while longer. I'd like you to help each other and be like a little family."

"That's what Jessica said."

"Awe you in ow family, too?"

Pressing the little girl firmly to his chest, he smelled her just-washed skin and cotton nightie... chocolate-chip cookies, and he snuggled his nose even further into her fine brown hair. "I'd like to be in the family, Sally," he said, "if you don't mind."

Quiet whispers and nodding heads told David that they didn't mind at all and his stomach turned upside down, as if he'd jumped into a world unknown to him, a world sun-filled and warm, but with no ground to catch his fall.

And then he smiled.

Nine

Eight p.m. Friday. David walked to the hospital conference room eager to give his news to doctors Jessica King and Gordon Bishop.

"The baby's name is Tammy," he said. David placed the obituary before them and slipped the thumb drive that held the death certificate into the desk top. "She died of SIDS. The parents are still married and living in Vallejo-Deli. Didn't have any other older children and none after Tammy. I've seen records from Clark and Talbot, the funeral home involved with burying most everyone at Oakwood. Every detail matches. I'm sure we know exactly who we're dealing with."

Jessica's smile grew wide, but the lilac shadows of her sweater captured David's attention more.

"We're lucky, that all but one could talk," she said.

He agreed…as his glance moved up to meet her eyes. "It, uh, made my job easier," he said, "especially where Tammy's involved. Had a date, a place."

"You say the funeral records are from Clark and Talbot, Sergeant?" Bishop asked. "Did they bury all five children?"

"All five. You got something?"

"Just hatching…maybe." The older doctor frowned. "Anyway," he said, "there are a lot of things I'd like to get through here tonight."

The three of them pulled their chairs to the small table and Dr. Bishop took his place at the head. He'd assigned himself as chairman of the group, obviously. David didn't mind. He certainly didn't feel qualified for the position. Now, if they were organizing a DIV or even a large scale evacuation, yes. Grinning at Jessica, who'd chosen the place opposite him, David doubted that she felt any lack of confidence.

"Sergeant."

Bishop called his attention as if sounding roll call off the lighted computer screen.

"How interested in this situation are you?" Bishop asked.

"Interested." David choked on the word. Did Bishop want to clean house already? Sure, he had most of the footwork finished, the investigation about wrapped up but, "Damn, Bishop, interested doesn't describe how I feel. I am involved and would very much like to stay that way. Now I realize there may not be much left for me to do–"

"David." Jessica grasped his tightened fist. "Gordon and I have had a chance to talk. We want to get a team together, a small group of devoted people with the children's interest at heart. We wanted you, *need* you, to handle the media, divert them off the track, contact the parents when it's time. If–"

"Count me in." David meant to interrupt and he could feel his skin grow hot again. He wondered if his face had turned red. The mere mention of the press and the disaster an uncontrolled story could cause rankled his bones. He sat up straight. "Who else is in on this?"

"The three of us for now, as the nucleus," Dr. Bishop said. "There will be the Adams's and the other parents, and I want to call in a scientist, Nevil Morrison."

"A scientist." David flinched. "What are you going to do with the poor kids, make them live under a damn scanner? They're human beings, remember?"

"Special human beings," Jessica said. "You're not being realistic, David."

"The hell I'm not."

"We can't send them out into the world until we understand every single inch of them down the last cell," she said. "For some reason their life underground was pure, germ free, their blood is rare."

"I know, Jess…." David stroked her thumb and along the side of her hand, a bit surprised and pleased that they still had hold of one another. "I didn't mean send them out," he said and stared at their fingers, how his tan and his calluses stood out against her delicate white. He looked up. "I know we've got to keep them, teach them and prepare them for obstacles ahead. But even if we make their lives as normal as we can during all that, do you know what it's going to do them inside?"

"We don't know," Bishop said. "That's the problem."

91

David rubbed his chin. He dug his fingers into the back of his neck and the air felt cold as it penetrated the puddle of sweat at the underarms of his shirt. He rubbed his chin, again. He didn't want to argue. So long as everyone held the children's future and wellbeing highest over it all, he wouldn't argue. "Then we've got to plan every move," he said. "I'll be point blank with both of you, if the media gets in on this we're going to have problems. They've screwed up one too many schemes of mine, already, and we're long overdue for a nosy reporter to worm deeper into this and try to get more than what we've already told them.

"Besides that," David said almost to himself, "I'd rather not involve the state at all if we can get around them and only at the last minute if we can't. When we begin to mainstream the kids, they'll need the usual records...BC's." His tone rose to question his own choice of words and he shook his head. "Would birth certificates work? God." David realized he'd stood up. He sat down.

"The complexity here is– is extraordinary," Dr. Bishop said. "Even the simplest detail as a BC becomes complicated."

"But what about birth certificates?" Jessica asked. "Can't we just reinstate the old ones?" She laughed before she finished. "If we did that, little Sally could apply for her driver's license."

David chuckled at the idea, too, and found that he could relax against the back of his chair. "Besides the medical and psych tests that I assume will be going on continually," he asked, "what's first?"

"Gathering the parents and telling the children the truth," Jessica said.

"Especially Steven." Gordon Bishop grinned. "He's already one step ahead of us and honestly, I think will be more settled with knowing. Not less inquisitive. No doubt more. The smaller children may not understand but the truth here is most important."

"We have agreed, David, that honesty is the best policy, inside the circle." Jessica paused and then referred to them all as family. "Lying to the children about their past will cause worse problems later."

Oh yes, David could relate to that –like a kid learning that he's adopted when he's seventeen. Changed his whole life. And David wondered, for a split second, if that moment was when he started to build the wall around himself, the barrier that appeared just the other day.

Appeared? He ran smack into it this morning. The kid's had tripped him up and he hoped his next dive in wouldn't make him feel so hot and strange. "I think this is a good time to discuss Tony and Tammy, their families," he said.

"Is there a problem, David?"

"I assumed you've located them," Dr. Bishop said.

"Yes. Yes, I've found them." He turned to Jessica. "And I don't know if there is a problem. I could be projecting dragons. Have you thought of the fact that the Alexander's might not want Tammy? They have no children at all. Now maybe it's physical, maybe they couldn't, but they didn't adopt."

In the quiet moment that followed, he realized Jessica couldn't possibly have thought of it, she'd just found out about Tammy. "And," he said, "there's Marie Rey. You know she's spent this entire time in prison for Tony's death."

"An unfit mother?" Dr. Bishop asked.

"Sixteen years ago, maybe yes. But I've had a nice long conversation with the warden and she talks like remorse and self-punishment are meaningless here. I believe Marie loved her son and I think they deserve a second chance. Do you realize the power we have?" he said. "We wouldn't have to tell the parents anything. We could keep their kids."

David knew his words had chiseled deep lines into his forehead; he could feel them and he stared straight at Gordon Bishop. "Can you trust, absolutely trust, this scientist, doctor friend?" When the word mad scientist popped into his mind, David closed his eyes. But when he looked at Jessica, his heart pounded. She had to feel the same about the kids as he did. Jess was strong. She had fight. Jessica wouldn't let anything happen. "I'm sorry," he said.

"It's all right."

She smiled that gentle sort of way but not like she smiled at the children. Her mouth looked softer, somehow. And she'd taken his hand into her own, again. Her fingers felt like velvet to him.

"Sergeant… David," Dr. Bishop said, "you and I are both aware of this subtle personality clash between ourselves which is fine, emotions in situations of this nature are sure to be magnified."

"It's not that I don't like you," David said.

"Just my quest for progressive research, the ultimate medical knowledge."

David grimaced− Testing the hell out of the kids.

"But I care about them, David," Bishop said. "I haven't a stone heart."

The doctor's words came in that same shallow tone but a light shown in his eyes, the extra David needed to get around the impasse. For now. Opposition was good, he decided. Questioning one another would create debates, new ideas. "So let's get back on track."

"Marie Rey," Jessica said, "the Alexander's."

"Besides it being her every right to be told, I feel Marie Rey should have custody of Tony." David looked at the two doctors who sat next to him at the conference room table. They'd invited him into this elite circle and he by God meant to take a turn to say his piece.

"I have no qualms about reuniting Marie and Tony," Dr. Bishop said. "The boy wants his own mother. He remembers her, loves her. I hate to say it this way, but we will be monitoring the families long after our immediate research is finished. If Marie is not yet responsible...." Dr. Bishop dropped the concept. "My mind is open towards Marie. I'll give her every opportunity to keep her son."

David watched Jessica nod and admitted to himself that the skepticism he'd once held against Marie Rey no longer existed, his mind was now open. He felt lighter in the chest, somehow. "I think I'll get hold of Marie first," he said, "if that's okay. Tony's anxious to see her."

"I'd like baby Tammy's parents re-introduced very soon, too, David," Jessica said. "The little sweetheart is already changing even after this very short time. Her weight is up, her muscles are strengthening. She should be building strong mental ties with her mother and father, learn to trust and depend on them for her care." Jessica looked at Dr. Bishop. "Tammy is going to grow emotionally to one person for her basic support system. I want that person, those persons, to be the Alexander's. And," she said, "if they for some reason don't want to be involved, someone else must be found."

When Jessica glanced down at her ivory trimmed nails instead of the two men in the room, David wondered. He wanted to see her blue eyes. He wanted to see if she entertained the notion that "the someone" be herself. He'd watched Jessica with the kids, he'd paid great attention to the gentle way she touched them, the cheerful way she smiled and the light in her eyes when she looked at them. He inhaled.

"What about Kurt and Sally?" he asked. "They're going to need someone too, just as bad if you ask me. Kurt is pretending to be so damn strong. Damn it anyway." David remembered how his own father used to crack him on the back and tell him to quit crying. He could still hear the barbed words and clenched his jaw against them. Good God, could he still feel them? "And Sally." David shook himself free of the memory. "She's a fragile little thing."

Pushing himself back into his chair, Jessica appeared at the edge of his vision. Did she wonder the same of him? Did she just ask herself if *he* were entertaining the notion? Her stare didn't drop away, as if she waited for his answer and David, once again, had to fill is lungs deep with air. He looked down at the nervous fidget of Jessica's fingers and then turned toward Dr. Bishop. "I would like to know everything and be kept up-to-date on your medical findings. I may not know what you're talking about a lot of the time but I'll learn."

"Learn with us," Dr. Bishop said, and he stood up to shake David's hand. "I'd like to agree upon a time to meet everyday, for now at least, while this situation is so new and with so much going on. You can fill us in on the parents, David, and of course you'll bring them here."

"I'd like all the parents to meet one another," Jessica said. "I'd like this to be kept intimate so we can build relationships between the families. The rarity of this phenomenon is going to isolate the children from the public. They're going to need the feedback and support from those who share this uniqueness."

"I agree, Jess." David leaned even farther into his chair and tipped back on the legs. "I've seen only good come from groups like that, rape victims, families of violent crimes. They have one specific thing in common and just knowing they're not alone is more help than one can imagine."

Dr. Bishop nodded, and as soon as they all agreed on a regular eight o'clock meeting time, he disappeared to leave David and Jessica alone. They soon found themselves in the direction of the five children. David hadn't planned to see the kids again tonight, but right now, as he walked down the hall with Jessica, the idea appealed to him.

He looked at his watch. "It's almost ten."

"They're probably asleep," she said. "They sleep more than other children their ages."

"Steven, too?"

Jessica laughed. "Steven, too. I like to think of it as hibernation, David. You know after the long slumber, bears do rest in their months of activity."

"Bears. Yes, I suppose."

"Or," she said, "we can compare the children to newborns who use their sleep for further development. Babies tire easily after birth from their new surroundings and need the long rests."

David felt welcome in the silent ward. Finally, he felt comfortable. The moon shone bright through the long narrow windows near the ceiling and dim circular lights glowed upon the walls. One could see the children and check them without disturbing the darkness with a more direct globe.

At the beds, they peeked over each cot in turn, each mass of rumpled white blankets, bulging knees and bottoms. Feeling warmth around his hand once again, David squeezed Jessica's satiny fingers as she guided him further into the room. The infant, Tammy, lay off by herself nearer the nurse's small station and David stood, spellbound, as Jessica took some time to tuck the coverlet around the baby's tiny shoulders.

"Daddy?"

As if called by name, David turned to the faint voice behind him. "Sally...sweetheart, you're supposed to be asleep." When he lifted her up, Sally's green eyes grew wide and she blinked to focus on his face.

"You not Daddy."

"No baby." Pressing her round little head into his neck, David rubbed her tangled brown hair. He squeezed her so tight to his chest that he felt her tiny ribs rise up in his hands. "You remember David, don't you?"

Nodding, Sally snuggled her face back against his skin and he turned toward Jessica, his eyes now damp, his throat cinched up tight. Clutching the girl in his arms, he swayed side to side, desperate to capture the essence of his grandmother's rocking chair.

Ten

"Something's going on." David slipped into county headquarters to start his Friday nightshift and glanced behind for a second time at the satellite station vans parked out front. "Shit." Forcing his mind to forget the serenity he'd left behind at Brigham, he came to full attention and controlled his pace towards his office to that of a leisurely stroll. In no time at all, the small crowd of people encircled him in the hall, people with microphones, notebooks and TV cameras.

"Sgt. David Straus? We're told you'll fill us in on the Oakwood victims, the ones buried alive at the cemetery."

"Are there only five?

"Were any more found?"

"This is for our eleven-thirty update, Sergeant."

Stopping, David turned to face the journalists. "At this point," he said, "there's not much to say."

"But they're still alive. What are their conditions?"

"Stable."

"Can the children talk? What are they saying?"

David hesitated. He chewed on his words in order to deliver them with the utmost care. "They can't remember much about the recent past." That…was not a lie.

"Do you have any clues of their identity, Sergeant?"

"Yes."

"Who are they?"

"Where did they come from?"

"I'm sorry. I can't tell you that. We have to locate the families first. We're handling this the same as always," David said, "families first."

"Yes, we understand, but what's holding up everything? Aren't the children asking about their parents?"

"Actually," David said, "the children are holding up the progress. They're too young to communicate well enough to give us many clues."

"They're no doubt listed as missing," a young woman said. "What about missing person records, Sergeant?"

"We're using every method we can to speed identification."

"Tell us their descriptions. We can transmit the information and bring the parents to you."

"No." David's voice boomed above the rest and

he massaged his eyes to shield himself from a vivid nightmare. "We would have every parent with a missing child on our doorstep to claim them. We would have a mob of people to turn away, and I absolutely would not set up a system for the children to be viewed, like a line-up." David shuddered at the concept. "If someone has a missing child, I will have a record of it and can sort through the data much more efficiently, more quickly, than excited families. Don't get me wrong," he said, "I'm very sympathetic to those who have lost relatives, but right now my main concern is the five children. I assure you…I assure you, they are well taken care of and shall be until a reunion can be arranged."

"Sergeant, you're talking like all the children are from this area."

"It's a place to start."

"What is your guess on who did it?"

"No guess."

"What if the parents are the one who buried them?"

David let the question and the silence, hang. He'd asked himself the very same thing not so long ago. "As we identify and locate we'll have more to go on. Believe me— trust me, every possible angle will be investigated." Sheriff Williamson's office door stood two meters away and David moved toward it, inching past the lights and people.

"Were there drugs involved? Is it a new cult?"

"I can't say. It's much too early. Please excuse me, I have a lot of files to run. I'll keep you informed."

"What doctors are on the case? We know they were taken to Brigham."

David halted, his hand steady on the door knob.

"Two very qualified, caring, physicians are watching over the children along with a full staff of nurses. We have joined forces to speed the process in both departments. Please, contact me with any questions. I am the spokesman and in contact daily."

Another pause, one that seemed quite long after the loud interrogation. David turned the knob and backed into the office. "Thank you," he said, "we'd all appreciate your cooperation."

An understatement.

David closed the office door. Darkness engulfed him.

Marie Rey lived in Potrero Hill, an older, residential area of San Francisco. David parked on a steep, slanted street to await her arrival home from work and stared at the row-houses that lined the block. The breeze felt dry today and smelled fresh off the bay. David rolled down his window to let the noises of cars and work trucks keep his mind occupied.

He tapped his foot on the break. He popped the radio stations back and forth to the news, music, talk shows. He tried not to stare at Marie's old police photo; he couldn't help but see Tony there, too. Marie wasn't pretty. No one looked good in those pictures. He hoped she hadn't changed much, that fifteen years in prison hadn't toughened her soft features. He hoped her face hadn't aged.

But David had to take a second glance when the young woman he watched get off the bus began to unlock the door of the blue apartment he'd picked as being Rey's. Springing forward in the seat, he clutched the steering wheel. "Good God Almighty," he said and stared a good solid minute before he opened his car door. In the photo, Marie had long, straight hair. The woman down the street had cropped hair −kinky hair, her cheeks were now hollow. Marie must have lost thirty pounds.

"Ms. Rey." Dashing across the street between vehicles, he caught her before she entered the home. How much Marie had changed. She had stooped to pick up her bags of groceries but left them on the cement to swivel around. He could see her face up close. "Marie?" David asked to be sure. Her face grew angular, unbelievable so, as she studied him and if it weren't for her almond shaped eyes, her son's identical wide eyes, he'd have turned away.

"I am Marie," she said. "What do you want?"

A hint of accent filled her nervous question, enough to remind David of her decent but at this moment, she did not look Latino. In the silence, her eyes were the only matching features, now narrowed with suspicion. But yes, this woman was Tony's momma.

"I'm Sgt. David Straus from the Sheriff's Bureau." When he displayed the ID and badge from his wallet, Marie stiffened. He wanted to rub her shoulders, hold her hand and give her comfort but he kept his arms straight down at his sides. "I'm off duty," he said, "you've nothing to...to worry about." His smile did nothing to put her at ease and with his shallow breath that followed, he decided that telling someone their child was alive, was as difficult as the times he'd had to do the opposite. "Could we talk privately somewhere, Marie?"

Oh, how she studied his face. Several seconds, maybe minutes passed while David let the woman stare at him. He analyzed her, as well. He watched her lips pinch into a hard burgundy line, her chin form into a knob of unpolished bronze. The breeze touched their hair, but not one of Marie's curls moved.

When she did open her mouth to speak, she gasped for air. "I will talk to you." Turning to push on her door, she stopped herself and yanked the door back shut. "There is a playground two blocks over." She pointed south. "I will put my groceries inside and meet you by the swings."

"That's fine," David said. "Good." Good for her to meet him in public.

Marie didn't open her door again until after David crossed the street and sat in the car. He watched her go in and then drove over to the park.

The playground was a crabgrass lot. Tires that hung from ancient eucalyptus trees served as swings and David sat on the only bench, about five meters from the sidewalk. He watched the gray squirrels, more active than the few children that tumbled in the sand pile but he didn't have to watch long. Marie approached him with steady short strides and he smiled again, to try to ease the uneasy vibrations. She didn't sit with him, just stared into his eyes.

"Tell me what you want."

Marie didn't evade the point and David knew from experience, he wouldn't have that privilege either. "I'm here concerning your son, Anthony." Lightening flashed from her eyes, suspicion and distrust that nearly flattened him against the back of the bench.

She spun around.

"Marie— no." He grabbed her arm. "Tony's alive."

"And you are the devil." She jerked her shoulders

to free herself. "Let me go or I will cry rape."

"We found him in the Oakwood Cemetery, alive. It's been in the news. Tony and four other kids who died in Dareing that very same day are all alive, Marie." Somehow, the run of his sentences eased her struggle. "I'm not here to hurt you." Releasing his clutch from around her arm, he stuck his hands out from his sides so she could see them. "Please," he said, "sit down. Let me explain."

So sharp were her eyes, so black and wary as she dissected his every breath and his every blink. David knew that nothing he did would go unnoticed.

"It still won't make much sense but I swear I can prove what I'm saying."

Another long, long pause where Marie didn't move. She remained an immobile statue, her stare so intense that it made David's neck and the back of his head warm when he turned to sit at the bench. He settled nearer one end and folded his hands together in his lap.

Marie sat down too, erect and balanced on the edge. Her hands were at either knee, clasped tight along the weathered board. She perched there, poised, ready to exit at the slightest sign of foul play. Her eyes never left David's body.

"You're aware of the earthquakes and storm of a few days ago?"

No answer. No nod, no flinch, no acknowledgement.

"Because of the quakes," he said, "almost the entire acreage at Oakwood Cemetery got ripped apart and many, many caskets came up. I went to the scene because a live infant girl was found and soon after, four older children were located. The older kids told me their names."

"What about Tony?"

David caught his breath. He began again. "A five-year-old boy gave his name as Anthony Llamas Rey. He spoke of a babysitter named Lori and a young playmate named Levi." David gripped the bench, too; the next part became the hardest of all. He looked straight into Marie Rey's eyes. "Tony told me about being left in the car at the drive-in to watch a movie and going to sleep."

She hid her face with dark shaking fingers. She hid her shame. Tears fell through her hands but she made no sound and still, David thought it over a good long time before he placed his arm across her shoulder.

"Tony is asking for you."

"And is that suppose to make me feel better?" She shot up to her feet, her eyes ablaze with shards of obsidian. "Why are you here?" she said. "Why have you told me this? No one will let me see him, even…even if what you say is true. Just go away. I have paid my debt to you. Why must you tear out my heart again?"

"Because Marie…Tony wants you." David stood up to squeeze her arm harder and to keep her from running. "He needs you. He loves his momma, just as you love him. Your debt *is* paid."

A disbelieving gape parted her lips. She tried to speak but she couldn't.

"You have second chance," David said, "if you want one."

Marie fell to his chest. "I do."

"You can't tell anyone about this."

"I would not."

"It must be kept secret Marie, for the children's

safety." David set her away to look deeply into her eyes. "Do you understand?" He gripped her shoulders, to both steady her and to make his point clear. "You cannot tell another living soul."

"I would never tell."

Her knees began to shake and her shoulders, her arms and her fingers so that David hugged her with all his strength. He pressed her quavering body to his chest and hugged her until all his strength disappeared.

"I understand. I swear to God."

Marie whispered so that the promise and the tears felt like they melted into David's soul.

"I would never hurt my Tony again."

Heat rose up to his face and his heart pounded in his ears with her remorse. He stroked her back and caressed the soft tight curls at her head. "We trust you Marie," he said, and she looked up. "You must understand that, too."

"I will not disappoint you." Her wet cheeks glistened in the sun. "I swear to God up above, I will not disappoint you."

David's gut, his heart told him that Marie would do her best to care for Tony now that she had a second chance. As they stood in the park, his arm still around her slender shoulders, he realized his own eyes stung with moisture. Something had hit him...at his core. "Are you all right?" he asked.

"Yes. I think that I am."

Stabilizing Marie with one arm, David walked her to the car. "We've gathered names and birth certificates, DC's," he said. "All the fingerprints match."

"You said there were four others?"

"Yes. All died the same weekend. I've contacted Mr. and Mrs. Adams," he said, "their son drowned that weekend in the Dareing canal. Two of the children are brother and sister, their parents are gone from the same fire."

"Fire?" Marie stopped as if the word triggered her memory. "I think I remember a big fire." Running her still trembling fingers through her hair, David helped her into the car. "Mister…Sheriff," she said and he turned to face her squarely when he entered his own side. "I have forgotten your name."

He grinned. "David Straus," he said. "I'm a sergeant." And in that second when Marie actually smiled back, he became David to her, the air around them softer, somehow.

They stopped at her home to gather a few belongings before going to Brigham Hospital. Marie picked up a sweater and faded yellow scarf, then put them in a drawer. She put her groceries away and filled the bag with a different sweater but the very same scarf. She swept up the three pieces of red onion skins that had fallen on the floor.

"Marie?" David watched her in amazement. "Something's bothering you, beyond the obvious. What is it?"

"I…I have changed," she said and her eyes glassed up all over again. Marie's bony fingers tugged at the tight black curls that now surrounded her face. She pressed both hands on her breasts. "What if Tony does not know me?"

David cringed −inside, the thought had certainly charged through his own mind and he found himself once again, choosing his words very carefully. "Before you see Tony," he said, "we'll meet with the two doctors who are caring for the children." Cheap answer. He knew it. But he also knew that Jessica, the pediatrician −the woman, would have a far better grasp on how to handle this one that he did.

Marie nodded as she stared at the grocery bag still in her hand. She inhaled and she sighed and she contemplated. "David," she said, "I have kept my Tony's little Bompa." She smeared the latest run of tears off from her cheeks. "Maybe he will remember."

"Bompa?" David frowned but agreed, with what he did not know and Marie disappeared into the bedroom to return with a small stuffed bear in her hand, complete with matted scraggly fur and four sagging legs. The bear sported a button nose of some pink striped flannel…and black Latino eyes.

"Sure." David nodded. He understood now and when he put Bompa into the grocery bag, Marie's smile grew wide. Her chin lifted.

The intimate group of doctors and parents accepted her that evening with no questions or comments of her past. David introduced Marie to the Adams's, Jessica, and Dr. Bishop, and they sat down. His nearness did not relax Marie like he'd hoped. Her arms stayed crossed, tight at her bosom.

Dr. Bishop spoke to the group first. He relayed the medical findings of the tests so far and David decided this was a good place to begin. Marie would have a chance to size-up everyone, unobserved.

"Our concerns about their immune system stood at the top of the list, and it seems now, that our fears were unwarranted. In fact," Dr. Bishop said, "my unofficial interpretation is that their systems are ultra in the important proteins. It is, of course, too soon to know for sure, and what the data means or why, is yet to be theorized. We've given all the children a basic mental and memory test that will enable us to compare them with others of their respective age groups, plus observe development within themselves."

"Their physical condition, blood pressure, respiration," Jessica said, "all remain stable, in fact, perfect. Psychologically, they seem settled, play well between themselves, but are growing bored with their surroundings. They want to go outside; want us to bring in a Nintendo." She shook her head and glanced at Dr. Bishop and the Adams's. "I believe it's time to tell them the truth."

"Steven's already questioned us about a lot of details," Sheila said. "He asks for things that haven't been popular in years. Of course, we answer him as best we can, but I'm afraid, most times we aren't too convincing."

Everyone nodded, all could relate, for each had faced the same problem. Jessica spoke again, looking at Marie. "It's doubtful that the younger children, Sally and Tony, will understand what has happened to them. We think they should be told, regardless. If nothing else, they will feel like a part of…our family."

When Jessica held out her hands to the group, David used all his restraint to keep from pulling her into his chest. He felt good inside, damned good. Jessica was determined to keep the family close. And she had a way of putting ideas into words for him, feelings into action. Yeah. Jessica had a way. So what if the kids didn't grasp the concept of death or life. They understood love.

"I do have one more thought," Jessica said, but

stopped as if the impression had not fully budded in her mind. "I think it's important that Tony and Marie be reunited a few days before we do tell the children. Tony is young and will need his mother's support and reassurance. If she is with him, as the Adams's will be with Steven, he may accept the facts better. Trust is involved."

"And I agree with Jessica," Dr. Bishop said. "The medical and psychological signs point positively in that direction." He raised his eyebrows. "Of course we've no histories to examine for reference in this area."

"Doctor...Jessica?"

Marie's voice came just above a whisper and her hands were so shaky that David wanted to grab hold of them, too. But he didn't.

"I have changed a great deal," she said. "I used to be fat. My face used to be plump, my chest much more to snuggle into when Tony felt sad. And what about my hair?" Again, Marie's lips quavered and the threat of tears hung in pools beneath her black eyes. "Tony has only seen me one way."

The silence that followed reminded David of his own speculations this afternoon. He heard Jessica sigh. He watched her breasts rise with apprehension and her shoulders straighten.

"You're right Marie," Jessica said. "There could be a problem. Tony may not rush to you. He may be frightened." Jessica stared at Dr. Bishop. "I think we should tell Tony ahead of time that David has found his mother. I don't think Marie should just walk in like Steve and Sheila did."

"You have a valid point," Dr. Bishop said. "The reason for a controlled reunion is no longer an issue.

Tony is much younger, more of a shy personality."

"Marie has a toy of Tony's." David reached for the sack and brought out the scraggly stuffed animal. "Do you think this would help if she had the bear with her?"

"Yes." Jessica's expression nearly lit up the room. "Absolutely…"

Her eyes turned so blue that David caught his breath to wait out the current of energy, his undeniable desire for her that swelled up through him and then settled back down –another damn wave. He watched her stroke the matted forlorn bear and he gripped the table to keep himself from caressing her the very same way. God. Did his expression look as desirous as he felt?

"It's perfect." She was quick to hand the stuffed animal to Marie. "I'm sure it will help. And Marie, I'm sure your voice is still the same. Talk to Tony, say things like you used to." Jessica's smile changed to an endearing grin and she checked her watch. "I see no reason why you can't see Tony now. It's eight forty-five. The children are in bed but it's doubtful anyone's asleep. We put them to bed at eight-thirty and the party begins. They chatter and make silly noises. We patiently remind them it's bedtime for about fifteen minutes." She laughed. "Then we get stern."

Dr. Bishop gathered his papers, the usual indication that the meeting adjourn, and the Adams's stood up, too.

Jessica walked over and put her hand on Marie's arm. "Please don't be afraid of Tony or what's happened to him," she said. "He's the same smart little boy you knew before. He's just been in a special hibernation."

"Yes, I understand." Marie held up her chin, just a little bit higher. "Sheriff…David has been very kind to me."

Turning toward him, Jessica held a gleam in her eyes that nearly made his legs rubberize.

"I think you would be our best messenger to tell Tony she's here," Jessica said. "Tony's expecting you to find Marie."

"No problem Jess," David said. "Could we talk about Kurt and Sally a sec, though? You say the parents should be there when you explain what's happened to them. I want to be there for Kurt and Sally." David shoved his hands down into his pockets. He'd made up his mind and didn't give a shit if anyone argued or if the idea sounded good or bad. Goddamnit, he just knew he wanted to be with them.

"I think it's excellent."

David spun around. Dr. Bishop agreed –Dr. Bishop.

"Good," David said. "I'll go tell Tony."

Eleven

David entered the isolation ward to tell Tony he'd found Marie. Dim lights, nameless aromas and the soft hum of monitors encompassed him as they had the evening before but he felt a difference, as well; he heard his name, whispers and giggles all being stifled for the nurse's benefit.

"I know you guys are awake," he said, and four heads popped up. A chorus of "David" filled his ears. "Close your eyes and I'll turn on more light." He touched the panel by the door until the room shone bright enough so that Tony would be able to see his mother.

"What's new, Sergeant?"

"What's new?" David smiled, surprised that Steven hadn't caught him off guard, again. He grabbed

Kurt's foot as he passed the cot. "Oh not much…
except that I found Tony's mom."

"Momma." Tumbling out of bed, Tony dashed
toward the door so that David barely captured him with a
wide sweep of his arms.

"Whoa there, tiger."

"Where is she?"

"She'll be here in a few minutes. She's talking to
Dr. Jessica. Can you wait?" For a second, David thought
the wiggly, excited child might not be able to wait. "How
about we sit down here on your bed and all watch for her
together."

Sitting beside Tony on the cot, David wondered
what the little guy could be thinking. Tony said nothing
past the first display of jubilation, his big black eyes
focused on the doors.

When Marie and Jessica did walk in, Tony did not
move.

"Aren't ya gonna say hello?" Prompting Tony to
his feet, David edged him along towards her.

"That's not my momma." Tony balked and
squealed like a pig. His toes dug into the floor. "You
cheatin' David. You trickin' me." Tony grasped David's
leg in a painful pinch but then he lunged forward to jerk
the stuffed bear free from Marie's hand. Speeding away,
he circled everyone to get back to his bed and to throw
himself upon it. Tony sobbed. "You trickin' me, David."

Marie had halted, her face ashen.

"Talk to him," Jessica said. "Go and comfort him
the way you used to."

Marie looked at Jessica. She looked at her son as
his hurt, confused cry chilled the air. "Tony…" Collapsing on his bed, she gathered him to her breast. "My

baby. I am your very own momma. We are not cheating you. My baby, my baby, my baby…"

The sounds of Tony's cry subsided as he strained to hear more words, more of the shy familiar voice.

"How would I know to bring Bompa if I were not your momma? I am with you now." Swaddling Tony up in the cotton blanket, Marie gathered him inside her trembling arms. She swayed back and forth to cuddle him. She cried. She prayed.

She sang a scarcely remembered lullaby.

Two down. One to go. David felt hungry for the final encounter, anxious to find John and Lynor Alexander, Tammy's parents, and he wasted no time to drive to Vallejo-Deli Saturday morning. He didn't prepare. He told himself that this time would be easy, but regardless, his gut twisted. He'd been prepared with Marie and her reaction had knocked him on his butt.

John Alexander worked as an executive planner for Vallejo-Deli and the streets to his home led David to an expensive neighborhood. Vallejo-Deli formed a union of two cities, one small, one large, Sunset Avenue a new addition to both. Walking up the brick pathway to the double doors, he decided that John had been paid well for his strategy in combining the two.

David rang the doorbell three times before he turned away. "Damn." He walked back and started his car. "Goddamn." He rubbed the dry from his eyes in an attempt to clear away the weary aftermath of Friday's shift and stared up at the two-story home. He would phone head next time and not waste a trip.

He planned that next time would be 11:30, right

before lunch, which meant, he decided with a yawn, no nap.

Once on the main road back to Dareing, a big new department store caught his attention and he wondered how he'd missed all the banners and balloons on his way over. "Good God." A clown stood on the street corner to wave at parents and children as they entered the parking lot and all at once a forgotten memo struck him, a note that David had written to himself.

"Toys." He pulled in, and within forty-five minutes, sat back in his car. "Shit," he said, "this'll never do." He knew about trucks and what made them interesting but not about dolls. David wanted the one he bought Sally to be just right, but hard plastic bands kept this doll tight against the back of the box. He wouldn't dare give Sally a doll and clothes she couldn't get out. There was a utility knife in his desk at headquarters. Yes, he'd cut out the bands there and head right over to Brigham Hospital.

Off duty, David pulled into the front lot used by the public. Entering through the main entrance, he stopped to survey all around him as he always did before his shift. His habit −a bad habit.

"David? Uh, Sgt. Straus. You're just the man I need to see."

Christ. A man and woman stood near the officer who'd called his name. David hesitated. He shifted the boxed doll from one hand to the other. He didn't want to talk to anybody. He just wanted to see the kids. Damn.

"What can I help you with?" David ran his fingers through his tangled hair and tucked his shirt in with his free hand.

"These folks are asking about the cemetery…

117

Oakwood, Sergeant. Would you mind answering a few questions?" Turning away, the officer left the couple to explain their needs themselves.

"We…" The man wiped the edge of his grayed temple to catch a single bead of perspiration as soon as it appeared. "We don't need to know about the missing children, Officer, it's about the others. We drove to Oakwood this morning but it looks to be all shut down. They have all the roads blocked off. We decided to come here."

The others? "Shut down?" David took a moment to follow them. "Oh." He nodded. "You mean the corpses." With his understanding the woman paled so that her tan faded to a color nearer the shade of her blond hair.

"We buried a child there quite a few years ago," the man said, "and we were wondering what was going to happen, if ours was uncovered."

"I know it might be silly, Officer," the woman said, "that we care after so many years, but it's very important to us that we find out if she's been disturbed."

A big tear pooled up in the woman's eyes so that David took a deep breath. He did feel empathy for her and it was certainly understandable that she be concerned but right now? This morning? Shit….

"It's not silly," he said, "not in the least, and I *am* in charge of the Oakwood incident but Sgt. Gable of Special Forces is handling the reburial along with Clark and Talbot Funeral." David took out his notebook and pen; he didn't plan to send them away empty handed. He gave them Gable's name and extension along with times best to call. "Now if you'll give me your name and number, I'll make sure Gable knows you're looking for him. I see him everyday."

"Yes, of course. John and Lynor Alexander."

Alexander. The name hit David like a fist in the nose. Sweat erupted on his face. His hand paralyzed. John began spelling the name, letter by letter, while David forced his fingers to move. He told himself this was coincidence, told himself to follow up, ask questions.

"We live in Vallejo-Deli, on Sunset Avenue."

"Mr. Alexander..." David looked over and swallowed his shock. "Mr. Alexander...I think I can help you after all."

The light inside Sheriff Williamson's private office came from the morning sun. John and Lynor sat on the padded bench and David rolled a chair from behind the desk to sit opposite them. He wanted to be less formal, and began his Oakwood Cemetery story at a different place. He told them, before hand, the details of their daughter's death, a mark of insurance that they were the correct parents of the infant at Brigham Hospital.

"My Lord she was uncovered. We want her immediately Officer, so we can, so we can..." John pulled his wife into his arms.

"Tammy's death has caused us years of heartache," he said. "She was our first child and we could never replace Tammy and...we could never live through it if it happened again."

Rolling his chair just a little bit closer, David nodded and he inhaled. So they lived through their careers. He rubbed the back of his neck where a square of sunshine rested on his bare skin and he wondered, once again, at how people accepted death, or didn't accept it, and how their lives would always alter. Somehow. Always.

He took an even deeper breath. "Our information to the media concerning the five living children that were found at the cemetery is false."

Again, he received curiosity. The Alexander's both stared at him, brows creased while they waited to learn how they were involved.

"What I am about to tell you must be kept secret," he said. "Under no circumstances can you break this confidence." David knew he could trust them and his explanation came very easily, the footwork and documents involved with the identification, the matching fingerprints and of course today, he would have some matching DNA.

His story ended at the same place as it had with Marie and the Adams's, the very same way, with silence.

David expected Lynor to cry. He couldn't ignore the wild energy that vibrated the air. But she and her husband just sat there. They just sat and stared at each other.

Lynor finally looked over. "So…is Tammy still ours? The way you're talking is—"

"Oh yes." David stopped her train of thought by a gesture with his hands. "Tammy is yours. We are by no means taking over custody of your daughter. In fact," he said, "I drove to your house just an hour ago to tell you. The doctors are urging a quick reunion so Tammy can continue the emotional ties that were forming before her death. You will have to share Tammy with us for sometime, but we are not taking claim, taking your rights."

Silence again. David watched John hover over his wife, Lynor still pale with both disbelief and wonder. He watched their knees shake and watched when then they began to pray. They folded their hands and bowed their heads and prayed until the tears ran down their faces. David knew the couple needed to cry; crying had been a healthy release for all of them.

Shifting in the chair, David tried to release his own accumulation of emotion, his own release to have these powerful reunions behind him, always amazed at how everyone accepted the idea. No parent he'd told yet had challenged the facts to be untrue, they just wondered at the motives of those involved. Had they all dreamed of their children coming back to them so often that acceptance was already there?

"When can we see Tammy?"

David motioned to the door and stood up. "I can take you to Brigham this minute if you like, introduce you to Jessica...Dr. Jessica King," he said. "I'll be just a sec, need to clip the bands away form this doll before we head over. Toys for the kids." Leaving the Alexander's in the sheriff's peaceful office, David found the knife and thought again how they hadn't asked many questions, but neither had Marie...or Steve and Sheila. Either his explanation was perfect or, he grinned, they're too damned shocked.

David and the Alexander's found Jessica in her office with two laptops running, several stacks of papers, a sandwich and coffee on top of it all.

"I've been so caught up with the little ones," she said, "my paperwork is suffering." But Jessica set it aside once more to speak to the anxious parents and take them to their baby.

"The sergeant has explained everything quite well," John said. "I guess this is just so unreal that one doesn't know what to ask or say."

"I have a question." Lynor's voice trembled and her hands were still a bit shaky as she twisted the strap of her purse. "Tammy died of crib death, but Dr. King, she was healthy, strong and alert. That's why we were so devastated. We had no warning at all, no clues to what would happen. And it could happen again, couldn't it? Tammy could just as easily quit...quit breathing now as she did then."

"Yes. Yes she could." Jessica squeezed Lynor's arm, Jessica's answer thoughtful and caring, as always, before she spoke. "I won't say that it can't happen again, but in our favor, Lynor, we have learned a lot about crib death since then. In ninety-nine percent of the S.I.D.S. cases, we've found that the victims have been born with a slight defect or underdevelopment in the central nervous system. Their ability to control breathing and heart functions, or both, are often limited. These infants, as possibly with Tammy, don't receive the signal to breathe." Jessica smiled and inhaled. She grasped Lynor's trembling fingers. "Minute, electronic devises have been perfected for babies who have other kinds of heart and lung disorders and, as a precaution, we have set the system for Tammy. If her heart quits, or she fails to take a breath, an alarm sounds to alert the nurses who can revive her. We have experts who train parents for the emergency, as well, and we have also learned that very simple precautions such as back sleeping and cool room temperatures for night make a difference. But so far," Jessica said, "Tammy hasn't missed a beat, or a breath."

Looking at her husband, Lynor sighed. Perhaps she'd not taken a breath, at all. And to David, she finally appeared more her thirty-eight years of age, not older. But her skeptical frown still remained.

"Will...we ever get to take her home?"

"Most definitely." Jessica's tone inched up higher to match her excitement. "We'll have to keep her for a week or two more while the major testing is taking place. I don't mean surgical type things," Jessica said, "in fact, most of our time spent with the children is just for careful notations of their activities. And often the same scans they have already received are re-taken so we can determine if there are any internal changes."

Lynor smiled, and when she took her husband's hand and closed her eyes, David saw the room exhale. He and Jessica excused themselves so the Alexander's could have a moment alone.

"So what do you think?" David asked as soon as they closed the office door. He grasped Jessica's fingers and led her to the sofa nearby.

"About the Alexander's?" Jessica said. "I think they've already accepted Tammy. Lynor seems pessimistic but that is expected. Negative thinking is a way of detaching from vulnerable situations so as not to get hurt –again. I'm glad you found them so quickly, David. Thank you."

She squeezed his hand in return; he could get very used to how the velvet felt along his fingers.

"I didn't find them," he said and a remnant of his surprise over their chance meeting seemed to flitter in his mind. "They came to the bureau to find out about Tammy, about the reburials. I don't know why, Jess, but I feel better about them for being upset that their child may have been disturbed."

Reclining in the seat, David did feel better, his brain finally free from the shadow of families to be found and as if played from a distance, he heard Jessica's melodic voice to where he allowed the gentle sound to settle around him like a hypnotic chant. Her touch felt soft on his flesh and David memorized all her fingers, her petite wrist and her smooth painted nails while he rubbed her hand. After closing his eyes for only a moment, he gazed at her body where the white skin of her arm nudged the generous curve of her breast. He wanted to lie there and take a nap; he wanted to sleep there for hours.

"What's in the sacks?"

"'What sacks?" David slipped the bags of toys behind him and smiled into each sunny face.

"Those. You know."

"These? Yes…well I guess we'll have to look." He laughed and winked at Jessica to tell her that he could keep the big kids occupied while she reunited the Alexander's with Tammy. He could hear the baby fuss. Tammy would respond with ease to her parent's attention, so like the Pied Piper of Brigham, David led the children to the furthest bed.

"Okay," he said and sat down, "first we have to be a little quiet. Those new people are Tammy's mom and dad and we don't want to disturb them."

"The lady has blond hair," Steven said, "they could be."

"What's they'a names?"

"Their names?" David loved the innocence. "Mr. and Mrs. Alexander," he said. Two proud parents…again. "Are you ready?" He rattled the bags and watched eyes grow wide. David felt excited, too, at what he'd chosen, and the kid's reactions said he did fine. Kurt and Tony followed the flashing police cars into the fort made of blankets and beds. Steven went off with his truck but with the science book in his hand, as well. David liked the idea that Steven enjoyed reading but could relate to the two boys inside the fort. If David were five again, even nine, an electronic vehicle of any kind would far out-weigh a book for entertainment.

"Put on her nighty." Sally climbed into David's lap and laid the blanket and clothes out on his arms.

"But it's the middle of the day," he said.

"I know but she went pee."

Groaning, and with lip curled, he lifted the doll from his jeans. Sally wrinkled her nose, too.

"Anyway, you do that," she said. "I'll go cook the bottles."

"Good idea." While Sally pretend at the other end of the cot, David felt thankful that he hadn't bought the tea set, too, but Jessica's blue eyes soon drew away his attention, Jessica's lullaby voice.

"This fits you, David," she said.

"The p.j.'s?" He knew exactly what she meant. Jessica had looked at him that way before when they'd spoken about Kurt and Sally's future. He couldn't quite describe the expression then, either. "How did it go?" He nodded toward John and Lynor. At one time he'd heard sobs from across the room but the kids didn't seem to notice so he didn't look over.

"Just fine, David."

Jessica sounded relieved, but when he looked into her face, sadness hovered there, an emotion she'd not been able to banish before she sat down. David took her hand. "You were thinking of keeping her yourself, Jess," he said, and she used David's own favorite response —silence. But as they observed the Alexander's across the room, Jessica's shoulders straightened. She watched them cuddle and love their daughter, the circle now complete.

David watched Jessica. He soaked in her blue eyes and the strands of blond hair that fell from her braid. He watched her breathe. Saw her blink. She smiled. Her ears moved.

And then they laughed.

"You know what's next, don't you David?" she asked. Jessica took the doll from his hands and turned the nighty around the right way.

David wondered if his life hadn't been spun around, as well. "Yes, I know what's next," he said. "Are you going to tell the kids or is Bishop?"

Jessica grinned. "You are."

She was teasing. Look at her face. "I suppose I've had the most practice," he said but still, the idea knotted his stomach.

"And you've done a beautiful job."

If she only knew. Each time had been hit and miss, hit the right words to keep them from throwing something at him, miss the others that would probably say it the best. Each time there had been a different choice of sentences that convinced them he wasn't crazy, that what he said really happened.

"I'm going to tell them," Jessica said, and in the morning David found himself back in the isolation chambers surrounded by the intimate family. The Adams's sat by Steven. David held Kurt and Sally close on his lap and Marie sat near them with Tony snuggled deep into her side. The Alexander's were present as well, to complete the group and acquaint themselves with everyone. The people they'd just met would be connected to the rest of their lives.

When Jessica finished, less than an hour had passed, even with her lesson on keeping promises and the few questions that Steven asked. The children's reactions were much the same as their parent's, calm and accepting.

"So you didn't save me after all." Steven walked over to David and looked straight up into his eyes.

"No." David reached over to squeeze Steven's shoulder. "Not from the canal, anyway."

Steven grasped the concept better than any of the children. Kurt registered it all in his young mind to be digested again, later. Sally and Tony listened and soaked in the family emotions around them, just like Jessica said they would.

And then the children ran off to play.

When the adults all gathered around Lynor and Tammy, Dr. Bishop caught David's attention and excused them to a corner of the ward.

"I'd like you to do a bit more investigative work for me," Dr. Bishop said. "You see…until now…I didn't have time or −or was unable to assemble all my disjointed thoughts."

Nodding, David wondered if the man had assembled his thoughts, even yet.

"There are two factors common with all the children," Dr. Bishop said. "They are one −that all the deaths were related to the respiratory system; they all quit breathing from direct lung failure."

"And the other factor?" David asked.

"The other…" The doctor paused. "Clark and Talbot Funeral Home."

"What?" David could see why Bishop hesitated at

the second common factor. "That makes no sense."

"Something happened there." Dr. Bishop rubbed his face and chin. "Something that holds the missing clue. Every one of the children has a faint scar at the base of the neck, a sign that they were embalmed but obviously, indisputably…." Bishop finished his thoughts with his eyebrows knitted along the top of his nose. "Those kids were not embalmed. They were only made to look that way."

Twelve

David drove to the Clark and Talbot Funeral Home at nine, Monday morning, and parked under the porte-cochere of the huge Spanish-style building. He'd driven by the stucco parlor several times over the years but never noticed that so much intricate iron work trimmed the windows and big glass front door.

When he got out of his car, David studied the grounds. No hearses waited nearby, so he guessed there were no funerals today, or at least this morning. Oleander hedges attended the front drive. Palm trees and tall Monterey Pines dotted the lawn −a strange combination of foliage, but rather nice. The front door sparkled squeaky-clean and the smell of the red geraniums greeted him from huge Mexican pots.

Inside the building looked as immaculate as the outside. Plush ivory carpet flaunted streaks from the vacuum and David hesitated. His shoe prints would show. And he stared at the three bronze, armored-up Spaniards looking at him. They did nothing to make him feel at ease, for in the mirrors, he stood among them, dressed in blue jeans and loafers. Still, David chose not to tuck in his shirt better or push over the tuft of hair that had fallen to his forehead, instead, he breathed in the polished smells and his uncomfortable emotions. He heard no sounds −no music, no footsteps and walking further in, David decided that even the depressing music they always played at the services would be better than this.

Down a short hall, a door stood ajar and he headed over to look for someone. He'd come without an appointment but that never stopped him anywhere before. He just always packed his ID. A woman spoke as he appeared in the doorway.

"Yes…" He introduced himself the usual way. "I'd like to speak to Otis Clark," he said. Sgt. Gable had informed David that Talbot, of Clark and Talbot, died a few years ago. Gable also said that Otis Clark was a conscientious businessman and very eager to clear up the mess at hand.

"Is this concerning Oakwood," the secretary asked, "the investigation?"

Nodding, David inhaled but he did not smile; he couldn't deny his apprehension being here. The secretary didn't smile either. She picked up the phone and touched a sensor of some kind, explained the situation, and got a fast reply.

"Mr. Clark is in the lab," she said. "He asked if

you'd mind waiting in his office."

David agreed and followed the woman, wondering, as he often did, what would happen if he said he did mind waiting. Someday he'd have to say it just to find out. The secretary showed him to a deep leather chair, disappeared, and David felt surrounded by a completely different atmosphere. He saw the same ivory flooring and dark furniture but he didn't feel stiffened by the elegance, indeed, he found he could relax enough to sit down. He smelled coffee here and sweet rolls. His footprints didn't mar the carpet nor did he smudge the shiny desktop when he touched it. He stretched his neck and arms.

The maroon and navy shades in the room coaxed his head back into the chair and he gathered his thoughts, mainly, Sunday afternoon's debate with Jessica and Dr. Bishop. The three of them had decided, after well over an hour of argument, to tell Otis Clark the truth about the children. The decision came with great difficulty but they could think of no other way. Vague questions would receive vague answers. The team needed to learn exactly what happened to the five graveyard children that weekend some sixteen years ago. To guess would be dangerous. And so David talked to Gable about Otis Clark. David wanted Gable's gut impressions of the man and he knew Gable would have them.

As it turned out, Gable felt good about Otis. David admitted that he felt better, too, in the office than at the front door and he rubbed his temples and the back of his neck with his slight relief. Ironic. The one who'd fought the idea to bring Otis Clark into their confidence became the one to do the job.

"Hell of a deal, anyway," he said and stood up to

131

stare out the big picture window. The scenery before him revealed a typical summer morning. Rains of the night glistened in the shade of the only Acacia tree and hints of a Pacific breeze worked in the leaves here and there.

David thought of the kids, Kurt and Sally. Their day wouldn't be typical; Jessica and Sheila planned to take everyone for a walk around the hospital grounds. He thought of Jessica and smiled. He remembered her dress and the way the shimmery flowered material caressed her thighs, the colors so alive that right now, he could almost smell flowers and he breathed in. He'd reached for her wrists once, to make his point clear and she felt so delicate to him that he couldn't help but imagine she'd be the same all over. He wanted to hold her to know for sure and crossed his arms at this chest as if to block the restless wave of awareness that swept over him. The woman. The kids. The emotion. "Sweet Jesus–"

"I'm sorry to keep you waiting."

Spinning on his heals, David jerked from the deep voice that destroyed the vivid image in his mind. He hadn't heard the office door open or close but there a man stood, materialized from nowhere.

"N…no problem," David said and cleared the gravel from his voice…from his brain. Otis Clark introduced himself, a tall bulky man, plenty big enough to handle the dead weight of any muscle-bound hulk who might have met misfortune. David noted Otis's round face; the red cheeks hinted shyness, a great contrast to the brawny body. His eyes held compassion.

"I wasn't honest with your secretary," David said. "My few questions might take up at least an hour of your time."

"You're in luck." Otis Clark motioned to the chair

where David had been sitting. "I've over an hour before any appointments and Sgt. Straus, I'm as eager to get Oakwood cleaned up as the county, get the press off my ass."

The two men sat down and David smiled; Otis's frankness certainly came as a nice surprise. He expected stuffy, like the gray tailored suit and fancy building. "Has the media been a bother, Mr. Clark?"

"Call me Otis, please, and yes, this whole controversy that ended up closing the cemetery three years ago is being dug up all over again. I'm sure you've seen the news. And of course, all my topographical findings, my technical maps and data that supposedly proved the area as stable are being put to the block." Otis ran his wide hand across the top of his head. A habit drawn from once having hair?

David felt sorry for the guy, the press could be vicious. For that same fact, though, David felt relieved; the journalists bit at Otis Clark's tail instead of his. Otis's cemetery maps became the primary reason David hadn't been hounded to death with questions about the kids. Oh, the children were in the news but had fallen back, a breather while the wolves gnawed awhile at Clark's twenty year old coat.

"Is Sgt. Gable off the case?" Otis frowned. "He's not ill is he?"

"Oh no. No to both questions. I'm working on a different end than Gable."

Otis's eyes grew wide. "Well sure. The five kids. Good God, you don't know how sick I felt. They're okay, aren't they?"

David had little time to nod.

"I haven't heard much in the news about them.

Tell me…" A smile crossed Otis's face. "How in the world do ya wrap up the media?"

"Under certain circumstances we can hold them off rather well," David said. "I have to admit, though, they're being pretty respectful as far as keeping their noses out, hindering our investigation, and such."

"Which I suppose," Otis said, "brings us to why you're here."

David agreed and wished again that he *wasn't* here. "I need to know your firm's position on embalming." Drawing in a deep breath, he knew damned well that Otis caught sight of his apprehension. "I know it isn't a law," David said, "you don't have to embalm anyone."

"It's our policy to embalm all corpses unless it's requested not to by the family, or sometimes before cremation."

"And how long has this policy been in effect?"

"For as long as I've been involved here," Otis said. "I joined Talbot as a partner when I turned twenty-five. That's about twenty-five years ago." Otis's eyebrows meshed together. His eyes narrowed.

And that, would include 1991. David thought to go ahead and tell Otis but he didn't. He wanted no doubts. He wanted to be positive. He had to convince himself he had no way out before he disclosed the secret. "What's the embalming procedure?"

Otis rose from his leather chair. "Harold is working on an elderly woman right now, we can–"

"No. No that's fine." David assured him with palms up. "A brief explanation is all I'm after."

"You get a stomach for it after awhile." A different smile captured Otis's face. "But I'm surprised,

Sergeant, you've no doubt seen a lot worse than I have. They're most often cleaned up by the time we see 'em. But," he said, "not always."

"You're lucky. And I know what you mean about getting a stomach for it."

"I bet, sure as hell, your gut was put to the test going down Oak Hill after the kids. At least Gable has a system going. Suits. You were first, weren't you?"

David chuckled and leaned back as if chased by the creepy memory. But in no time he put his foot on his knee, hands in his lap.

"Embalming is simple, really," Otis said. "It's only used as a preservative to keep one's color looking... alive until the burial. A small incision is made into an artery at the groin, base of the neck, or sometimes under an arm. The solution penetrates tissues, the blood drains out a vein at another small cut."

"And the solution is?" David asked.

"Formaldehyde, alcohol, salts, dyes, basic stuff to prevent dehydration."

"Otis?" David placed his hands on the desk in a hot tight clench. "Would there be any reason why a mortician might make his incision and then not complete the routine?"

Otis shook his head. Then his mouth dropped open. He motioned his hands through the air as if taking off for flight. "Sgt. Straus, what did you find on those five kids, if, in fact, we are talking about them."

Shit. "We are."

Otis's chest expanded so quickly that it jerked his broad shoulders. "Then there is evidence of cult involvement." A grim expression changed the big man's face; one couldn't imagine some things, couldn't develop a stomach for it. "Maybe I don't want'a know," he said after a second. "You did say they're okay."

"Yes. The kids are fine." David stared into the brown eyes opposite him to hunt the depths of Otis's soul, and Otis stood still to let him. No one moved for a good solid minute. No one said a word and the vibrations, the emotions and the fear soon settled at David's feet. He shuffled through them to be nearer the desk. He rubbed his widespread hand over his face and the back of his hot neck. "I believe I can trust you Otis," he said. "There is no cult involved, no crime or misdeed by anyone, but something out of the ordinary did happen. Do I have your promise of secrecy?"

"Sergeant. Absolutely." Otis pinched the top of his nose. "If you knew the secrets I have to keep, the shit a dead body can tell ya…you don't need to ask."

Otis smiled and so did David and David began his story like he had before to relate the facts of his investigation first. But then he ended his tale in a different way. "These five kids were brought to your mortuary on June eighth and ninth, nineteen ninety-one, dead, and were all buried at Oakwood Cemetery within six days where they have lived in a state of hibernation."

Otis Clark stumbled around his desk. His eyebrows worked up and down as his mouth tightened into a thin red line. David wondered if Otis read a lot of science fiction.

"Are you positive of this?"

"Positive."

"I'm dumfounded."

"I understand."

"And you say we've been a part of the phenomenon?" Otis waved his hand. "Clark and Talbot?

We did something?"

David stood up so he could look into Otis's eyes. "We have no hard evidence that you did anything, just sniffing…on a sixteen-year-old trail."

"That led here."

"Yes," David said. "Now there may be other trails we've not picked up on, going a different direction, but…" David hesitated. "This particular trail is quite… odorous."

"But not," Otis said, "one that smells like embalming fluid."

"No."

"From your previous questions," Otis said, "someone made an incision on the bodies. Where?"

"Base of the neck and groin. All of them."

"And obviously," Otis said, "they didn't complete the procedure."

"Oh no. Those kids have blood inside them, but its type has yet to be decided. There is a chemical, a drug —something that caused this rejuvenation to occur."

"And you're here to find it. Damn Sergeant." Otis hit the desk with his fist. "I don't know what to tell you. All the chemicals we have around here are common things you can get anywhere."

"But how about in ninety-one," David asked. "What then?"

"Same thing." Otis sat on top the desk. "I remember who you're talking about, at least the date and the deaths. There aren't many people around Dareing that won't recall it. Seven people died that weekend in a fire, a drowning, some kind of car thing." He frowned again so that the creases in his forehead became red canyons. "We were gone that weekend. Talbot and I went with our families somewhere. We only had one employee then, Don Talbot and I did most all the work in those days. Harold, I'm sure, set the kids up, embalmed them." He struggled some with his choice of words. "Harold was on part time but a good worker, had good credentials. When we got back late Monday night he had everything taken care of."

"You've mentioned a Harold before. Is it the same one that's working for you now?"

"Mrs. Day...." Otis glanced at the door, or beyond it to another room. "Yes," he said, "that Harold, same one. Last name's James."

"So he's been with you over sixteen years."

Otis nodded.

"What kind of guy is this Harold?"

"Quiet," Otis said. "Lives alone as far as I know, always has. I don't think he has any family close by, even far away, for that matter. I'd like to say that I know my employees. Some of them I do." Otis's cheeks puffed out with his deep heavy sigh. "But some people are just more giving of themselves, will let you get to know them."

"But not Harold James."

"Not Harold. And...I suppose you get used to how people are after years of the same and accept it. Like I said, he's a good employee, very conscientious. In my business, Sergeant, you don't let a guy go just because it makes you nervous that he keeps to himself. Not everyone can work with a stiff."

David's understanding didn't ease his gut, that twinge he'd grown used to feeling when something didn't hit just right. "Do you like the guy?"

"Yeah, I like him fine. He's not one I'd pick to socialize with but we get along good here, easy to work with, polite. Sticks with business, though."

A weary ache took over David's neck and back. His brains. He rubbed his shoulder. "Shit." He sat down in the chair and put his elbows on his knees, face in his hands. "Is there anyway possible to get answers from this Harold and not tell him anything?" David lifted his head. "I'm going to be honest, lay my heart on the line, these kids mean a hell-of-a-lot to me." As he made the confession, Kurt and Sally appeared before him but he blinked them away. "Their futures depend on the secret that I've told you and only a small, selected handful knows it. And son-of-a-bitch," he said, "the number is growing too damn fast. We have to learn things and haven't time to investigate beforehand when we should."

"Investigate your confidences?" Otis asked.

"Yes." Goddamnit, he suspected everyone. He had no choice.

"I've no reason to expose this secret." Otis made a wide gesture with his hands. "In fact," he said. "I'm better off if it were planted outside with Mrs. Day, tomorrow. If a rumor started that I buried some kids alive —worse yet, that I could bring them back to life. God—" Otis gasped to catch his breath.

"I wasn't worried about you, Otis," David said, "but I'm going to be point blank, I don't get good vibes from what you say about Harold James."

"And I'm sorry about that. Harold has never been in trouble with the law that I know of. Like I said, keeps to himself."

David rubbed his temples, he rubbed them hard to try to compress his scattered thoughts. "I guess I'll just have to punt from here," he said, "say as little as I can and see what happens."

Otis moved toward the door but stopped and turned before he opened it. "Don't know how familiar you are with the decomposed."

David pointed easterly, to Oakwood Cemetery. "Just down the hill."

"Anyway," Otis said, "the stages of decay, per specified time, Sergeant, is something I can't ever remember and I doubt very much that Harold can, either. Beyond that, bodies decay at different rates depending on how well they're embalmed and how good the casket seals. Many variables are involved. We could approach Harold with the idea that these certain bodies you're asking about seemed abnormal compared to the rest, see if he might recall what he did."

And what choice did David have but to agree? Motioning toward the door, he followed Otis to the end of the hall and through an exit. They entered a large garage area with hearses where two young men vacuumed the interiors. Across the way stood another closed door, oversized in width, LAB-NO ADMITTANCE marked on it in red. That's where Otis went.

The room they entered resembled an operating theater, the temperature much cooler than that of the office. A bread box shaped machine on the wall emitted a faint hum and a pressure gauge danced as orange embalming fluid pushed through the long tube attached to Mrs. Day.

Out of respect, David looked away from the half-naked body. He didn't feel uneasy being here, the room was clean, the chrome tables and stretchers were shiny. But he didn't want to look at the woman.

He looked at the walls instead, at the stainless steel instruments that hung on them, things he'd never seen. Some of the tools were thirty centimeters long and thicker than a pencil. He guessed them to be what went inside the veins during the embalming process he now witnessed.

David didn't ask for sure, he directed his attention to the stranger of the room, Harold James. Harold didn't turn around to acknowledge their presence, he continued to work on the deceased and pull a small, faucet devise from her neck. The room's odor grew strong and David took a second to identify it –formaldehyde, blended with the other solutions Otis mentioned, not a hospital smell but maybe antiseptic, a doctor's office.

"Harold," Otis said, "if you have a minute, I have Sgt. Straus with me to ask some things."

Harold drew the sheet that covered Mrs. Day's mid-section up over the rest of her so that only strands of gray hair were visible. "Yes sir," Harold said, but he still didn't face them. When he did, he looked at David just a second, if that long, then over to his boss to await instruction.

David filed away his first impression…odd way to act for a man in his forties.

"How familiar are you with the situation at Oakwood as it stands now?" Otis asked Harold.

When Harold pushed up his thick glasses, his mouth opened at the same time, as if the action helped the weighty spectacles further along his nose. To David, the guy looked like a bass gulping water.

"You're not being investigated," Otis said. "The sergeant's just found some unusual things at the cemetery."

"Well, I suppose I'm as familiar about it as anyone who watches the news, reads the papers."

Harold straightened his shoulders, as if to add height to his stocky frame but he still stood inches shorter than David. Then Harold tightened the belt of the leather apron he wore.

"I'm working with Sgt. Gable," David said, "trying to match bodies with names."

"I've talked to Sgt. Gable. I know what he's doing."

"Yes." David glanced at Otis. "We've, uh, matched up some kids, ones that were…abnormal." He used Otis's word. "They all seem to come from a time in June, nineteen ninety-one."

"How are they abnormal?" Harold directed his question to Otis.

"The bodies are very well preserved," Otis said. "They're in far better shape than average for that length of time."

"Interesting." Harold pushed up his glasses and contorted his mouth. "Always a lot of factors involved, you know."

"Some doctors and scientists," David said, "are involved with the case and asked me to see if you used anything out of the norm to embalm them."

"When *I* embalmed them?" Harold's chest puffed out. "You said you matched up names…times. Who were they? How did they die? You say ninety-one, I worked part time then. Talbot could have worked on them…yourself, sir."

"Yes," Otis said, "but from the facts I've been presented, it looks as though you handled all of them."

Harold stiffened and he fidgeted with his glasses.

Otis looked at David. David chewed on the inside of his cheek.

"And what, exactly, are the facts?" Harold asked.

"Excuse us a sec, please."

As if they'd planned ahead, David followed Otis out of the lab and the door snapped shut behind them. "I'll be honest with you now, Sergeant." Otis looked David straight into the eyes. "Harold James has a good recall on names," Otis said, "better than most, even. If we tell him the truth, give him the situation, the kid's ages, I'm sure he could relate word for action what he did that weekend."

Otis's broad shoulders, his round face and red cheeks, all captured David's full attention. Otis's big eyes. He didn't blink. Nor did he smile. He just offered his right hand.

"I'll vouch for Harold's integrity."

David stared down at Otis's fingers, at his gesture of good faith, and he saw the biggest step of all right before him. He felt as if his guts lay wide open and he felt that familiar stab of pain right below his heart. His insides were exposed all over again, and to someone like Harold James who wouldn't even look at him for more than a second at a time. Shit.

Why did he even come here? Because Dr. Bishop insisted? Because Jessica touched him? Because her fingers trembled in his hand? David held his breath.

He came here for the kids, to protect their lives. Oh, the doctors and scientist could muddle through, but no one knew how much time the children had. The kids could go on forever, or they could fade away right before his eyes tomorrow, if the answers were not found.

This final decision rattled David, goddamn rattled him to the core and he hated every minute that he stood there to assault his alternatives and come up outnumbered every time. Sure, he could take a day and investigate Harold. He could take a goddamn month. And what if the guy turned out to be a total asshole? What then? They still needed answers from him. They still had to learn how the kids were embalmed.

No one but Harold James could teach them.

"Okay." David inhaled, as if he'd held his very last breath and he grasped Otis's hand. "Okay," he said. "Damnit. We'll goddamn bring him into the circle."

David prayed then…prayed that the circle wouldn't fall around his neck as a noose.

Thirteen

Otis told the story to Harold James. David watched Harold's reaction. He counted the times that Harold pushed up his glasses and shifted his weight from one leg to the other. Harold's fingers squirmed. His lips twitched as if he wanted to speak out but when the story ended he just stared at Mrs. Day. David stared at the dead woman too, wishing she would leave. He'd grown uneasy from her presence, or lack of it.

"I...I did exactly the same thing that I always do."

David hung his head. What a liar, a goddamn kiss-ass liar. David could see that clear as day and he'd only just met the man.

Otis grasped Harold's arm. "You are by no means going to be reprimanded for doing something different to those kids. This story must be kept secret. I swear, there will be no repercussions from me."

Removing his glasses, Harold wiped the sweat from his brow and then he collapsed forward. The color of his cheeks turned white. Harold didn't faint like David thought he had, just clasped his hands to rest them on Mrs. Day's hip, his forehead upon them. David started to speak but Otis waved his hands.

They all remained there, frozen, for what felt like an eon to David.

"I know exactly who you're talking about, the names, the date, everything." Harold stood up straight and spoke only to Otis. "I got a call very early for the Latino boy –Rey. The coroner wanted to know if I could come get him. Course I did, then barely got home and Alexander came. The baby. Crib death. They'd found her early in the morning. It was Saturday, you and Talbot had no funerals Monday and had gone inland for a long weekend, the first weekend I'd been left in charge completely on my own. I didn't embalm the kids right off, went back home again for some reason, sir, can't remember why."

"That's fine Harold, go on."

"Well, I thought I'd do it in the afternoon, do them both at the same time and have it all done. I thought you'd...be proud of me, sir."

Otis nodded.

"Well, things were slow then, if you remember, and Talbot only kept a small supply of solution on hand. I was supposed to order some." Harold put on his glasses. "I didn't get to it. I'm sorry, Mr. Clark. It never happened again. I learned a good lesson. I was young then."

"Harold," Otis said. "Harold, for Christ sakes,

that's sixteen years ago. I don't care now."

Otis sounded like David felt but he kept his mouth shut. Harold took long enough to tell the story without being badgered.

"There wasn't enough to do the baby, I was pretty sure about that, so I went into the storage room hoping to find more, enough to at least get one done. Well, I came across several vials of LS_5. They were sealed."

"LS_5?" David said.

"It's a fairly common fluid," Otis told him. "Was back then. We used it externally to revitalize flesh and tissue cells. We used to spray it on arms and faces right before an open casket memorial."

Otis and David looked at Harold, their eyebrows raised high.

"I just injected a whole bunch into them, rubbed a bunch on, didn't figure anyone would know the difference then cut them to make it look like I'd embalmed them then those two, the brother and sister came in, early Sunday, the next morning from the fire that killed the whole family Saturday night and the Adams boy came. They'd found him in the canal at five a.m. I did the same to them all and ordered more solution Monday. I thought I could go back later and do it right but they held up fine. No one said a word. I...I used LS_5."

"Holy shit." David could barely breathe. "I need to take some back. You said that you *used* to use it. Do you have any of this LS_5 around now?" Some kind of weird, vibrant electricity pulsated straight through David's body so that he could hardly stand still. "I need to take some back to the lab."

"Hell," Otis said, "I haven't ordered any in over

ten years. Have you, Harold?"

Harold shook his head, but an odd strained expression seemed to pull at his mouth so that his lips moved over to one side. The more he tried to compensate for it, the worst it became.

"Harold...Jesus Christ." Otis stepped up beside the table. "If there's something else," he said, "for Christ sakes, say it."

"The vials were in a box." Harold shifted his glasses so they sat back center upon his nose. "I opened all of them," he said, "used all nine bottles. There might have been some in one container left."

When Harold began to rock on the balls of his feet and push up the glasses, yet again, David wanted to shake him.

"Mr. Clark, Otis, sir, I realized I was...." Harold looked down at the floor. "I put all the vials back in the box, even the empty ones, and returned them to storage. I thought if you or Talbot went there you'd see the box and not know any difference. I thought if you needed some later, you'd go down and find them, thinking a foolish mistake had been made."

David frowned. Harold's logic didn't seem all together...logical and he wondered why Harold didn't order a few at a time to replace the empty ones. "How about this storage room?" David asked. "Do you think this box might still be around?"

"What?" Otis grimaced. "After sixteen years? No. We do a good job of keeping up, cleaning things out. Empty bottles would have been thrown out."

"It was the old cellar, sir."

"The old cellar? Is that right?"

"What is it, Otis?"

"When we built on the new chapel and office, we closed up the old section. Nothing much in it if I remember right, nothing of value. We just put a heavy lock on it and planned to clean it out later. Come on." Otis waved toward the door. "I'm a great procrastinator at some things. Why do today what you can do in sixteen years."

The old storage shed stood at the farthest end of the sprawling mortuary and as David followed Harold and Otis across the grounds, his optimism grew with his every step. They walked, single file, to the very back but paused, three abreast, at the top of a narrow wooden staircase that descended along the cement wall to the basement. Rain and heat had blackened the wooden rail, broken plaster chips and paint, dirt and leaves, littered the steps. This part of the establishment hadn't been remodeled with the rest. David shook the wobbly handrail. Had Otis even been near this end in sixteen years?

"Cost too much," Otis said as if he'd read David's mind, and descended the stairs without hesitation. He looked over the rusted padlock only to wrestle with his key to get it in. "No one ever sees the back of this place, anyway."

David agreed. The fence around the acreage ruined any visibility from behind or on either side. "Are you sure that's the key?" he asked.

"I'm sure." Otis checked it again. "I've threatened to clean out some of the keys on this cussed ring, too."

After fighting several minutes with the mechanism, Otis muttered, stepped away, and then he

149

kicked the closest panel near the latch with the flat of his foot. The door burst open with a bang but slammed back shut, cracked down the center.

"Geez," Otis said, "must have hit something." He pushed the door open and poked his head in. The shed looked pitch black. Otis tried the light switch.

"I could get a flashlight, sir."

"Yes, Harold." Otis turned around. "That would be good, thanks."

When Harold disappeared up the steps, Otis and David sat down on the bottom one.

"You know this is damned hard to believe, Sergeant."

David's eyebrows shot upward into distinct thoughtful arches. "Call me David, okay?" Resting upon his elbows, the official title all at once sounded formal to him, stilted. He inhaled. "For some reason," he said, "I feel like we've know each other a good long time. What do you mean in particular −hard to believe?"

"Everything," Otis said. "Harold for god sakes. The LS_5." Otis glanced over. "No one that I knew ever injected it, never held the qualities of embalming fluid. I imagine if Harold shot enough in it would, I don't know..." He struggled for words. "Keep a body hydrated, keep one from shriveling up. It's gonna smell real good in there."

In one breath, David understood. The mildew in the cellar had crept out into the daylight and slithered up their noses.

"What'd you keep in there?"

"Just chemicals," Otis said, "boxes. Junk." He stood up and scuffed his shoe in the dried mud near the door. "It's been flooded a hundred times I bet, rotting

150

wood."

"No light at all," David said and by the time Harold came down the stairs they'd about talked themselves out of going in. Taking the flashlight, David pushed the door open with his foot until it stopped about one-quarter wide.

"I guess if you can go down the hill," Otis said, "you can go in there."

"If you'd rather...." David chuckled, turning to face him but Otis's dark eyes said no, like David felt when asked to see Mrs. Day. Well, he did see the old lady and damnit, Otis would have to see this stinking room. "Son-of-a-bitch." The light revealed a disheveled disaster and David's good humor vanished with his next inhale. Wooden storage shelves, ripped from the wall, were all he could see, bins and crates broken beneath them from the weight.

"The quakes?" Otis said. "We had a problem before but always kept an eye on the shelving, made sure they stayed secure."

"Small tremors over the years undoubtedly loosened them, sir, and the last one, as we are all aware, hit pretty hard."

David stepped back to study Harold James, to try to decide if Harold had made the comment to cover-up. Maybe the man had done the damage himself.

Harold James stared back in return.

Swiveling around, David flashed the light inside small black room. "Shit," he said, took a deep breath, and wiggled inside the room.

"Do you remember what area you put the box in, Harold? David, breathe through your mouth."

David listened for Harold to answer. The room

wasn't huge but a general place to begin would help.

"Left wall near the second switch. I remember turning the second one on and seeing the box about eye level."

"You've a hell of a lot better memory that I do." Otis poked his head inside. "I don't even remember a second switch. Move that wood so I can get in, can you David? I'm not so thin like you are. I'll find the switch."

David obliged and handed him the flashlight. Otis climbed over the first set of collapsed shelving that blocked the way and shined the beam around. They could see somewhat of an order to the chaos. The center rows had fallen like dominoes, all piled up to face one direction.

"Damn lucky," David said from behind. "Left." He pointed. "They've all fallen away from that left wall."

"Are you coming, Harold?" Otis didn't wait for any reply, just began to kick and push the bins and boxes for a passageway. David followed right behind.

All the containers sounded empty. A spongy slick moss grew on the shelving, slime that lived off the damp boards, and David felt sure that his jeans caught on every soggy splinter. He inched along, regardless, and after the first few times, paid little more attention. The slivers broke away with the next step. He could feel his legs get wet. He felt a chill despite the film of sweat at his forehead.

"Can ya get up that, David?" Otis stopped to point at the shelves and David jumped onto the second row of framework to walk along the top of the boards so he could get to the opposite side.

At the count of three, they heaved on the last giant rack. David and Otis pushed the saturated wood upward until it stood like before, against the left wall.

"Now where's that switch?" As Otis panted, the beam of light pulsated upon the wall.

"About there, sir."

Standing nearest the area, David hopped down onto the cement floor to where his shoe scraped along something hard. "Wait," he said, "wait a sec." He could only move his foot maybe at inch, if that much, but whatever it was had already buried itself halfway into the hardened muddy residue.

Otis moved the light to reveal a large chunk of glass. Smaller pieces lay nearby it, along with a metal screw-on cap with the jagged edges of bottle neck still attached. "The vial?" he said and trotted the light around the general area, creating figures of deep browns and greens. One thing could barely be distinguished from another.

"There it is," Harold said, "by your foot."

"That?" Otis moved the light so a flap of streaked cardboard peeked out from the mud, the rest of the box lodged beneath some kind of upper support column, fallen with the rest of the structures. "Are you sure Harold? Be sure."

"Give me a hand," David said and Otis grasped one end of the huge beam. Both men grunted with a hardy upward yank and the pillar broke away with a mournful cry, a crack that sounded like the ceiling gave-way.

"Duck −"

Dropping the beam, David hunkered down to protect his head with his arms. The support landed on the floor with a thud. "Damn it to hell," he said. "Get this bastard off my foot."

"You okay?"

153

"Son-of-a-bitch."

Otis hefted the column alone this time, just enough to roll it over until the huge wooden post rested tight against the shelves.

David couldn't breathe, amazed at the man's strength, amazed that his foot hurt so much. His toes throbbed and burst with pain clear up to his knee. If the elusive cardboard box weren't right in front of him, he may have allowed himself the pleasure of passing out.

"You okay?"

Otis shined the light on David's foot. David opened the flaps of the box.

Harold reappeared from the darkness. "That's it."

Otis and David both stared over.

"That's the case," Harold said, "I remember the bottles."

The paper labels, still stuck on pieces of glass at the bottom of the carton, were too faint to read, too faded from years of moisture. But two of the vials lay unbroken, frosted with white finger-crystals from the liquid once inside.

"Let me get it." Otis said. As if working with a bomb, he peeled cardboard from the floor as best he could and wrapped the two vials with what remained. Then he flashed the light toward David's feet. "Need a piggyback ride?"

"No. Shit…." David waved toward the door. "Let's just get the hell out of here."

David could move his foot around at the ankle but nothing more. Shelves and boxes jutted out to grab his shoe and test the pain, and the least bit of pressure on his toes sent red hot needles straight up through his shin. He leaned on boards, hopped on one foot, and when out, hobbled like an old man.

"It'll be okay," he said and rested against the wall. His vision adapted to the sun fairly quickly and then settled upon Otis's worried face.

David could see Harold, too, perched at the top of the stairs with the two wrapped-up vials of LS_5. Harold wore a grin, a smirk that twisted David's gut in pain far worse than his foot. Something burned in Harold's eyes, a daring, foreboding ember, intensified by the distance between them…and the glasses. Harold no longer looked guilty and dog-beaten, he looked calculating. Diamond hard.

Fourteen

"Damn it anyway." David sat on a counter in the Brigham Hospital laboratory to pull off his shoe. After much debate between them, Jessica had left. She made him promise to remain in the lab while she went to get an elastic wrap for his foot and to locate Dr. Bishop. Bishop's scientist colleague, Nevil Morrison, had arrived earlier that week and would come, too.

David looked across the bleached room at the cardboard-wrapped LS_5 that waited on another table. "I hope you're worth it," he said and inched off his sock to reveal a mound of puffy flesh right above his toes. His foot throbbed with deep blue color and he told his toes he wouldn't mind, so long as they turned the shade of

Jessica's eyes. A minute ago, when they argued over his injury, her irises had brightened to Persian crystal. David smiled. He really didn't mind her attention. He loved her attention; he just didn't like to be fussed over. He'd been hurt far worse than this before. So why did he give in?

Noises from the hallway caught David's ear and he swung his leg over the edge of the counter. Dr. Bishop introduced him to Dr. Nevil Morrison, a thin man in his late fifties with a wild batch of black curly hair. Morrison had few wrinkles and looked to David like he kept himself in good shape. The two doctors walked right over to the mangled carton and removed one of the unbroken vials. Jessica examined David's foot.

"You say this is LS_5?" Dr. Bishop held one of the tall, oblong bottles to the light and peered in.

"Yes," David said, "but that particular batch is sixteen years old. That is the exact chemical used on the kids."

"Just how big was that board, David?"

"What? Jessica…no, a beam, a–"

"Sergeant." Nevil Morrison spun in a half circle. "LS_5 is nothing more than Lytensol, a base solution. It's in products for fortification but has few uses on its own. Do you see what I mean?" The doctor's brown eyes narrowed. "It's filler, Sergeant…hydrant. Nothing more. I believe you have been played for a sucker."

"Now wait a damn minute." David hopped off the counter and limped over to the scientist. "The funeral parlor used this LS_5 potion to wipe over a corpse before an open-casket funeral," he said. "I don't care what it's made of. All I know is that this dude, Harold James, shot the kids up with it, over a bottle a piece and from those exact bottles."

Dr. Bishop held up his palms, or did the deep lines etched in his face halt David's argument?

"Nevil," Bishop said, "to my knowledge, LS_5 is used strictly as a foundation, never used, even in its earliest experiments, for medical reasons, no basis for it."

"Toxic, if not handled correctly," Morrison said. "No one ever injected it and lived."

"But if one were already dead?"

The lab fell silent. David could feel Jessica's warm body as she came up close beside him. He could feel her, but he didn't hear her steps nor did he move, even as his toes throbbed from his weight.

They all watched Nevil Morrison, watched him turn the bottle around and around so the sunlight refracted off the crystallized liquid inside. Muted prism colors danced on Morrison's face and shoulders. He stood mesmerized, contemplative. And then he walked away.

Dr. Bishop spoke after another long silence. "I'll let Nevil do some private research," he said, "get his basic theory structures down. What happened to your foot, David?"

"A post," he said. Bishop didn't seem to want any more information, he'd already turned to leave and so David hobbled back to the counter and tried to act like his foot didn't hurt as badly as it did. Jessica inched right along with him.

"Have you seen the children?" she asked

"No Jess." He shook his head and hopped back upon the lab counter. He'd much rather talk about the kids than his foot, his foot and the LS_5.

"Are they okay?" he asked.

"Oh yes. You know we went outside."

"I didn't forget...honest." He wanted to call her sweetheart. He wanted to touch her soft blond hair. "I planned to come and meet you," he said. "I wanted to see how they reacted. It was a good day but damn." Wincing, he sat straight up when she touched his bruise. "Got tied up a lot longer than I thought. Don't wrap that too fat, I have to wear a shoe, you know, work my shift tonight."

"David." Jessica jerked up to stare into his face. "You can't work with this swelling. Your foot has to be elevated, iced, or it will hurt much worse than it does now."

"Maybe I can't, but I'm going to."

When Jessica looked into his eyes, she said no more. Her shoulders sank.

"Sweetheart...." He said it. He inhaled. "I have to." Clasping her fingers, David urged her over so she stood between his legs. He ran his hand along her braid and he could smell the apple blossom or honeysuckle or some kind of exotic, intoxicating flower that stole his senses and clouded his brain –turned his goddamn knees to warm butter. "Have dinner out with me tonight," he said and watched her expression soften, her lips relax into a pink satin oval. Her eyes grew wide, specked with azure and sapphire and....

"Absolutely not. I just advised you to keep off your foot and then you –you invite me out?"

"Jessica...." Brushing her with his thumb, he traced the translucent silky skin along her cheek where it had blushed with red. David wanted to kiss her so damn bad his hands shook and his arms and he leaned forward so that her lips brushed against his as she spoke.

"You're staying home," she said. "I'll fix dinner

for both of us. I can come to your house."

Caressing her face one more time, he stroked her with the back of his fingers. He'd agree to anything. Anything. Just so he saw her again.

Jessica arrived at David's apartment around seven. He greeted her in his rolling kitchen chair and the unmistakable aroma of chicken fried steaks and gravy. Sheila Adams had fixed a meal large enough for them all before going to the hospital for her last visit of the evening.

"Sheila seems to be doing fine," Jessica said while she settled David at the table. She elevated his foot on another chair and placed the ice pack, twice, to get it just right.

"You know I hate this fussing around." David squeezed her arm so she would turn to face him and he smiled. Who was he kidding; he couldn't get enough of Jessica fussing over him. "Thank you," he said. "And yes, I think Sheila's doing fine. Guess her old man trusts me, leaves her here alone."

"But can you be trusted?" Jessica laughed, and when she bent to dish his plate, David rubbed her hip with his hand.

He watched the steam rise off the potatoes. He soaked in the softness at his fingertips. His stomach tighten. "Only with some women," he said, and to his surprise, she didn't remove his fingers. They just slipped from her side when she sat at her place.

"And Marie...." Jessica said as if they'd been talking about her all along, "the Alexander's. They're visiting as much as their work will allow. Did you know

Lynor has put in her notice at work? In two weeks she'll be a full-time mother."

"I hadn't heard," David said. "That's great. Good for the Alexander's. All the families are making the adjustment. But what about Kurt and Sally?"

"I know." Jessica's cheeks puffed out with her sigh. "We have to find them a home. I'm going to ask Paula Reynolds to do it."

"The same gal that's going to help get new ID's for the kids, right?"

"Yes." Jessica nodded with her fork poised at her mouth. Then she put the fork back on the plate. "I've been thinking about that quite a lot, getting new identifications. I agree, it's the simplest way and hardest to trace. But the concept always seems funny to me for a second, that the children will be adopted by their very own parents."

"The feds hand out new ID's all the time, Jess, give a person a new name, occupation, home. Life. It's best, sweetheart. The kids know who they are. You can't take that away from them."

Looking down, Jessica stared at her plate but then she agreed and a quiet grew between them. David wondered about Kurt and Sally. They'd been on his mind all afternoon, and now, with this Paula Reynolds in the picture. He closed his eyes and braced himself as his muscles tightened, one after the other, up from his legs to the top of his head. What if Paula split up the kids and destroyed the only family connection they had left? Jesus. What if Paula split up the kids? "I want to meet the prospective parents that this public representative brings in," he said, "be in on the screening."

"David?"

Jessica's frown, her oval-shaped lips said she'd read his mind, again. He swallowed.

She touched his hand. "I assure you, Paula is more than trustworthy. She's qualified, respected, and rightly so. The work she's done for the county is marvelous."

"You don't need to sell me on Paula, it's the...." He didn't finish, he just stared into Jessica's eyes. "Damn it," he said, "I'm scared, okay?" He clenched his fist around his napkin. "For some reason I get these feelings; I hurt for those two. It's like I'm feeling what they are and I can't help it. I just can't. Damn." He ran his fingers through his hair. "Believe me, I've tried to stop. I look at little Sally, she doesn't understand. She feels lost and alone and− and Kurt. God." David pressed his fist on the table. He saw his own white fingers. "I just want to take him and shake him and say cry, damn it. Let it out. He's trying to be a man and the little shit isn't big enough to have that laid on him by anyone, least of all himself."

Jessica knelt beside David and he held her in his arms. He pressed her to his chest, stroked her hair, and weaved his fingers through the long blond strands that fell down her back. He'd never seen her hair out of a braid, never felt the satin. The kitchen light drew golden glimmers through the waves and the sight of it made his arms tingle, touched somehow by the electricity. In some ways Jessica looked like Sally. Their hair was the same. Kurt's mouth curved up at the edges like Jessica's. All their eyes were shaped by innocence.

"Jessie? Hon, are you crying?" David inched away to wipe a tear from her lashes.

"No."

"Tell me what's wrong."

She shook her head. "Nothing's wrong."

"Please Jess, tell me." Hugging her tighter still, David kissed her hair. He kissed her forehead and her temple and he turned so their lips were but an inch apart, so she could see deep into his eyes. If she could just see into his eyes, he knew she would have to tell him the truth.

"I don't know, David," she said. "It's everything, a-and…nothing." Threatening again, her tears hovered at the edge of her eyes and she buried her face into his chest.

"The kids?" he asked and she nodded. "Jessica, are you falling for them, too?" David squeezed her tight for she had nodded again. He could feel it on his heart.

David didn't know why, but resentment crept up his spine when Nevil Morrison asked that Harold James be brought to the Brigham laboratory for a conference. Waiting at the mortuary, David admitted to himself that Harold made him uneasy –that look in Harold's eyes, the one that David had yet to analyze. Maybe that's why he felt irritated, he couldn't fit Harold into a category.

A box.

"David." Otis stepped into the office. "Don't tell me something else is going on. I don't think I can stand anymore excitement so soon after yesterday."

"No Otis." David laughed. "No. I think enough has gone down here lately to last a decade." They shook hands, like two buddies who'd gone through the war together. "Came to see if I could borrow Harold for awhile. This doctor scientist character, Nevil Morrison, wants to speak to him first hand."

"Harold's going to be quite the hero, eh?"

David's mouth dropped.

"Good thing this is hush-hush," Otis said, "the old boy might run for the high country if too much notoriety came his way. Don't believe Harold's one for a crowd. You okay, David?" Otis stared over.

David forced a smile. "Sure. Just tired. Haven't been home to sleep off the midnight shift yet."

"Have a lot to do today?"

"No." David straightened his shoulders. "No I haven't, actually. Need to fetch Harold if I can. That's about it."

"Well, come on." Otis made a motion with his big arms out wide and a silly grin on his face. "How's your foot?"

"I can walk, thanks, if you'll slow down. Where are we going this time?"

"The new and improved storage room, David. It's not far."

This time down the wide mortuary hallway, David looked around as they went. Pictures of Otis's family were tacked up, along with the various physical changes that the building and business had progressed through. The atmosphere felt warm and serene and David never dreamed in a million years he'd find solace in a morgue. "This is sure a nice place, Otis," he said, "you've built an excellent business here. Lot of hard work."

Otis stopped. "Thanks." He paused at the doorway and ran his hand over the top of his head, his chest puffed out to its full expansion.

David stared, once again, at the look in Otis's steady brown eyes. He'd *felt* that look before, some kind of intense primordial connection that he couldn't even begin to explain. The back of his neck broke out in gooseflesh but then with no more comment from either, Otis pushed open the door.

"Harold," Otis said, "a scientist at Brigham wants to talk to you about the LS_5. I'll finish up."

"Yes sir."

Catching his breath in his throat, David pinched it tight and he wanted to do the same to Harold −keep the little man from scurrying around the room to get ready. No shy little mouse worked here. No. David smelled a stinking rat and a chill of the complete opposite slithered down his arms. God…he shivered from the contrast of emotions and the disparity. Something had him cornered and completely on the edge.

"I can't tell you enough how serious this situation is, Harold," David said as they headed back down the hall and Harold turned just long enough to pushed up his eye-glasses and give David that strange facial contortion. "Secrecy here is very important to−"

"You," Harold said.   "And the others. I haven't forgotten, Sergeant, nor will I."

Harold's smile looked genuine −genuinely malevolent, if that combination was at all possible and David memorized Harold's square face, the squinted eyes, the creased lips. The film of sweat at Harold's nose. David secured the picture in his brain.

Starting his car, he pulled ahead of Harold so he could lead the rat to Brigham. "Shit." During the drive through traffic he told himself, over and over, that he was projecting dragons, a bad habit. He needn't fear Harold James. There's no crime in feeling like a hero. Is there?

He'd have to check into it.

Fifteen

David left Harold in the lab with Nevil Morrison, left all his troubles there for now, and headed straight to the isolation ward. When Sally ran to greet him, the first to receive his long awaited embrace, the world seemed to right itself in an instant. "How's my girl?" he said and picked her up to hug her snuggly to his chest.

"Oh pwetty good," she said, but before he could stop to read her expression, Kurt appeared, his eyes big and green.

"David. Wow," Kurt said, "Jessica told us you wouldn't come and see us today."

"She did?" David knelt down to be Kurt's size but jerked up from the shot of pain in his foot. "Why wouldn't I come?"

"Cause of your toes."

Ruffling Tony's black hair, David chuckled.

"Jessica said you couldn't even walk."

"I bet she said I *shouldn't* walk, Kurt. How about we sit down."

They all gathered around. "Well?" Steven said.

"Well what?"

"Yo owie, David," Sally told him. "Don't we get to see it?"

Sally made him laugh. He was truly surprise at their concern. "Why in the world do you want to see my foot?" he asked. "We've got to find you guys something more stimulating to do if that's the only excitement around here."

"Come on." They begged. "Jessica said it's bumpy and green."

"Monster foot. Monster foot–"

"Okay. Okay." David waved his hand. "Lordy, what have I got myself into? Hush down now and I'll show you, just so you can see I haven't a monster foot." Laughter sang throughout the room, David's the loudest of all. "We'll wake up little Tammy."

"Baby's with Jess'ca," Sally said.

"Remember though," David said, "Jessica told me not to come and be on my foot. Now if you kids tell that I came here, I'll get in trouble."

"We won't tell," they said. "We promise."

"Won't tell what?" The question came from behind him, from across the big room.

"That he's hew, Jess'ca." Sally pointed. "You not s'pose to know so you won't give him a spanking."

David grimaced. The situation was funny, hilarious, according to the children, nor could Jessica

167

keep a serious face, even after her persistent instructions to David the night before that he go straight home after work. "I'm sorry Jess," he said and she walked over, his voice loud in the suddenly quiet room. All four children had quit laughing, aware of Jessica's vibrant blue eyes. "I had to bring Harold James down," he said and in an instant the weight on his chest returned. "Morrison."

"Yes, I know, David. But did the man need an escort?"

"No, sweetheart." He exhaled. "Harold didn't need an escort." David didn't tell her why he came with James, that he'd become obsessed by the need to have a talk about secrets.

That Harold James didn't give a shit about secrets.

"So what did Morrison say?" Jessica stared a good long moment into David's eyes before she placed Tammy into his arms and knelt down to pull off his sock.

"What did Morrison say to Harold?" he asked, "I have no idea. I didn't stay. The swelling's gone down some, Jess, and I can curl my toes this morning."

"Yes, I can see." When she smiled, and as if by invitation, the children crowded in closer to join in a chorus as she wiggled each digit. "This little piggy went to the market..."

Their voices danced in the antiseptic air, an odd combination.

"This little piggy—"

"All right, already." David groaned but they continued the rhyme as Jessica moved each toe up and down to check the mobility...as she took her sweet-ass time. "Okay you guys." David tried again. "You've had your fun."

Smiling even wider, Jessica looked satisfied with

her revenge and David even thought he heard her hum when she placed the wrap back around his foot. Steven went to his cot to finish a story with Tony. Jessica put Tammy in bed for a nap but Kurt and Sally remained very near David and he snuggled them against his sides.

"Been sleeping good?" he asked. "No more bad dreams?"

"Pretty good," they each answered, pretty good being their usual reply.

And, as usual, David nodded. He wished they'd say more but he had no idea how to draw anything out of them. He had zero experience with children, and with a frown, he thought of the home they might go to. Pulling them up closer, his heart twisted to a complete three-sixty. Hopefully, the new couple would know more than he did. And it would be a couple, damnit. And it would be one home for both kids. "Christ," he whispered, he'd make damn certain.

"David? You okay?"

"Yeah, Kurt…" He inhaled, slowly. "I'm okay. Are you okay?"

"Yeah, I'm okay."

Each one knew the other was lying. Each one knew the other knew and David stared into the big eyes opposite, green eyes filled with doubt and fear, with anger and love. He lifted Kurt upon his knee to squeeze him and to stop the deep dull ache in his own chest.

"We love you, David," Kurt said, and his eyes spilled over with a rush of tears. His little body shook. His voice rang high. "You're like my daddy was, David."

"And Mommie." David swept up Sally to bury her against his heart, too. "I want Mommie to come back. I want my bedwoom."

"Can they David? C-can they ever come back like we did?"

The questions poured out, the expectations, the needs of ones so young and with their innocence and faith already destroyed, David could barely say the words, the cruel hard truth. "No, son," he said, "I'm sorry. They'll never be back. God. I am so very sorry. Please forgive me."

Forgive him for what? For saving their lives? For falling in love?

For wanting to give them the life he never had?

Instead of sleeping that day, David tortured himself, uncertain that he should have told Kurt and Sally that he loved them, too. The confession just came out. He didn't take time to consider the consequences. What if they put their trust in him now and he disappointed them? What if that disappointment broke their already fragile spirits, all they had to their name?

But what, dear God, would he do when they went to live away with someone new?

David turned over and kicked the wad of blanket onto the floor. He buried his face in the pillow. A picture of Jessica popped into his mind and her intense blue eyes as she watched him struggle to comfort Kurt and Sally. He'd begged her, silently, for answers, but she never replied, he just saw that now familiar expression on her face as she listened. David learned about Kurt and Sally, how life once had been for them. He heard about their playful father. They remembered Momma.

Jessica stood there the entire time but said not a word, just guarded the small circle as they absorbed one another. David dug around at Kurt's guilt. The boy believed that he could have saved his parents if he'd awakened sooner. David chipped and axed away at the notion until Kurt understood that he'd done all he could, understood, that David had once dealt with the same guilt when his own father died many years ago.

"You can do it, David," Jessica had said after he'd tucked his exhausted children back into bed. David thought he knew what she meant. But she could mean so many different things.

"Sheila?" At the sound of the front door, David jumped out of bed and pulled on his jeans over naked skin. "Is everything all right? Kurt? Sally?"

"Yes, David." They met in the kitchen and Sheila studied his face, his eyes, the stubble on his chin. "You haven't slept at all, have you?"

He turned away. Running his fingers through the tangles in his hair, he opened the refrigerator door to look at nothing.

"They went outside, again. Marie got to come this time."

"Good. Good." David removed a pitcher of tea. "Join me?"

"No thanks. I'll wait and have some with dinner."

David looked at his watch but couldn't find it on his arm. He rubbed himself there. "Tell me about your kids, Sheila."

"Steven?"

"Steven…yes," he said. "Kristy. All of them. What's it like raising kids?" This time he stood still and allowed her to study him just a little closer, but for a moment only, before he turned away to the table to sit down.

"It's beautiful," she said. "And it hurts."

David understood the experiences through Sheila's smile or wobbling chin. Her emotions, not her stories relieved his tensions and relaxed him so he didn't feel so torn apart inside. Because of circumstances in David's life, he never thought of children, never thought of raising a family and yet, here he stood. He'd asked Sheila.

David felt back on top of things −himself, when he and Sheila went to the eight o'clock conference that Tuesday evening. All the parents and doctors gathered together. Dr. Nevil Morrison waited at the head of the table, and to David's great relief, Harold James didn't show. But for a moment he wondered if he'd rather see Harold than the new face among them. Paula Reynolds, the county social worker, stood next to Jessica, deep in a conversation.

Hesitating a moment before he approached the two women, David studied Paula, a pretty black woman, about thirty-five years old and almost as tall as himself. He liked that. He could look her straight in the eyes.

"I've explained to Paula about your feelings toward Kurt and Sally…your closeness," Jessica said after she introduced them. Jessica grasped David's arm. "Paula will be happy to work with you on this."

"Have you talked to the kids?" he asked.

"Yes." Paula nodded. "They're delightful. Kurt and Sally seem as though they're already beginning to adjust. I am nicely surprised."

David's breath caught snug in his throat. Could this mean that Paula would try to run them through the system too fast? He shuffled his feet. Might she settle for parents less patient? Might she settle for less than his heart demanded? Sweat broke out at his brow. He hadn't spoken to Jessica since morning and knew nothing of what had happened with Kurt and Sally after he left. "Could we talk outside for a sec, Jess?" Forcing a smile, he shook Paula's hand before he excused himself and Jessica from the room but when the door closed against the inside conversation, he squeezed her arm, tight, to feel as much of her bare soft skin as he could. He needed more and so he pressed her against him, his hands widespread at her spine to search for the warmth he knew she possessed, her warmth easily found, always, when he reached for her. "What did they do, Jess?" he said, "Kurt and Sally. What did Paula tell them?" Jessica buried her face into his chest. She wrapped her arms around his back, he knew, to avoid his eyes. He closed his own eyes and they burned.

"I explained first, that their time at the hospital was coming to an end," she said, muffled against his shirt. "I told them that I'd asked Paula to help me find a new family for them, some new people who would care for them like a mom a-and dad."

"Damn Jessie, don't choke up now." He pulled away so he could see her face and he heard her sigh…he could feel it. "What'd they say?"

"Paula asked them about their parents and they were quiet again, you know, just said a few things, like what they looked like, not things like they told you today. David. They only opened up to you."

"Shit." He tightened his grip at her shoulders. "Son-of-a-bitch."

"Except for one thing…."

In Jessica's moment of hesitation, in that moment

where the air seemed to pulse with his heartbeat, her eyes turned to a vibrant intense sapphire, color that pulled his insides straight out from his chest.

"Except," she said, "that Paula asked them if they had any ideas, anyone they could remember who they'd like her to call."

"And…" David held his breath. He stared into her guarded expression. "What'd they say?"

"They want you, David," she said. "Kurt and Sally want you for their father."

"Son-of-a-bitch." Releasing Jessica's arms, his hands felt wet with his sweat and he clasped the back of his fiery neck. "I knew I should never have–"

"Never what, David?"

"Never said I love you, that's what. Never reached out to them at all just so I could drop them to the ground."

"But you meant it, didn't you? You meant every word that you said, didn't you?"

"Of course I meant it," he said. "Hell yes, I meant it and they know it, and now I'm gonna turn right around and let some strangers take them away. Jesus–" David turned and grabbed the door casing to dig his fingers into the metal. Never in his life had he felt "like a stinking pile of shit," he said out loud, and faced Jessica again. "I'm no better, worth no more after this."

"David."

Touching his jaw, she held him where the blood pulsed beneath his skin…his angst. She stroked his hot flushed face.

"You can do it," she said. "I know you can."

"You keep saying that, Jess, but damn, you don't tell me what you mean."

"You know exactly what I mean."

Jerking his shoulders stiff, he stared into the clear depth of sapphire once again. She sounded so positive; she looked so confident that he breathed and contemplated and counted the times his heart pounded hard in his ears.

"All right," he said. "Goddamnit, I know what you mean but let me think, Jess. I have to know for sure so, so I'll only let them down once if I—"

"David...."

Encompassing both of her hands in his own, David pressed her fingers to his lips. He read her eyes and delved into her trust. He searched her self-confidence...her soul. "Don't say it," he whispered. "Please...don't say another word about it."

Admitting that he considered adopting Kurt and Sally struck David with a jolt of lightning. He wanted the children, of that he felt sure and he knew, now, that they wanted him. He could make a strong family with them; David knew that, too. Something held him back.

Something. He ran his hand over his face. Kids need a yard and a house, pets and trees. Kids need a mother. David looked straight through the metal door of the meeting room, straight through to see Jessica King, as clear as if she stood right before him.

His job. Only an idiot would take on kids alone and remain on the police force. A week didn't go by without some kind of hazard standing along side him. No officer ever knew when tragedy would strike, coming in the ribs from a hidden blade or just plain getting blasted away. When you're single, no family at home... If he took Kurt and Sally, the odds for them losing another father would triple, at best. And if they loved him, cared enough to put their trust in him, just to be let down again, feel the pain, again. "Damn." He'd be dead, but knowing they were left alone, he'd never rest in peace. The decision loomed around him, gray, black… overwhelming.

Returning to the meeting, he sat in the chair next to Jessica. He took her hand and held it in his lap but he didn't look over at her, not yet. One last question plagued his mind. Would Jessica marry him? He could think of nothing sweeter. Would she want a child of her own? She would have to know that he couldn't father a child, that his time in the Persian Gulf took a precious gift from him. David inhaled. Oh, he could be a man for her; he could make love to her, something he longed to do but Jessica would have to accept that part of him as well and take Kurt and Sally as David would, as his own flesh and blood. God…

He squeezed her hand with both of his and with his thumb, traced the top of each of her long smooth fingernails. Her skin reminded him of a rabbit's fur, a velveteen rabbit and he felt sure Kurt and Sally felt it, too; they understood the feel of Jessica's fingers, her caring, her knowledge.

Noticing that his breath had slowed and the tight clench in his chest had finally disappeared, he glanced over at the woman beside him, his dear sweet Jessica, and watched how she observed those around them. She absorbed everything, he could tell by the way she held her mouth, how her lips turned off to one side, how her eyes narrowed. The sounds of the room, a voice, filtered into his brain. He felt better. Maybe, because he'd organized his thoughts and removed the emotion. Or just maybe, he was being honest.

"David."

Startled from the sound of his name, from that voice again, he shook away all the fog in his head. "I'm sorry," he said, "I didn't hear you, Paula."

She smiled. Did she know why?

"I have a small debate going on in my mind and I wanted your opinion."

Paula hesitated. Was she waiting for his full attention? For his eyes to focus? He rubbed them to hurry the process.

"I need a judge to help me on this new identification for the children," she said. "I have two in mind, A.L. Crenshaw, or Elvin Bailey."

"Bailey, by all means." David sat up in his chair. "And if that's good for you, Paula, I want to come along."

"Love to have you come. Thank you. When is a good time?"

"Anytime." No way would he be left out of this one, left out of Kurt and Sally's future. He took the few minutes right there to decide on some possible appointments, two minutes where Nevil Morrison fidgeted in the head seat, anxious to continue.

Morrison began the second Paula closed her weekly planner. "There have been some very interesting findings these past few days," he said, "and because of that I hope you've forgiven my absence from the last conference. I have met Harold James, the man responsible for beginning this miraculous chain of events."

When David's stomach clenched into a hard molten rock, he pinched Jessica's fingers for counterbalance. His neck turned to fire. Talk like that wouldn't get Harold off the high-horse the man had climbed onto and the more David stared at Morrison the more sick he became, the scientist's words never heard. Why did he dislike Harold so? Did he resent the fact that Harold stood out, did something good? No. Hell no. He just didn't trust Harold, plain and simple. More than anyone else, Harold James could benefit if the secret were exposed.

"Oakwood Cemetery," Morrison said, "the hill is now officially in an active geothermal area, as you are all aware. The bodies buried there were warmed at the two meter level, insulated by the dirt surrounding the caskets. That temperature accounts for the harsh odor that accompanied the upheaval.

"I'll be honest," Morrison said, "I don't know what all this means, but I am certain that everything I've mentioned is a part of the complete picture —the geothermal burial area, the LS_5 injections and lung related deaths." He tapped his finger on the table. "If any one or two of these children would have died from a car accident, say head trauma, or leukemia, I'd bet money that the solution would not have done a single thing."

"So Harold James isn't a hero," David said.

"No, not a hero. He didn't set out to bring back these kids but…." Morrison straightened taller. "He is the cause."

"If the children would have been buried somewhere else," David said, "cold earth."

Morrison shook his head. "I can't be sure yet, but yes, I believe the warmth had a great deal to do with their being alive now."

"So all you have mentioned, the cemetery,

circumstances of death, are as equally important factors as the LS$_5$. I mean–"

"Mr. Straus," Morrison said, "what, exactly, are you getting at?"

"I mean…." Holding his breath, David stopped a moment to reconsider his jumble of thoughts only to wade though them again with his self-examining pause. Jessica stared at him. Everyone in the room stared at him. How could he explain his feelings, the indescribable need to put Harold James in one spot, behind everything? Not in front. How could he relay the fact that he found Harold so obnoxious?

He couldn't. Not today, anyway.

With his silence the subject changed and the meeting was adjourned. Remaining seated, and with his hold still tight around Jessica's hand, he leaned back in his chair and propped his foot upon his knee. But only his countenance appeared relaxed.

"David," Sheila said, "were you going back to your apartment?"

"Yes." He sat forward. "I can take you home anytime you're ready. Did you want to peek in on Steven first?"

Smiling, she looked down at he and Jessica's hands. "Shall I come back here when I'm done?"

"Sure." David glanced at their hands, too. "I'll be here," he said. "I told the little guys goodnight earlier." Besides, he didn't know if he could face them just yet, he didn't know if he could look into their expectant green eyes.

When Sheila left, David and Jessica were alone. The door stood ajar a fingers-width or two and the room grew silent. He could tell Jessica watched him, his skin

179

felt warm from it, like his hand from her touch and he wondered if she counted the times his jaws clenched together or how often his thumb stroked her wrist.

"Something's bothering you," she said, "about Harold James."

He nodded. "But I guess I'm the only one that's apprehensive." He inhaled. Had he stalled on the word a little too long? "Morrison seems to think the man is all right. Have you met Harold?"

"No. Tomorrow."

"Tomorrow?"

"He'll be at the meeting tomorrow night, David."

"Shit." When he dropped her hand, his own felt unusually cool, like his back, where his shirt stuck to his skin from the heat and frustration. He rubbed both his palms against his face and into his hair. Turning away, he stared at the small blackboard, the word $LYTENSOL_5$ written in bold white letters. But he'd not escaped Jessica's reach; she touched him again to massage his shoulders.

"It's okay to feel that way," she said. "I-I'd rather you follow your intuitions now than be sorry later."

"Intuitions?" David gripped his knees. Did that word even fit? Nothing fit. "Damnit, Jessie, you don't know how I hope that I'm wrong. Am I just being over-protective? Am I making any sense at all?" Swiveling around, he saw her eyes, her irises crisp with blue. She understood. But could she, really? He pulled her against him. Right now he didn't care. He just needed to feel her near him. All of her.

Jessica's lips melted into his own, soft and warm, but the sweet moisture inside her mouth did little to sooth his raw emotions.

David met with Judge Elvin Bailey and Paula late Wednesday afternoon. David, as usual, became the one to tell the children's story. He explained the amazing events to the gray-haired judge.

"We need your help, Vin," he said. "We need a complete new batch of ID's for these kids, new birth certificates and school records for two of them."

"And I feel it would be easier…better," Paula said, "if the information remained in this county." She removed a file from her briefcase and picked out several papers. "Here is the list of names, Judge, as they are now –Steven Adams, Anthony Rey, et cetera. These children, as named, shall be left on our discs as dead. Their new identities, as I have projected, shall somehow be shuffled in, as if they'd always been around. I have a schedule that brings each child up to date." Paula handed over those pages, too. "As you can see the infant, Tammy Alexander, is set up as being born February of this year, Anthony Rey's year of birth 2002, and so on."

Elvin nodded. And then he shook his head. "This is mind swelling," he said. "Unbelievable. And I'll say this just once, if it wasn't you, David Straus, telling the story, I'd have everyone involved committed here and now."

The two men stared at one another. A test? A strip search? David's eyes fixed on the man opposite and he didn't look away. He didn't blink. He didn't dare, just did his best to allow the judge inside him. Goddamnit, anyway, David owed Vin his life and here he sat, again, with his heart stretched out on the table…again. The judge had saved him from hell, got him in the service and on the right side of the law. But did Vin still remember every single detail? That night unfolded like yesterday in David's mind and he smiled to where the judge smiled back. Yeah, Vin remembered. Somehow, David knew from Vin's eyes. David had never asked what it felt like to beat the shit out of a punk kid, to jerk that kid up from the dirt, have a gut to gut talk, and then kick his ass one more time.

Elvin swiveled the chair more toward the center of the desk. "Let's get busy." He cleared his throat and straightened his shoulders. "The adoptions shall be handled by me in closed chambers," he said. "I can notarize and officiate for any papers you will need, Paula; I do have first hand knowledge of how this process is managed. Did you know that?"

"We came to you, Vin, because *I* trust you —with my life."

Nodding, and once again, Elvin looked over and smiled that certain smile, the one for David's benefit, only.

"Which, I suppose," Elvin said, "brings up a crucial point —parents. Have you anyone in mind to adopt the real orphans, this brother and sister, Kurt and Sally?" He looked toward Paula. "These will have to be very special people. You say there are no relatives?"

"No close relatives, Judge," she said, and Paula flashed a glance toward David before she continued. "I've found a very distant vein of family living in Tennessee but it's a great-great uncle. He's seventy-five. I don't think so." She looked at David, again. "The children have requested someone that I am considering."

Considering. David shuddered. He knew she spoke of him, her expression was unmistakable. "Tell me," he said, "what all do you consider?"

"Financial status," she said, "mental stability, current family structure."

"Might you place them in a home with other children?" Elvin asked. "These two may require a good deal of attention."

"Lots of attention," David said, "but not that they should be spoiled."

"So are you serious about it?"

Paula turned in her chair so she faced David, squarely, and he opened his mouth. He closed his mouth for the next moment that passed…a moment to think and to breathe. "I'm very serious," he said. "There's a hell-of-a-lot to be serious over." A mountain. "What would hold me back, Paula? I have no wife. I live in a tiny apartment in the city, nice and safe, but kids need a good place to run."

"But it's not essential," she said.

"And my job." David didn't finish the thought, he just looked at the judge with all the questions he'd asked himself, now in the open for all to see. But if he did apply, as Paula said, the same would be asked by others.

"Do you want these two, David?"

"Yes." Vin's eyes, his scrutiny nearly sucked the truth, David's heart, right out of him and just like no years had passed between them, David sensed the hair at the back of his head and on his arms rise up on his skin. He rubbed his forehead and the perspiration on his temples. "I want them bad," he said, "but damn, Vin, I want to be good for them. You know I don't know a thing about raising kids."

Elvin Bailey chuckled. "If that were the prerequisite for starting a family, no one would be able to.

What's bothering you, son?"

"Besides everything already mentioned?" David waved his hand. "I didn't like being a kid, couldn't wait to grow up, you know that. Dad made some big mistakes with me. Mom…" David blinked. "I don't blame them, don't get me wrong. I loved my folks, but how…tell me, how do you know if you're doing right or wrong until it's too late, like with me?"

"Sometimes you don't?"

"But most times you do," Paula said, "if you just stop once in awhile and be present, observant. Parenting isn't a blind alley you head down when you have a child, David. It isn't a treacherous journey that has trap doors and quicksand at every turn.   There are plenty of obstacles," she said, "but it's a lighted path, you can see in front and behind you. Learn from your mistakes. Benefit from the mistakes of your parents."

"Should I apply?" he asked.

"Yes, David," she said, "I believe you should."

Her words hit him right below his ribs and he had to get up from the chair. Walking to the huge office windows of the Courthouse, he could hear Paula and Elvin whisper…not whisper, their voices turned to a monotone drone in his brain. He thrust his hands into his pockets.

Something told him that Paula would endorse his application and he felt that Vin's presidency over the adoption would prove in his favor, as well. So what held him back? His apartment? He'd threatened to get a home of his own a hundred times. Marital status? No. He would take the kids whether Jessica took them all or not. His spirit would be devastated but he'd survive, he'd have Kurt and Sally. No problem with the financial end, he had plenty of savings, a good income from steady years on the police force.

The force…his stomach dropped to the floor.

Sure enough, Harold James showed up at the family conference just like Jessica had warned and David pulled his chair up very near her to sit down as if he could stake a claim. Harold's eyes wandered all over the blond doctor, eyes with an unreadable expression that rankled David's bones.

Nevil Morrison called for attention. "I have asked Mr. James to be with us tonight so everyone could meet him."

Morrison looked at Harold and smiled –one more stab to David's heart.

"Why don't you stand up," Morrison said, and Harold did; he pushed up his glasses and nodded, kind of, more of a nervous bob while being introduced. "Harold is the mortician, who, lucky for us, didn't embalm our little friends down the hall."

Straightening tall, as if enabled by the compliment, Harold looked proud of the act that he kept hidden from Otis Clark for sixteen years. David held his breath.

Morrison put his hand on Harold's shoulder. "I have had some in-depth, interesting conversations with Harold. He's been very helpful in my basic research, a very well-read intelligent man and I wanted to take this opportunity to thank him publicly." Morrison chuckled with an encompassing gesture. "As publicly as I can," he said. "I'm selfish. I realize that this information we all hold secret could –should be told to the world, but," he added, "I want to figure it out. I want to be the one that finds the answer." Morrison rubbed his chin as he watched Harold sit down. "But I have to be honest with all of you, everyday, as each test is taken and analyzed, I don't get much closer. It's as if I'm testing perfect, healthy children. No different. But I'm far from giving up, you understand. I won't give up." Morrison tapped the papers in front of him as he sat down. "I may eventually call in another scientist, but not until I have exhausted all my resources."

"When he says resources," Jessica said, "he doesn't mean the children."

Dr. Bishop laughed. "He couldn't exhaust them, they have unlimited energy. Besides, we don't perform the same test on everyone, we divide the studies among them."

"Which brings me to our next subject."

When Jessica sat up closer to the table and glanced at David, he forced a smile to his already stiff expression. He forced himself to breathe.

"The time is approaching when we feel the children should go home to their parents," she said. "They need stimulation. They need their families. We'll have them come back quite often for check-ups and progress reports but we may be stifling them by keeping them here much longer." Jessica rolled the hem of her blouse between her fingers. "Paula, would you care to finish, tell us what you and David found at Judge Bailey's today?"

"It looks as though we'll be able to run everything through quickly and quietly.   The judge…" Paula acknowledged David with a nod in his direction, "is very familiar in the processes we must go through.   He'll preside over all the adoptions in closed chambers as soon as everything is set. This is also a top priority measure so we can hide the children as soon as possible."

From the corner of David's eye, he watched on as Nevil Morrison squirmed in the chair and David, literally, felt the struggle, like sharp quick jabs in his butt. He shifted too, and cursed the idea, once again, that the children could be exposed. Damnit. David had tried to ignore Morrison's little comment about the secret but there were so many lives at risk. Could Morrison be trusted? David had asked himself that before. "Let's by God get them raised." Standing up, his deep voice hung on the air and his six foot frame grabbed everyone's attention. Looking down, he stared over at Morrison and Harold James. "Let's get them raised…first," he said. "Then, when they're all grown up, functioning, sensible adults, and you still want to tell the world, you can consult them on the subject. If the kids want to come out with their secret, it's their life, fine, I won't stop them. But I swear to God, until that day comes, I'll do everything in my power to keep this lid shut." David's fingers turned white on the edge of the table and he stared at everyone in turn, the scientist, the doctors…parents. Rodents. He challenged anyone to go against him.

"You're right, David." Dr. Bishop's words sounded soft in comparison. "What you have just said is correct. I'll admit I have considered what might happen if we bring all this to light. Some of the aspects are frightening. I agree that it is our moral responsibility to protect the children while they are young but if, as you say, one or more of them decides to come forward as an adult…." Dr. Bishop nodded. He leaned back in the chair.

Everyone looked more resolved to David, like he'd picked some intangible words from the air and made sense out of them. He surveyed those around him, Marie, the Alexander's and Sheila. Nevil Morrison nodded, too.

Harold James stared at the table and cleaned his fingernails.

Sixteen

When David's shift ended early Saturday morning, he felt anxious…he felt excited about Kurt and Sally's weekend visit.

"Sgt. Struas. The press."

"The press?" Frowning, he swiveled around with his hand still gripped on the back doorknob. "Bradley, you sure know how to shoot a mood."

"Were you in a good mood?" Bradley asked and David paused to glance, again, at the exit door.

"Hell, I don't know," he said. "Where are they? What about?"

"The missing kids from Oakwood, Sergeant."

David started to say he already knew, but he had asked, hadn't he? "Thanks," he said and released his grip and by the time he entered the main lobby, a scowl had darkened the lines of his face. Still, the day looked brighter to him now, with the daylight, but no sun had yet poked through the morning fog. Jump-starting his mind, he gathered the handy, side-step answers that he'd planned in advance but he spotted only one reporter, no television camera, no microphone, just one young man with a pad and pen. The media had kept their attention from the kids to the geothermal mess up the hill, but this lack of interest surprised him.

"Sergeant, I'm doing a follow-up report on the living children found at the cemetery. There is a...rumor, that these are not normal children, that there is something very special about all five of them."

David's mouth went cotton-dry. His heartbeat shot up to his ears.

"I'd like to hear what you have to say about it, Sergeant."

"Bullshit." Did the guy say rumor? Rumor my ass. Coincidence? Good guess? Not hardly. Too close to home to be a guess. David's eyes fixed on the eyes opposite. "Where do you get your information from, kid?"

"Grapevine."

"Sour grapes." David chuckled. Or tried to. "You best get a new vine."

"I'm following all the leads," the reporter said. "I'm sure you've had your share of dead ends...or not so dead."

David grimaced from the kid's use of words and he prayed that his deep breath of air had camouflaged the uneasy shift of his stance. "You haven't heard anything from me because there is nothing new," he said. "Unfortunately, things of this nature take a long time in sorting through. Our only clues of the abductors are from the children, and I'm afraid things aren't too clear. The rains and earthquakes ruined anything we might have found at Oakwood."

"Are you saying their descriptions of the kidnappers don't match up with one another?"

That deduction sounded good to David. "Until we can sift it all out we're stuck with next to nothing."

"Then you're going on the assumption that just one person did it."

"Not necessarily." David smiled. "We're following all leads, all possibilities."

The reporter smiled, too. "The children are still at Brigham, right?"

"Right."

"For how much longer and have you located their families?"

"No idea and yes but that info is confidential. The children's safety is at risk." While the reporter checked over his notes, David reflected aloud. "Maybe your... your rumor is more an opinion," he said. "The kids *are* special, damn *lucky* would be a better word. Mother earth saved their lives. Maybe they have a guardian angel or something."

"Yeah." The reporter looked up from his notes. "Yeah...when you think about it, they'd almost *have* to. Thanks Sergeant." He backed away toward the door.

"Listen...." David stopped him, and at the very same moment, told his own heart to relax. He placed his arm around the reporter's shoulders. "We've all hit dead ends, right, and I know how frustrating they can be. Trust me," he said, "I've encountered more than my share of them on this one." David forced out his best put-together laugh. "You get anymore rumors, just come to me and we'll clear them up here. You'll be off to chase a tail somewhere else. I mean that."

David did mean it, with all his heart and soul and when the young man's eyes lit up, David released a long controlled breath. The pup had fallen for his line, happy with the story in his book and the promise of the continued support. But as the front door clanged shut, David could feel himself go pale; he could feel the gray, moist morning air surround him. His feet couldn't carry him fast enough to the back exit, to his car, and Brigham Hospital. Something told him the reporter's grapevine wasn't sour at all but grew sweet and pure and right in his front yard and by the time he arrived at the hospital, depression had eaten away his once pleasant mood.

"David, don't look so worried." Jessica took hold of his hands as he perched on the edge of her desk. "I think this is a wonderful idea, that you take Kurt and Sally for the weekend."

"I'm not worried over that." Inching Jessica nearer, he buried his face into her soft shoulder. "Nothing's worrying me." He saw no reason to tell Jessica about the reporter. Or the rumor. Even so, as he squeezed her tight, he decided to visit Otis Clark later and get some feedback. He wanted to see how Harold acted at work now.

"You're still coming over tonight aren't you?" He set her away from him but not too far, and when she smiled, he found that he could smile, too. He brushed a wisp of blond hair from her temple.

"Yes," she said, "I'm coming."

"I'm just going to lay it on the line to them, Jessie. I know Sally's too young to be asked if she wants a cop for a father. Hell...Kurt's probably too young, too."

"But you're talking to them, David, including them. They'll know they're important in your life."

"My parents never talked with me, Jess, ever. They talked at me. Mom and Dad had troubles of some sort or another all the time that I remember, but never once explained to me or asked my feelings. I just always thought I caused the turmoil."

"David, that's awful."

Hugging him, she stroked the glimmer of smile that touched his lips again. She made him feel important in her life. "Do I sound like a broken record sweetheart?" he asked. "Christ, I don't mean to; I don't dwell on the past," he said, "hell, I'm always more or less looking ahead. It's just that lately...all this has been on my mind, trying to understand, I guess."

"I want to understand too, David. I want to hear what you're thinking, please..." When she studied his face that way, when she caressed his skin, David felt sure she could see what he'd hidden away from her and so he kissed her, full and deep on the mouth so that the tender images would block everything else from his mind. Squeezing her tiny waist between his hands, he explored the warmth of her mouth with his tongue, he searched within until her lips calmed his disjointed turbulent thoughts. When she gazed up again, his worry had vanished.

"Are the kids ready?" he asked.

"They were ready last night."

David never looked at his modest apartment beyond its solitude and its convenience in keeping the small rooms neat. One bath and two bedrooms led off a short hall and that was about it. He didn't have much furniture −less to dust −and he'd gathered few souvenirs over the years. But today the home fell under his rigid scrutiny. He looked at it, now, as he imagined Kurt and Sally were; they took all of thirty seconds to breeze through and check the new surroundings.

David met them in the hallway and pointed to his spare room.

"You two can sleep together in this big bed, or one of you can have the sofa."

Without discussion they chose to sleep together. Kurt claimed the side nearest the door; Sally settled her doll on the other.

"Your room's in there, right David?" Kurt turned to see a direct path into the other bedroom, something, David decided, that would earn a lot of points for the small place.

"Yes indeed, that's where I sleep," he said. "Remind me to get one of those LED sensors, today. You know...a nightlight." He grinned at the thought...a nightlight, for god sakes, whoever would've imagined. "We'll put it in the bathroom so if you have to get up at night...do either one of you wet the bed?"

"No," they chorused.

"Sally does."

"Nuhuh," she said, but the disagreement stopped short when Kurt stared over with his hands on his hips. "Only sometimes, maybe."

"Mom gets her up and has her go."

"Great. How about we do that too, Sally.   And we have to go to the grocery store," David said as they walked to the kitchen.   "But there's something very important that we all have to talk about."

"If we're gonna be your kids, huh David."

"We'll be good. We pwomis neva to do anything eva bad."

"Sally honey. Kurt...." He picked up both of them just to see their green eyes, and then plopped them on the sofa next to one another. David took the place opposite, to sit on the coffee table, and dive into the situation like he would a cold deep swimming hole. The sooner one gets wet, the better. "First, and most of all," he said, "you must understand that I want you to be a family with me. I love you guys." He grasped their bobbing legs. "I love you a lot and want what is best for you...no matter what that is. And we all know that there will be times when you're going to be bad," he said, using Sally's own remark. "But that's okay, it's part of being a kid and growing up. I'll do things you won't like either, but we have to learn about each other and we're bound to have troubles sometimes. It's okay." He smiled but straightened tall and pressed his hands back down on his own knees.

"What's bothering me is that I'm a policeman," he said, "and policemen, you know, go after criminals –people who have broken the law or done things to others and hurt them. There is a good chance, Kurt...Sally... that something might happen to me someday. A criminal could...make me die and you'd be left without a daddy – again."

Their faces said his explanation...failed to explain and David closed his eyes. What he must say, the mere idea of it, filled his throat with gravel. "What I'm trying to get at is, that you might not want me, a cop, for a dad because the chances of me dying are big. Do you see what I mean? What I mean is, you might rather Paula find someone else." He choked. "Someone like a mailman or maybe a doctor, or−"

"Daddy drove a truck."

"What Kurt?" David frowned. "I'm sorry."

"Daddy died and he drove a truck."

"Yes…." David stared at the little ones as they watched his face change, as his eyes widen with comprehension. They watched as he just sat there with his jaw dropped open. Kurt had made a simple statement; the interpretation staggered him. "Yes," he said, again, "I guess what you're saying is that it doesn't seem to matter what a person does." David's own father ran a wrecking ball but booze destroyed him. And his mother? She stayed at home and she died, too. All at once, his chest, his heart swelled with the understanding. With his humility. His love. "Well…" he said in a breath, "I −I guess it's all settled then."

Kurt and Sally knew what that meant and they tumbled off the sofa to tackle him with a double embrace. Giggles filled the rooms, laughter and loving that David had subconsciously yearned to hear for a very long time. He prayed to God it would always be.

The discussion lasted just five minutes but accomplished a great deal and the good strong feelings that came from it followed them out the door and through the day as they shopped for clothes, food, and played in the park. Driving along the streets to Clark and Talbot's, they looked over houses and neighborhoods to discuss their next, bigger home and David listened intently to their suggestions. Sally wanted an orange swing set. Kurt wanted an oak tree, a dirt pile and a cat.

While making some plans himself, David smiled, the picture of blue eyes always present. Jessica...if they were lucky, she would have some ideas for a home, too.

"You kids like Jessica, don't you?" David's question came from nowhere but the children took no time to figure where his mind had been.

"Oh yeah. You like her too, David." Kurt looked at his sister and they both giggled and wiggled in their seats.

David wiggled too. "Yeah," he said and his heart, as always, picked up a beat, "I like her a lot."

A smile still covered his face when they walked hand in hand up the steps of Otis's funeral parlor. They met him exiting through the narrow hall from his office.

"There's the man," David said.

"Well, if it isn't the sergeant. What in the he—world brings you over?" Otis eyed the youngsters with great interest. They, in turn, edged near David's sides, dressed now in new summer outfits and their hair just combed. "Did Syl tell you I'd be here?"

"Syl?"

"My wife," Otis said. "Didn't you call? How'd you know I was working today?"

"I didn't. Hell, I never thought about it being Saturday, just drove over. Am I keeping you from something now?"

"No, course not. I was just heading home."

"Keeping you from your wife then."

"She'll thank you." Otis bent down to be eye level with the children. "And who might you two be? I didn't know Mr. David had kids."

"Sally. My butha is Kut."

"Sally and Ku…rt. Well, how about that." When Otis stood up, his eyebrows stood up, too. Kurt and Sally. "What did you need to see me about David? Nothing's…wrong I hope."

"No Otis, just need to gab, get some feedback."

"Feedback I got." Otis grinned, again. "Let's go out front, you kids can run around and give the lawn some exercise while we visit."

Kurt and Sally darted out the door for an instant game of tag. The sun had broken through the clouds, along with summer's afternoon temperature, and so David and Otis sat on the steps in the shade of the porte-cochere.

"You'd never know those were the kids, would you?"

"No," David said, "you wouldn't." He'd thought that a hundred times today. They'd played and ran and argued like any two ordinary kids would and if no one tried to screw with their lives, he may always get to see those beautiful wide-eyed smiles.

"It's even harder to believe now that I watch them," Otis said. "More reasons than ever why this needs kept secret."

Some kind of deep-set honesty filled up Otis's brown eyes and David soaked in every bit of the phenomenon. He held it in his hands, in his heart –his gut. "Do you have children, Otis?"

"Three," he said. "They're grown now but you know, David, they mean more to me than anything on the planet, and in a few months I'll be a grandpa. Let me tell ya, I'm looking both ways before I cross; I don't want to do anything stupid and miss what's in my future.

"Yeah..." Otis leaned forward and exhaled. "This needs kept secret. Those two will blend in so fast no one will know the difference. Are the others as healthy, David?"

"Every bit," he said. "They're keeping a closer eye on the baby but even she went home this weekend."

"And how did you get elected parent of the day?"

"I elected myself."

"Is that right?" Otis smiled and then he tipped his head. "I'll be damned. Temporary or what?"

"I'm going to adopt them —unofficial at the moment but..." He didn't finish, just smiled and rested his elbows on his knees and listened to the chatter now coming from the side of the building. "Anything they can get into over there?"

"Sprinkler's on the hedge."

"Oh shit." David stood up but halted before he went very far. "I'll just wait." He sat back down. "See what they do. I'm not going to spoil the kids, Otis, but I hate to stifle them too much. They need to have a little fun, get things out of their system."

"But you know," Otis said, "to them, it probably doesn't seem like they've been just...lying around for sixteen years. It probably only seems like a day. Maybe just an hour."

David had no time to respond, Sally's wail captured his attention, and he stepped across the lawn. Kurt had pushed her into the water. "Young man..." His deep voice brought green eyes wide; all the scolding necessary came in those two words. "I think you're right, Otis." Laughing, David rested on the steps again. Kurt and Sally resumed their game. "But I didn't come to talk about raising kids. I...need to talk about Harold."

"Harold?" Otis stared over. "Has he been

bothering you?"

"Shit...." David shook his head. "Just in my mind. And I don't have a thing to back up the way I feel. Harold hasn't *done* anything to me. It's just that I get these vibs from him." David looked straight over. "I'll be blunt Otis," he said, "I don't trust the man. I'm sorry but–"

"What's to be sorry for?"

David held his exhale. "I have a lot riding on this secret," he said. "Those kids are mine now, my heart, my gut says they are. I'm being over-protective, I know, and I'll be that way for a hell-of-a long time. You see, a reporter came to me this morning with a rumor he wanted some facts about. This...rumor, Otis, hit too damned close to the truth to be coming from anyone outside."

"And you suspect Harold."

David's shoulders sank. "Yes," he said. "But I've nothing to back my guess. Has he been acting different at all?"

Otis took time before he spoke, as if he meant to review the past few weeks with a greater awareness, just for David. "No," he said, "I'm sorry, not really. I have noticed he's more talkative. He's buddy-buddy with this Morrison, the scientist. But David, if anyone else is around Harold is very careful how he words things or just quits speaking altogether until we're alone."

"Well...shit again." David stood up and shoved his hands deep into his jeans pockets, an invitation, it seemed, for Kurt and Sally to come swing on his arms. "Hey, I'm not a gym. You two about ready to go?"

They ran to the car, answer obvious, but instead of following, David turned to see Otis Clark's face. "Do you think I'm–"

"A screwball? No." Otis smiled, and when he rose, he placed his wide-spread hand on David's shoulder. "I'll be more observant when I'm around Harold."

Once again, David saw sincerity in the eyes very near. He saw a deep sense of pride in Otis, pride that few men these days dared to carry with them, no matter what their stature.

"Boy oh boy, looks real nice." David praised the dinner table that Kurt and Sally had set with plates and silverware. "Jessica's going to be real surprised. All we need now are some candles and a roving minstrel."

"Candles. Yeah, David," Kurt said. "Where are they? I can get 'em."

"I'll get the moving minsel."

"The moving –Oh Lord." David chuckled as he went to the storage closet in the hall. "Gee Sally, I'm fresh out of moving minsels, we'll have to do without tonight." He searched for the candles when the doorbell rang and before he thought, before he could have stopped them, the children opened the door.

"David."

Trotting down the hall, he smiled, ready to see Jessica but he halted and stared straight at Harold. "Mr. James…" Freezing and without a step further, he watched as   Harold pushed up his glasses as a greeting. "Would you excuse us a minute?" David didn't wait for a reply and he grasped the children by their shoulders. "Do either of you know this man?"

"No, David…."

"You cannot let people in if you don't know them. Is that understood?"

"Yes, David."

He rubbed their arms. "Look out the big front window next time and see who it is."

Without instruction, they paddled off to the bedroom and David waited until they disappeared before he spoke. "I apologize, Harold, didn't mean to put you on the spot."

Harold looked everywhere except at David. He examined the living room and studied every piece of furniture. The table set for four. "Can't be too careful."

Too careful my ass. "What can I do for you?" David didn't invite the curious man to sit and so they remained in the middle of the apartment. The room grew smaller with every silent second and with every silent second, David felt his pulse beat at his temple.

"Nothing you can do for me…today, Sergeant."

Again, the glasses. David stood near enough to see that they'd slipped along a fine bead of perspiration.

"I was just in the neighborhood." Harold didn't expound and turned to look behind him.

David struggled for conversation. "Do you live around here, Harold?"

"I drive a lot −came out to get a newspaper."

"Newspaper." Did David echo the word out loud or did his instant bile burn up the exclamation? And in contrast, ice had stiffened his spine so that the frost curled his fingers in his pockets. "Anything interesting?"

"The usual." When Harold sat on the arm of the sofa, his in-depth surveillance settled on David's face. "I read a small piece about the five children," Harold said and pointed down the hall. "You're camouflaging quite well."

"Isn't difficult. I just answer questions." David

selected his words carefully. He thought them through, slowly, while he analyzed every flinch and every movement that Harold made. "Have you been approached?" he asked. "I know reporters have been badgering Otis quite a bit."

"They have," Harold said, "I remember a young reporter with Otis." A malicious smile darkened Harold's face and words. "But no one's...*called* me about anything."

"Harold...you–" Stepping forward, David dug his hands down deep into his pants to insure they didn't clamp around Harold's throat.

Harold sprang to his feet.

The doorbell chimed and started the children in a race to the kitchen but David stood there, motionless. Everyone froze while he dissected every tick, every blink, every breath in the room.

"That must be Dr. King," he said, and with nerves on the razor's edge, his vision did not shift from Harold, even as he found the doorknob. "Jessica." Plastering on a smile, David did his best to mask the disorder inside him and opened the way further to let her in.

Harold acknowledged the doctor with some kind of shit-eating grin and made some pleasant comment about the grand summer weather. All the while, David gnawed at the urge to trip Harold's feet right out from under him. Harold ogled Jessica again, her blond hair, her breasts and hips, the bouquet of colors in her dress that wrapped the sensual package. The package meant for David.

"I was just on my way out." Harold nodded as if the uncomfortable silence never occurred. "I can see your dinner's about ready."

"Yes, you're right." Jessica glanced at the range and the steam that rolled from the pans. She stepped away, quick to take Kurt and Sally with her to peek under the skillet.

"Have a nice weekend, Sergeant, maybe we'll run into each other again." Making a gesture like he'd tipped a hat, Harold said goodbye.

David closed the door.

Then his eyes. They were all that moved. This left no doubt in his mind. Harold James started the rumor. Harold James was up to no good.

"David?"

He heard Jessica's voice from right behind him and he turned around to wrap his arms around her. "I missed you, sweetheart." He buried his face into her hair and in her shoulder, into the light fruity scent behind her ear.

"I missed you. David?"

"Can you make gravy, Jess?"

She nodded. "David…."

"Good. Good, I'll get those steaks out of the pan." He brushed his thumbs along her silky lips. He stared into her eyes. "Sally honey, there's a big platter down in that cupboard, can you get it?"

"Did you find the candles?" Kurt asked.

"Almost." Smiling at Jessica, David filled his lungs with the vibrant air and he begged her with his eyes to understand, to relax and enjoy their time together. They better enjoy it now. This time, he allowed her to study his face and she stroked the lines at his temples and eyes. Ever so slowly, she did finally smile in return.

"It looks like everyone's been busy today," she said in a breath.

"Oh yes," Sally said. "I didn't even take a nap?"

Cowering, David realized he'd forgotten all about nap instructions. "I'll get those candles." He ducked out of the room with Kurt right behind him.

"I see you went shopping, Sally," Jessica said.

"We got shoes, and jamas, and a coat." Sally recited the complete list. "But not a dwess and we got mo stowies and a twacto and some dishes fo my baby."

"My goodness."

"But..." Sally straightened her shoulders, "we have to keep that stuff home."

"Home?" Jessica swiveled from the steamy food as David came around the corner, the word still formed on her lips.

"Home," he said.

"We decided it was okay fo David to be a cop daddy."

"And about that simply, too, Jess."

In the light of the kitchen, and from the bit of western sun that yet hung in the evening, David caught a glimpse of a tear that edged onto the sapphire rim, Jessica's eyes bright with her relief and her joy. She allowed but one drop to fall away just as Sally and Kurt jumped into her arms.

"I'm happy too, Jessie." David watched his family embrace and he felt his heart fall into his hands. He paused to breathe and to clear his voice of the emotion. "These candlesticks were my mothers," he said and David placed the porcelain holders on the table. Arranging them to the center, he wiped a light film of lint from the yellow roses.

"They're beautiful."

Jessica touched the candlesticks; she touched his

insides in a way he'd never imagined and he stepped back, his heart slow to follow as though suspended for the moment in mid-air. "Those two things are about all I have of my mothers." He looked at Kurt and Sally. They had nothing of their parents, nothing to cherish but memories and Sally only kept a vague few of those. Helping the little girl atop the pile of pillows in her chair, David promised himself they'd have all that he could ever give them. He made a fair living and now…now he had something to work for….

"I think we should all say blessing," Jessica said.

David nodded. They settled around the table and he wondered…how could she see so clearly into his mind? The worry of Harold James returned to his spine, right dead-set behind his heart to where it pressed back into his chest and he could feel Jessica stare over when she started the quiet devotion.

He prayed along, out loud, something he'd never done, ever, before.

Kurt and Sally were tucked into bed at 8:30 and asleep before David read the last page of <u>Munchie the Cottontail Rabbit.</u>

"I didn't know it took so much to get a kid to bed." Turning out the bedroom light, he grasped Jessica's hand to lead her down the hall.

"If you hadn't had the water war with them in the bathtub, it wouldn't have been all that hard."

"Ah, come on Ma," he said and the words sped his blood, the thoughts of Jessica as a mother, a wife…his lover literally raced his desire to every part of him. David gathered her into his arms so she stood between him and the wall…so that their bodies matched up and the air escaped his lungs. He closed his eyes and buried his face into her neck and her shoulder, her silky blond hair that caressed his skin. Gardenia and almond? Christ. Pressing his hips against hers, he ran his hands along her waist until his palms rested at her breasts and when he breathed in again, he melted further into her body. He brushed his thumbs over her nipples until they grew hard, until his breath grew shallow and he found her lips, parted and inviting him to come inside, to share the moist heat. He kissed her eyes, her temple…her ear.

"David…" Her breasts rose up, full, into his touch. "We'll wake up the children," she said but she didn't move; her fingers pressed at his hands to keep them locked tight against her.

"God…." He groaned and again, tucked himself deeper into her, further into every curve of her waist and her hips to where every breath seemed to knead and mold her body to match his own. "Baby," he said, "I never, ever thought I'd hear those words." Stretching back, she moved just far enough so that David lifted his head and he gazed into her eyes. They sparkled like blue cut diamonds or some kind of rare translucent sapphires and he couldn't get enough. Her fingertips roamed through his hair and along his temples and his jaw. And then she laughed at him.

"What kind of a man have I found?" she said. "How long have you been out of the circuit?"

"The circuit." He frowned and laughed, too, and he pressed his hand over hers along his face. "What?"

"The dating circuit," she said. "Trust me, what I just told you, that's rated right under, honey, I have a headache."

"Jesus…Jessica…." Turning, he danced them along so his back touched the wall and he could get both his arms fully around her, both his hands to glide along her satiny dress and firm curve of her fanny. "I know," he said. "I know…God." He snickered with her again. "But it sounded so good, sweetheart, you just don't know. Jess, baby, I have to talk to you."

Talk seemed the furthest from her mind, he could tell by the way she ran her fingers along his skin and pushed her thighs up even further into him…how she teased his earlobe with her lips and her tongue.

"If it's about Harold James," she said, "I don't want to hear about it, not now, after this precious evening."

"No kitten, he'll not ruin our evening." He'll not ruin our life. David led her to the sofa and coaxed her into his lap. "The man just dropped by, no reason that I know of." He said no more about it, thankful that Jessica was cuddled to his chest and that she didn't see into his eyes. He hated lying, loathed deceit, and if he let himself dwell on it very long, he'd soon hate himself for lying to Jessica. But he had to. Tonight, he had no choice.

"So tell me," she said, "did I miss a special day?"

Her tone sounded light…the warmth of her breath that tickled his neck. "I'm afraid you did," he said. "We came right home after leaving Brigham and had our little talk. Jessie…Kurt is one perceptive kid, let me tell you. He's got things pretty much figured out." Tucking a strand of blond behind her ear, David drew in one more deep breath. "After I went through this long spiel to explain the hazards of being a cop, that I could die and leave them alone again, do you know what Kurt said? 'My dad drove a truck'."

"Really?" Jessica shook her head. "Doesn't matter what a person does, I guess."

David laughed. "That's what I said and they tackled me with a great hug like everything's all settled. It is Jess. Sit up here, sweetheart." He tipped her chin and she moved so they faced one another. He couldn't avoid her blue eyes now. "I'm going to apply Monday morning, officially. Have you talked to Paula? Has she said anything?"

"Against David Straus? No." Jessica stroked his cheek. "You were the only thing holding it back."

"I had to think. I had to be sure."

"I know," she said, "you being sure is important to me, too. I asked Paula to wait a few days before she approached anyone else. You three belong together, David, something told me that a long time ago."

David tapped his chest. "Probably me. I can be a stubborn bastard."

"But don't ever change."

Nodding, grateful to soak in her every nuance, he watched her eyes darken to that exquisite indescribable color he'd come to love from the moment they first met. Yes. He owed these five kids more than they may ever realize.

"I wonder how Steven is doing with his family," Jessica said.

"Oh, I bet they had an emotional day." David had been thinking of Steve and Sheila too, but in another way, their marriage. The union looked perfect, at least by his view from the outside. Steve and Sheila had been married a long time, some of the years were no doubt hell, but they'd pulled through, still in love. Still strong.

"You know, David, it's going to be most difficult

for Steven."

"What part?"

Jessica sat up further in his lap. "Steven used to be the eldest child," she said. "The people he's meeting this weekend are his younger brothers and sisters. They're grown, strangers to him now. I can't even begin to imagine what that must be like."

"Did Sheila talk to you about it?"

"We had a very good talk," Jessica said. "I'm not worried or anything. Steven is prepared; it won't be a complete shock. I think he'll be fine."

"If anyone can pull it off," David said, "that family can. I like Steve and Sheila, I like what they have together. Trust," he said, "depending on someone and by God knowing they'll be there when you need them." When he cupped Jessica's face in his hands, his fingers trembled along her cheeks, her ear and in her hair. He kissed her once more, to breathe the sweet smell of her skin deep into his lungs. "I love you, Jess," he said. "I want that with you." He caressed her eyes and she stared at him in disbelief, her lips parted. "I want to marry you. I want you to be my wife, Kurt and Sally's mother."

"David…."

"Don't answer baby, not yet." Pressing his forehead onto hers, he needed to touch her even more –to give himself a moment more to gather his senses. "I have to tell you something," he said. "It's something very important you'll have to consider, if…" He glanced up again, for a second, only. "If you're even interested." The glimmer in her eyes, as he played with the button at her dress, said that she was definitely interested and he tucked his finger inside the material to help search for the words. "I guess there's only one way to say it." Fixing his vision on her thick golden lashes, he swallowed. "I'm sterile, Jessica," he said. "I can't father a child. If you marry me, we'll never have a baby together." He could tell his confession surprised her and he squeezed her shoulders. "I'm sorry sweetheart," he said. "maybe I should have said something sooner."

"Before I fell in love with you?"

But did she love him enough? Her smile, the dance in her eyes, said maybe, and David held his breath. "You've got to think about it, Jessica," he said. "Search yourself. Know your needs and dreams." Brushing her cheek once more to trace her lips, the silence between them swelled. Some kind of weird childhood panic surged up inside him so all at once he could hardly sit still. He wanted her to be sure. But could he accept her decision if she said no? He thought so earlier. But now… now she sat right next to him; she bathed him in the blue tropical depths of her eyes. Her heat. "Can I get you something to drink?" Stumbling, David crossed the kitchen. Never had he cut himself open so far, revealed so much of his heart as he had today. What the hell…. "There's water on the stove," he said. "Hot tea?" He gripped the kettle handle hard. But he could still feel. He could hear Jessica behind him.

"Have any champagne?"

"Champagne?" He swiveled around.

"To celebrate, David."

He stared to make sure. He analyzed her eyes, her voice, and the way her lips held his name the moment after she said it. "Baby…."

"I don't need to think or search myself." She buried herself into his chest…his heart. "I know I love you. I have for a long time."

"But Jess...."

"No buts, David." Stepping away, she coaxed him back to the sofa to settle beside him, again. To secure his full attention. "I want children," she said, "yes. I want them very much. I want a family." She looked down and rubbed his fingers with her palm. "The thing is..." She pressed his fingers to her face. "I can't afford to take the time I'd want off from my career and have them now, while I'm still young. David...I haven't been head pediatrician very long, earning decent money. I have a lot of loans to pay. I'm handling it fine, and each few months it gets easier. But–" She laughed and threw her arms around his neck, her excitement out into the world. "I thought when you began to explain about yourself, that you were going to ask me to give *up* my career. I thought you were going to ask me to have *your* child and add to the little family we already have. But I wouldn't. I couldn't."

"I'd never do that," he said, "you love your work... Jesus. I've seen you be a doctor."

"I do love it, David." She sat up. "I love you, and now that I have a chance I want both. I don't need a child that's from my own genes," she said. "If Kurt and Sally are all you'll ever have as your own, then they'll be mine. I'll accept them the same way. Yes." She shivered with her unmistakable excitement. "Absolutely, I'll marry you."

"Baby...Jessie, don't cry. Good God, you'll have me doing it." But David didn't cry even though her tears didn't stop and he stroked her hair to let the soft weeping on his chest fill him up with strength and good new memories to offset the old. He trusted Jessica. She would be happy with her decision.

212

"David?"

Smiling, he heard her question, just from the tone of her voice. Dr. Jessica King. "The Gulf War," he answered but not before he wiped the moisture from her cheeks and kissed her nose. "I had just finished my tour on the desert when all hell broke loose. Some British choppers had pitched equipment and water, food, to this satellite base where I was waiting for my papers. We all scrambled out to pack in the new supplies when a damn Hummer came tearing over the dunes. Nobody thought much about it, had an American flag on the side."

"It blew up," Jessica said.

David nodded. "Shit and sand flew everywhere, honey, you couldn't see a meter away. Boys dropped like flies. I was one of the lucky ones, just far enough away. I picked up some metal, though." David stood up to show her. "I got a load through my thigh, across here and into my groin, over about there. If it would have entered a little higher, I wouldn't be here today. Lower...."

He shrugged, eyebrows raised. He'd given up, ages ago, thinking about what might or might not have been. "I'm alive Jessica, and damn glad now."

Seventeen

"You dirty, son-of-a–"

"Sergeant." Harold James straightened his shoulders. "Let's not start name-calling."

"Name-calling." David gripped the chair at his kitchen table, seconds from hurling it across the room as hard as he could. "I knew you were up to something three days ago."

"You should be thankful that I've come to you first instead of proceeding with the press."

"Thankful for the opportunity to be blackmailed." David inched toward Harold, hands clenched into hot white fists.

Harold removed his glasses from his face. So much sweat had piled on his nose that the hefty frames could not stay up. "Blackmail is a bit harsh," he said.

"Maybe you'd prefer extortion, either way, it's illegal. I should know, I'm a cop." David groaned at his own stupid statement. "You are a thick-gutted bastard. I could have your ass in the can so damn fast you wouldn't know where you were for a week."

"My word against yours."

"Until I pay you off."

"So much for being an officer of the law." Harold slipped his glasses back on and magnified the proud smirk on his face.

"You'd be stupid enough to take the money, too. Once it's in your hands–"

"You could arrest me," Harold said. "But people can talk in prison. Why I believe they can even write books. The process wouldn't get that far though, would it, David? A man's innocent until proven guilty; your little secret would all come out in court. But why wait that long? Why I'd spill my guts, as you say, so fast you wouldn't know where you were for a week. And to think, a man of your stature trying to jail a hero, a person who brought five people back from the dead."

David stared as the room spun around him. He studied the brave man in his apartment and recounted Harold's facts, logic the man used to twist the story and make himself a demigod. No. The details didn't matter, the secret –his children, would be at mercy to the world.

"I plan to write about this," Harold said. "I'll be on all the satellite radio stations, make the news show circuit. I figure my royalties could hit the five-hundred-thousand mark within six weeks. I've merely given you the opportunity to buy the rights."

"Five-hundred-thousand?" David swallowed away

the hot sick taste that climbed up from his gut. "You are a stupid son-of-a-bitch. What makes you think I have that kind of money?"

"You no doubt have something in savings," Harold said, "enough for a down payment, and say in a month, you can buy a little more, ten thousand worth and so on. I know Kurt and Sally are very important to you now."

"If you ever –"

Flinching, Harold stepped backward but David hadn't moved, just his hands toward the man's neck.

"I've come to you, David, because you have the greatest opportunities for a regular…" Harold smiled. "Income. We all know of the graft and corruption in our police department and the problems just get worse every year. Why, you're such a righteous man, you no doubt have your eyes on a few of these lowly officers, already. I'm sure if you befriended them, only as a set-up of course, they'd help you learn the routine."

The nausea turned to magma and began to burn David from the inside out. He was so near killing Harold that it felt white-hot on his face. He moved closer.

Harold took another step back. "And if, perchance," Harold said, "you can't come up with the payment, you might ask your friends. But I doubt the wealthy Alexander's would help you. Besides, how would it look to them?" Harold puffed out his chest. "There's Nevil Morrison, of course, but he's not as stubborn about this secret as you are. Given the choice, he could be persuaded either way. Then there is our lovely Dr. Jessi–"

Thunder shook the living room. David slammed Harold up against the wall in a storm that knocked the wind from both of them. "If you ever touch Jessica, talk or look at her, Kurt or Sally again, you'll not be able to in the future."

"A murder sentence would be far worse on your little family than anything I could ever do."

Murder. The word exploded behind David's eyes. His body shook from the aftershock and pinned Harold further against the wall in violent jerks. Murder. He would never do it. Not now. Not in this house. Not while Sally's baby-doll watched from the sofa. Not in the living room where he and Jessica had made love. Kurt would sense the crime in an instant. "I've got seven thousand."

"Cash," Harold said, "and I want it tonight. Meet me at Oakwood Cemetery at eight-thirty. Sharp."

The smile David had seen so often came back to Harold's face. But Harold could not push up the teetering spectacles, not until David let him to the floor, several seconds later. When the front door slammed shut, David promised himself that $7,000 would be all Harold ever got. David bought in, yes. For time. He needed precious time to think, to plan and trip-up Harold.

David scrubbed the sweat and filth from his hands. He threw the soap as hard as he could against the wall to shatter the sickening silence. He couldn't stay. Jogging to his car, he sped out into the morning. His mind raced, the scenery around him a concrete blur. Violence and hatred and bile boiled up from his churning gut. Never in his life had he been threatened like this and to think who did it twisted every nerve. David could handle his own life in danger, that would be easier to accept. But those he loved were being taken, being used by a nauseating parasite.

217

David sat in the bank's parking lot ten minutes before he realized the significance of where he'd driven. He didn't go into the building. He remained outside and forced himself to concentrate.

"Think damn it." David hit the steering wheel with a blow that jolted the whole car. He had to keep Harold James from talking. No question. "But how?" The words hung in the air. Something told David that Harold had thought out every angle.

He could arrest Harold for extortion. He could go to Judge Bailey and explain the situation. Vin could hush the proceedings. But…. David's eyes closed down. It wouldn't shut-up Harold. Once he started through the system, the man would have access to a lawyer, someone he could convince to tell the world and reap the money with him as a partner.

"Money," he said out loud while he stared the bank ahead. "The goddamn root of all evil." If David turned his back today, the secret would be out tomorrow. Scientists and reporters would besiege his kids and steal their precious childhood right from under them. The hierarchy and cults, and everything in between, would try for a crack at their rebirth.

"Jesus–" He groaned. He ached. Harold wanted to be wealthy and it didn't matter from where the money came, a publisher, talk shows and specials. Or from David.

He depended on David to be there for the long haul.

Money. Harold knew where David could get his hands on a steady supply. David knew the men on the take in the county. He and Sheriff Williamson had been watching a small handful of officers right in their own company, waiting for the perfect moment to pounce. They were there, all right. David was there.

A weight settled over him like a strength sucking sponge. What kind of husband would he be? What kind of father to Kurt and Sally if he turned to corruption? Lord, what kind of a man would he be if he screwed up and harm came to them?

David had wrapped his fingers so tight around the steering wheel that they turned numb. Had he taken on too much? His desire to protect the children would never go away. A lot of angry years lay ahead of him if he were going to feel this way, vulnerable and open to every opportunist that decided to take advantage of his family. David wondered if he could handle it, his emotions, at this minute, so intense that the stress would kill him in a year.

"But dear sweet God in heaven somebody has to do it," he said and at that very same instant, he knew that person was he. No one else.

The scene looked different to David when he drove up the narrow road to Oakwood Cemetery. His mind went back to the weeks past, to the mist, the upheaval, the strange stillness that had hovered all around him. Stepping out of his car to walk along the road, he remembered the stench.

"Sergeant, you're smart to be right on time."

He nodded —keep the rat calm.

"You see," Harold said, "I called that young reporter, Jackson Miles. If you hadn't shown up on time, he would have gotten the story."

David looked over the area; he could see no cars

in sight and so he studied Harold's face. He searched for that give-away expression. Harold stared back.

"Where's the cash?"

"In my front pocket."

"You can get back in your car in a minute and I'll take it then."

Swiveling away, David headed toward an uprooted tree hauled near a pile of tombstones that had been gathered from the rubble. He thought of the Gulf. At least there he knew what to do –shoot or be shot. He fought a different battle now, only the enemy held the weapon, a pistol shoved right in his mouth.

No. David stared at the broken arm of a marble angel. The gun wasn't aimed at him, it pointed straight at Steven, Kurt and Sally, Tammy and Tony. David had to stand by and watch the hammer go down, or stand in the way and take the bullet himself.

Harold walked over. "You know why I've chosen the cemetery to meet, don't you David?"

"I have a good guess."

"Anyone coming by," Harold said, "will think you've asked me for help because I know so much about Oakwood."

"And you've answered all my questions, thank you." David turned to leave Harold behind. The longer he remained, the weaker his control became and he told himself, with every long stride, that he had to keep a clear head, doing anything rash would work against him. Harold James stepped at his heels.

"You're certainly taking this well, Sergeant."

Whipping around, David grabbed the base antenna of his car instead of Harold.

"You're not so moral after all, are you?" Harold

said. "No longer the perfect, law abiding citizen, the all-knowing sheriff's big-deal sergeant."

"Don't try to drag me down into your stinking pit." David knew that every single cell in his body recoiled at what he had to do. "You're of no more use to this earth than snake shit."

Harold smiled. He opened the door of the car and motioned that David get in. "Very good, Sergeant." He took the white folded-up envelope from David's hand. "Now there's one more item that needs to be settled," he said. "Next month's payment. I'll expect one on this same date in September, and as they say, David, same time, same place. Don't try to find me in the meantime; I may take a short vacation, not too far, you understand."

"Of course not," David said. No such luck.

"There's our good friend Jackson Miles." Harold's eyes narrowed behind the thick spectacles as his attention turned down the hill. "Right on time, just like everything else."

David checked his watch. 8:40.

"You run along now, I'll handle the reporter."

"Harold, I swear–" David lunged out the window.

"No need to worry Serg…" Harold chuckled. "So long as you hold up…hold up your end of the, uh, contract. And I certainly hope your savings account doesn't look too poorly for the adoption. Oh Serg." Harold waved his hand as David popped the car into reverse. "You won't miss tomorrow's paper, now will you?"

Bearing down on the accelerator, David spun the car in a half circle and sped out. He passed Jackson Miles, the same young columnist that had approached him Saturday about the rumor.

The hours felt like an eternity to David before the next evening's news appeared.

"My goodness..." Sheila came down the hallway of his apartment. "You must be looking for something very important."

Startled, he sprang from the sofa. Newspaper fell in sections at his feet, all but the one David gripped in his fingers. "Sheila, yeah..." He sat back down. "I think there's going to be an article about the kids. I've been keeping an eye on what comes out." David's attempt to laugh barely succeeded to put a smile on his lips. "I'm comparing what I say to what gets printed or...or what anyone else might say."

David looked away. He didn't want to see the worry in Sheila's eyes. He couldn't talk and reassure her with lies, not now with this wild, trapped feeling inside him. When she sat next to him, an impulse flashed –he should move.

Run.

But if the truth had been printed, it would be here for all to see.

"Is that it, David?" Sheila pointed to a small paragraph at the top of the third page. "Straus Requests Aid?"

His mouth fell open.

"Sgt. David Straus of the San Francisco County Sheriff's Bureau has asked Harold James, employee of Clark and Talbot Funeral Service, for help in his search for clues concerning the five live children unearthed by July's quakes. Straus says that James is a well read, intelligent man. With his knowledge of the cemetery, its controversy and geothermal environment, they can collect the information needed to complete the investigation. Is that right, David? I don't understand why you'd have to do something like this."

"Camouflage, Sheila," he said and David walked to the kitchen in hopes that the hot, angry rush didn't show through on his face. Harold James knew how to cover his ass, and the more David realized it, the more smothered he felt.

"Didn't they say what you wanted?" Sheila came up behind him. "I mean, it was smart that you chose someone like Mr. James who works around the cemetery. People will more than likely see you together every now and again, that will make your story seem all the more real."

Son-of-a-bitch. David tried to breathe through the fire in his chest. Sheila was right. Harold thought of everything. David pressed his fist into the refrigerator.

"Something *is* the matter, isn't it?"

"No. No, Sheila, nothing's wrong." He spun around and clasped her shoulders, only to stare into an unconvinced, ruddy colored face. "Please believe me," he said. "I'm doing what I can, what I have to."

Gathering the woman into his arms, he pressed her against his heart. He needed the comfort. David closed his eyes. He needed goddamn deliverance and he told himself to breathe. "You about ready?" David's voice sounded just above a whisper and he set her away, only to have her search his face while he rubbed her arms. "I'm sorry," he said. "I guess I'm feeling real inadequate, you know, damned anxious, with so much riding on what information I give the media. If I screw up, Sheila–"

"You won't."

She hugged him again but he'd caught a glimpse of moisture in her eye; she was scared, too. If the truth came out, she'd lose her son. Again. Her loss would happen in a different way, but hurt even more. It would have to.

"You're doing fine, David," she said. "Thank you. No one has ever said thank–"

"No Sheila, good God no." He shook his head. "Please don't start now."

"Steve and I were talking this weekend about how glad we are that you're the one handling the reporters," she said. "You care about the children as much as any of the parents."

He couldn't goddamn deny that and with the words came some faint glimmer of release from inside his clench of emotions…his body. "It's funny how quick I got involved." He nodded to breathe in the truth of it, his own surprise. "I've been a cop a long time. Christ," he said, "my entire adult life. I've seen a lot of terrible things happen to families, but for some reason, I just never reached out like this. I just never did."

"Then it must have been meant to be." Stretching up, she kissed his jaw to thank him, regardless, and David smiled. Odd. Sheila made him feel better.

"Kurt and Sally are very lucky," she said. "And Jessica.

Frowning, he set Sheila an arm's length away. "And what does that look mean?"

"I was supposed to let you tell me," she said, "but you're not going to are you?"

"Tell you what?"

"That you and Jessica are getting married."

"That's supposed to be a secret?" Scooting out the dining chair, he loosened the shoe lace at his sore toe and pulled up his socks so he wouldn't have to face

Sheila. The idea that he should back out of the marriage kept popping into his head; Jessica deserved far more than he could ever offer her, especially now.

"Jessica didn't know if you wanted to tell anyone," Sheila said. "She's very excited. I'm sure that's why she told me. Jessica has become a very good friend."

"I know the feeling well. I hope I can do right by her."

"My goodness, David, don't look so serious. You two are in love, anyone can see that. Just always talk to one another and always listen. It took Steve and me a long time to learn but communication is what's held us together. It got us through the hard times, losing Steven." She took David's hand and he stood up straight. "You'll have career challenges," she said, "a new ready-made family to cope with, but as long as you let each other know what you're thinking…what you're dreaming about, you'll be just fine."

David regarded the woman's words like law. If anyone could give sound advice for obtaining a good strong marriage, Sheila Adams could. When her fingers slipped from his hand, he sat down and put his elbows on the table, his chin atop his fingers. He watched her disappear down the hall. Always talk, always listen. Was there some kind of rule in there about masking the truth, concealing it to protect the ones you love? There had to be or he'd soon be over-run with guilt. Guilty because if he were in Jessica's unknowing shoes, he'd want to be aware of every incident, good or bad, and be fighting to learn. This situation with Harold was definitely bad but be damned if he could bring himself to tell her, cause her to feel the unimaginable strain. He could see no gain in telling Jessica.

Anyone.

"David?"

He had to squint and to focus his eyes to see over; he had to struggle away from his mental debate to answer. Sheila waited at the door, ready with her raincoat and umbrella.

"I want you to know that we think you'll make a wonderful father."

"What?"

"You've already helped Kurt start to feel good about himself. Steven really likes you, accepted you right off, which is unusual."

Nodding, David gathered his wallet and keys for the drive to Brigham. Steven was one smart kid, he'd go far in his life and no doubt accomplish anything he set out to do. Steven's the one he should tell about Harold. That brain would click in right away and in no time, spit out a quick sharp answer to solve all the problems. Even Kurt would find a solution but sensitively, slowly, with inner strength. Kurt wouldn't think of himself, either. He'd say to let the secret out, save the heartache and bear the repercussion himself.

Turning to face Sheila, that intense sharp ache sped through his heart again, like his ribs cracked in two with some kind of pure deep love that he never thought was possible. Pressing in on his chest, he closed his eyes and held the doorknob for support.

Good God Almighty, Kurt *was* his son.

David and Jessica planned to tell Kurt and Sally of their wedding during a nice   restaurant dinner.

Neither felt apprehensive over the children's reactions. They'd each received obvious hints that David needed a mommie and that Jessica was the perfect choice.

No, David didn't feel jumpy tonight. Having his family around the candlelit table made him feel better than he had for some time. Anxiety struck when Kurt and Sally asked when.

"We were thinking the end of this month."

Jessica's words added a good hard twist inside David's stomach, his guts stretched out in the middle. He could hurt Jessica and postpone the wedding with no good reason, just some stupid flimsy lie he could dream up, or he could marry her and entangle her in a union of deceit and corruption. Son-of-a-bitch.

"Plus..." Jessica glanced at David. "We thought if you two didn't mind, that we all might go to Disneyland for a few days."

"Fo ow honeymoon?" Sally gasped. "Oh boy."

David's heart flipped over, yet again, and he promised himself he would have this thing with Harold all sewn up before he went anywhere. With the end of August just three weeks away, he had to, one way or the other. Looking over, he worked to push the conflict out from his mind and squeezed Jessica's hand. He saw her innocent eyes, those rich irises of blue, hopeful and looking forward to their lives with child-like eagerness.

"I love you, Jess," he said, "always know that." Her head tipped to the side like it did so often but her smile shifted somehow and softened; she nearly glowed in the candlelight. Christ...she looked prettier to him than ever before. He should get her a ring, at least ask her what she wanted, for god sakes.

He hadn't given Harold all his money and he

227

vowed the man would never get another cent. So why couldn't he just forget it? By three weeks a break would come and he'd settle this situation once and for all. Why couldn't he forget it for just one minute?

"David, what are you thinking?"

The expression on his face, the plastered one −the awkward one became painful. His lips ached after smiling but two seconds. "I guess I'm skeptical whether we can get it all done," he said and Jessica stroked his arm, as always. He knew she wanted to erase the weary creases, the ones that made his forehead hurt, the lines she didn't understand.

"We'll just make a list later and decide what is most important," she said and they did, that evening in her office after they'd tucked the children into bed in the isolation ward.

"Only a few more days of that."

"Yes." David nodded.

"Next week we'll tuck them in at home."

Jessica's cheery voice, as always, found a way to creep into David's soul and ease his worries some and he rested his head against the tall leather chair. With the kids home he could watch over them. And knowing that they were his very own would set a purpose to the whole disgusting mess with Harold James. The adoption wouldn't be final then, but there were no hitches. The documents were very near completion; he and Jessica would sign them together as husband and wife.

"So what's bothering you the most?" she asked.

"That you're way over there." Without hesitation, Jessica cuddled into his lap to where he could hold her close and shut his eyes. "I had a good conversation with Sheila," he said. "She couldn't stand that I didn't tell her we were getting married. I assumed you would, that's why I didn't say anything."

"I couldn't stand *not* telling her," Jessica said. "You don't mind?"

"No kitten, God…why would I mind?"

"Do you know how I feel inside, David?"

Nuzzling her face with his lips, he caressed her long trim waist and curved his fingers along the sides of her rounded breasts as they rose up with her sigh. "I remember exactly how you feel inside."

She snickered. "I'm trying to be serious," she said and he had to snicker, too, but she allowed him one more kiss, his hand spread wide against her hip. "I feel like I did at Christmas when I was a little girl," she said. "I would lie in bed, all excited about the big day. I haven't felt like that for so many years."

"I'm glad baby." With one finger, David tucked her satiny hair behind her ear and traced her smooth, ivory skin, her curved thighs and the silhouette of her breast against his arm. "But you know what you're getting on this big day." He pet her hair and relaxed into the chair just a little bit more to listen for the rain taps on the window. The smell of this woman always reminded him of a distant garden of flowers, subtle, where he could never quite get enough and always drawn in further to try to find more.

Paula Reynolds decided that Kurt and Sally should be known as David's shirt-tail relations. Supposedly, their mother, a cousin of his, died last month and left them as orphans. Paula and David both thought it might bring questions if he just adopted two children from nowhere.

David had the story straight in his head for the new dayshift, Monday morning.

"Hey Straus."

"Hey Gable." David didn't look behind him, he knew from his buddy's voice that gossip had traveled fast.

"Hear you're gonna be a daddy."

Few people knew of David's mishap in the war, Gable was one of them. The fun-loving tone brought a chuckled from David, but he'd yet to turn around; he just stopped inside the crowded office.

"Damn miracle if ya ask me," Gable said.

"Don't think I asked."

Gable draped his arm over David's shoulder. "You don't look too strung about getting some younguns dumped in your lap."

"I'm not. It's about time I got some family one way or another, don't you think?"

"Yeah, but let me tell ya, I was shocked."

"You were shocked?"

"Sure. Guess I have the right. Now all you need is a wife and you'll be all set."

David looked Gable straight in the eyes. "I'm going to get one of those in a few weeks, too." Walking to his desk, the conversation hung in mid-air, just like David knew it would and he snickered at the surprise on Gable's face.

"And you're fulla cow pucky."

"I believe he's speaking the truth."

Bradley spoke from across the room and as David swiveled around, he faced the young man, squarely. "And how the hell did you find out?"

"Grapevine."

Jesus. The word hit David like a brick, full-on against his chest. "Don't give me that shit, how did you know?"

"I...I came in the office when you told Sheriff Williamson, Sergeant. I'm sorry, I didn't realized you wanted it kept a secret."

Secret? Son-of-a-bitch. More words, more ache and it all caught inside his throat in some kind of tight painful clench. And did he look as foolish as he felt? His mood had just snapped. From one minute to the next, he could barely hide the turmoil inside. Shaking himself just a bit, he tried to calm himself so no one could tell. "I am a little touchy, I guess," he said. "Hell-of-a-lot going on in a short amount of time."

Bradley smiled. "I think I understand what you're feeling, sir. I got married about six months ago."

David could only nod. No one would understand what ate at *his* guts. His love for Jessica grew stronger everyday, his devotion to Kurt and Sally had become unequaled, yet on the opposite end of the spectrum, matched with intensity, boiled dangerous unstable hatred toward Harold James.

"So it is true." Gable eyed David. "I can't believe it. When?"

"When what?"

"When are ya getting hitched?"

"End of the month. Is that okay?"

"Hey...." Gable looked around. "If Williamson says it's okay, I ain't gonna tag ya."

"Williamson says it's okay." Bradley added his last bit before leaving.

David drew in a long slow breath as he watched the young man go. He exhaled the same slow way, to calm his insides to a tolerable keel. Damnit, he'd have to get used to Bradley. They shared dayshift now. "I'll get the kids tonight Gable, and in about three weeks, Jess and I'll get married."

"Jess?"

"Jessica King," he said. "Doctor."

"Doctor? Are you shittin' me?"

David shoved his hands into his pockets. "And when you see her, ole boy, you'll doubt it even more. She's beautiful, Gable, intelligent…soft. Has the most gorgeous blue eyes you ever saw."

As David spoke, his mind drifted away so that the others in the office disappeared right before him. He thought about what Gable might be thinking, wondered himself at times, how a woman such as Jessica could see anything in him. But he believed her, with all his heart, when she said she did see something. He just prayed to God she saw enough. David also knew, with all his heart, that nothing but hell loomed ahead of them if he didn't find a break soon. David had dug his brain ten times and again and still could find no way out from under Harold James.

Eighteen

The children had been released from Brigham, and Kurt and Sally awaited David's arrival to pick them up. This day held a special glimmer in their eyes, barely matched by Jessica's own excitement. Inside these moments, David could look ahead with an optimism that appeared when his new family stood near him and he felt more than relieved to get them home. Sheila had helped him fix the bedroom with comforters sporting the latest movie characters, bear-shaped pillows and a few more toys and clothes. All awaited on the bed for the children when they walked in.

"Now don't you two expect something every time you come home." He patted their heads. "Today is just special."

"Cause you ow daddy now, huh David."

"I sure am, sweetheart." David squeezed Sally snuggly to his thigh and he wondered if his kids would ever call he and Jessica, dad and mom. He didn't expect it under the circumstances, but the words would sound great if he ever heard them.

"Kurt." He waved as the boy ran by. "How about getting the mail from outside. I forgot all about it."

Disappearing in a flash, Kurt returned but a few minutes later with a confused frown. No letters. "There's a whole bunch of mail boxes out there and they're all funny and stacked up."

"It's the black one," Sally said.

Kurt turned around, and when he shoved his hands down into his pockets, he looked just like David. "That's the *other* house, Sally."

"No problem. Ours is by the end closest to our apartment, son, second box from the bottom. You'll have to read the name on the front. Plus...." David winked. "You'll need this key."

"You don't have to spell it." Kurt took the silver ring from David's finger. "We were practicing today. S-t-r-a-u-s."

"We?" David asked.

"Jess'ca and us," Sally said. "We all wote ow new names."

"Is that right?" David pictured the three of them writing Straus behind their names and he nodded with a grin. Damn, he did like the idea. "I didn't realize you could write, Sally."

"I can't," she said and paddled off to find her brother outside. She met him at the front door; Kurt held their mail in his waving hand.

234

"Can I open this one?"

"No…" David walked over to open the envelope. "That's a bill."

"This one?"

"Sure." He paid no attention to the one in Kurt's hand, instead, muttered about the electricity costs and went to the desk in the living room to pull out the file from beside the computer where he'd stashed his last bill. He heard giggles across the room. He smiled. There were children in his house.

But as a certain set of words met his ears −the distinct way Kurt's voice became high− illness crept upward from his insides.

"This is a funny letter," Kurt said. "David don't forget."

"Give it to me, son." David's tone chilled his own neck and arms. Or did his change of expression erase the children's smiles?

"What does it mean?"

David held a classic extortion letter, a reminder in his case, where the name and message had been cut from pages of a magazine and glued to another paper, unimaginative as hell but effective in rattling the recipient, and in David's frame of mind, rocked him to a near violent rage because Kurt and Sally saw the letter, controlled only because they stood right there, gazing up at him.

"It's just a joke," he said, but innocent green eyes told him they didn't believe it. "Some people think they're funny when they're not."

That, the children understood and so David tuned in a cartoon to occupy them while he went to his room. He closed the door, locked it, and forced himself to breathe.

He heard Kurt laugh.

He smelled the watermelon bubble gum that Sally had left on his night stand.

He saw the sweater that Jessica hung over his chair.

"Son-of-a-bitch."

Collapsing on the bed, he managed to turn the long envelope over and over in his hand. He ran his fingers across the top of the letters and read the words, the postmark dated the day before out of Dareing, California. Harold hadn't left on his little vacation.

The rotten pile of shit had him high-centered and spinning his wheels. He should have killed the bastard. He screwed that up, too. Damnit. There's the $7,000 withdrawn for no reason. Evidence. Never should have paid the shit-head.

"Jesus Christ–" Sweat broke out at his face. Every part of his body knotted up with his astonishment, the disgusting nauseous bile that claimed his throat to even think that way at all, and he tucked the note between his mattresses, a gesture, as it were, to do the same with his emotions…for now, with his family only two rooms away. "Evidence." He wiped the sweat from his brow and walked away to join his kids.

The rest of the week passed without occurrence and if he wouldn't have had the constant black shadow of Harold James, David's life might have felt normal. But just as he began to crawl out of the stagnant hole, a neat reminder would come in the mail. And then Otis Clark called early Saturday morning.

"Sorry David," Otis said, "thought I'd give you a ring before you had a chance to go to sleep."

"My new shift." David yawned. "I've had the kids since Monday, I'm working days now."

"Decided to join the human race, eh?"

David chuckled. "Guess I'm not quite used to being a human. Anyway, I always thought it was a big deal to sleep in on the weekend." David rubbed his eyes. He frowned. "What's up, Otis? You don't sound so good."

"I'm fine, David." Otis sighed so loudly that it resounded over the receiver. "You remember our last visit? I said I'd keep my ears open about Harold?"

"I can't come right now." David shot straight up in bed. "The kids–"

"No. No it's not the end of the world."

End of the world? Holy Christ... David could barely breathe. "Jess is coming by around ten," he said. "You going to be at the mortuary?"

"I am," he said. "All day. And I'll be in the lab where we were that very first time. Think you can find it?"

"Otis?"

"I'll talk to you then."

When the phone went dead, David closed his eyes and the exhaustion that settled over him felt like he'd not slept at all. "What? Sally?" He heard his name from afar, then again, as she came into the room. He still held the receiver, aware now of his white-hot clutch around the plastic. Hanging it up, he wiped the sweat from his face with the back his hand. "It's too early to get up, honey," he said, but she just stood there, her eyes green and wide. "Are you sick?"

When she shook her head, her tangled locks tossed about her shoulders and she hugged her doll with one arm while her fingers tugged on the nightgown she wore. "I kinda don't feel good," she said. "I think I need to get in yo bed."

"Did the phone wake you up?" David flipped over the covers and Sally climbed inside them.

"No," she said, "You did when you talked."

"I'm sorry, sweetheart." Resettling beneath the blanket, he felt her tiny arm across his chest and she tucked her feet beneath his legs to where his heart seemed to warm with the toasty temperature.

"Aw we going shopping today?"

"I don't know for sure, Sally, why?"

"Cause you need to buy some jamas, David."

"I do, huh," he said and a smile inched along his lips so that he closed his eyes. What in God's name did he ever do without this sweet family? And if Sally noticed he needed more on, perhaps he'd better buy some jamas. Or at least some boxers, for god sakes. Grinning, he brushed a strand of tawny hair behind her ear.

"Did you wun out of money?"

"What?"

"Fo to buy jamas."

"No honey, I have money. I just never liked to wear them." In the silence, and the way her fingers tugged at the hair on his chest, David could sense the workings of her mind. Daddies were supposed to wear nightclothes.

"Well, if you liked them and didn't have any money," she said, "we could get some fum my otha daddy fo you. He liked jamas."

"Except Sally…" David filled his lungs as best he could and pressed his lips onto the top of her soft tangled hair. "Baby, though, remember…."

238

"I know," she said, "they bunt didn't they."

"Yes." He didn't know if she referred to the pajamas or her parents, but he just let it pass and squeezed the fingers that twisted his hair. "Sally do you think about your other daddy?"

"And mommie," she said, "at night, a lot I do when I can't sleep."

"Well sweetheart…please come and talk to me then and tell me what you're thinking. I want to know about your other daddy. I think he must have been a very smart man." Sighing, he pressed Sally tight against him to feel her tiny heart thump strong at his ribs. He smelled her cotton candy hair and the warmth of her milky-scented breath. "Your other daddy would have be to awfully smart to get such a good little girl."

"Does that make you smawt, David?" Sally's head popped up from off his chest. "Cause you got me now, don't you."

David's lips parted to speak. But his answer barely sounded. "I hope so baby," he said. He sure as hell hoped so, because if Sally could see in his mind right now she might think him far from intelligent. Only an idiot would do what he'd done, let a life sucking snake wrap itself around his neck so that the longer he left it, the tighter it became.

Like the ember that grew in his gut and quite literally flamed up with red hot anger into his throat as he walked down the too-quiet hall of Clark and Talbot's. As he headed for the lab, he hoped to find Otis alone.

"Why the hell don't you pipe some music into this place, Otis?" David meant his greeting as a joke. Neither man laughed.

Otis looked up from the corpse. "If this bothers

you, David we can go out."

Otis inserted a long silver instrument into the dead man's groin and for a moment, David wondered if it might bother him. "No. Shit. Just tell me what's going on. I thought you didn't do this anymore. I thought Harold did all the embalming."

"He did." Otis stared down at the body as if he saw nothing there at all and then all at once, he flipped the sheet to cover it up. "Come on, let's get some coffee." Grabbing an antiseptic towel to wash his hands, he headed to his office. "Harold came up to me late yesterday, just after Malcolm's funeral, and said he was quitting."

"Quitting?"

"Just like that." Otis snapped his fingers. "No notice. No explanation. No nothing. What the hell's going on?"

"You're asking me?" David stepped back to catch his words. "The bastard quits and you're asking me? How the hell would I know?" But he did know, and now he had to lie and cover-up with Otis. Or he could just walk out.

"I read the paper, man," Otis said. "What's this scam about you needing an assistant at the cemetery?"

"A scam. What did Harold say?"

"Nothing." The big man's eyebrows knitted so closely together that a single dark line crossed his forehead. "Why do you need a scam?" Otis stared at David. He stared hard. "And whether it's a phony story or not, I know as sure as we're both standing here, that you'd pick anybody but Harold James. Harold James would be the last one you'd put with your name on the printed page. Especially," Otis said, "especially when you know damn well you could have put my name."

David walked to the office window, blind to the outside scenery. But he could still see Otis's eyes; he could feel them penetrate the back of his head.

"Didn't have a choice."

"Balls," Otis said, and David whipped around.

"Damnit, Otis, don't push me."

"Push you for what? Information? Hell, I'm suppose to know all there is. This is me..." Otis poked his own chest. "The jackass who said you could trust Harold. Well by God I'm telling you now, something's going on, and I want to know what it is." Otis looked as if an earthquake had rocked his insides. "This secret just cannot get out. Do you realize what it would do to our lives?"

Clenching his jaw down tight, David knew damned well what it would do to their lives and the knowing shown clear in the sweat that dripped from his temples...the strain that he felt at his eyes. David knew he'd turned pale.

"Harold told me he's going on a vacation," Otis said.

"When is he going? Where?"

"I don't know."

Otis's vision locked onto David and he couldn't break free. He tried. He could not turn away and the tension literally breathed down his spine like fire from the gates of hell.

"How can I help," Otis said, "if you won't–"

"Help. Who the hell said I needed help?"

"No one. You don't have to."

Spinning away to face the window again, David crossed his arms at his chest but he could still hear Otis behind him; he could hear him shuffle papers and mess with his pens to make noise.

"I couldn't sleep last night, David, thinking about this."

"Forget it."

"The hell I'll forget it."

"The hell you'll do anything but." David walked over and stood beside Otis at the desk. "Harold quit. No big deal, right? People up and quit jobs everyday."

"People, yes. Not Harold James."

"Drop it, Otis." Anger rocked the room and the two powerful men within it. Electricity collided like lightening shards and yet cradled in the confines of the office, a clock ticked. David had never heard one here before. Strange. It kept perfect time with the blood that pulsed at his temples. He forced himself to breathe and closed his eyes for one second only. "You told me what's going on and I thank you," he said. "I'll just keep an eye on Harold, watch him."

"Good God, David, Harold's leaving. How can ya–"

"Alright. Damnit. The man's leaving." David backed away, his composure blown. "I sure as hell can't stop him." Trying to convince Otis everything was square, was like pulling teeth from a mother bear while she watched you stuff her cubs into a goddamn sack. "I gotta go." Jesus. "I gotta pick up the kids." He turned around to face the door.

"David."

He halted. But he didn't dare look over at Otis, again. "There's nothing we can do, okay?" When he heard no reply, David moved ahead.

"How are we going to stop Harold if he decides to

talk? This just can't...."

"I know." David's answer brought a red, hot rush to his face, his fingers white and ice cold on the brass doorknob. "I know," he said but the whisper left an echo through the mortuary so that it taunted David clear down the hall. He knew he hadn't convinced Otis one iota. The man felt too guilt ridden, too nervous, after Harold's sporadic move. David only hoped that he'd relayed the emotion of fear to Otis, fear that Harold may talk, not that Harold had already approached with extortion.

Otis was a good man, had a heart of gold and plenty of remorse for bad advise, but, "Damn–" David shifted his car into drive. "Damn if I'm going to drag someone down with me. Even you, Otis."

They had all misjudged the cunning Harold James. Too late to cry about it now.

Four days later, David received another personal letter. No longer permitting the children to get the mail for him, he picked it up himself. The typed envelope looked the same but had been postmarked from San Diego.

TWO WEEKS SHERIFF SERGEANT STRAUS

Nausea struck as he tucked the third note between his mattresses with the others. Harold liked schedules, a cycle of two letters a week and David knew where his money went during the little vacation –magazines, postage, and the San Diego Zoo. With any luck, Harold would fall into a hungry lion's pit.

When Jessica and the children were around him, David kept his emotions on a tight leash. He didn't dwell on the situation as he often did when alone and allow the intensity to grow inside with an acid that ate him alive. No. Determination kept him lying to Jessica. She had no idea of the extortion, until the reporter, Jackson Miles, came over to them as they left the hospital for a quick sandwich.

"Sergeant. Sgt. Straus, I've got to talk to you." Miles ran to their car while he flagged a white piece of paper in the air. "I've got a letter here, Sergeant."

Letter. The word hit David's ears with an explosion and he grasped Jessica's arm to spin her around but Miles shoved the note in front of them both.

STRAUS BEWARE!

Jessica gasped, as if the air had been knocked from her lungs.

"Your boss said I could find you here."

"Did you show this to Williamson? This is private, damn you."

"David—"

"It's the same type of letter I received about the rumor, Sergeant. You remember before, about the five live—"

"I remember."

"David—"

From the corner of his vision, Jessica reappeared and David's heart crumbled inside his chest; she looked like he'd punched her in the face.

"Have you received any letters of this sort?" Miles asked.

He studied her eyes and her white damp flesh. He stared into the irises of vibrant turbulent blue. And then he turned away. "Yes," he said, "I've received some letters. It's from the abductors, if you haven't already guessed."

"I've figured that out, but why are they sending things to me?"

Good question. David shook his head. Damn good question. "My only thought would be that they, the cult, know I am very near. They know I'm trying to keep the story under wraps. That's no secret. I suppose it's a way to stress me out and rattle me to hinder the investigation."

"What kind of notes have you gotten, sir?"

David pressed his lips together. He didn't blink. Or move. Or swallow.

The reporter shifted his shoulders. "Am I to assume that your work with Harold James has developed significant findings?"

David's mind whirled. It raced. He had to out-jump the rat. But what in God's name was Harold trying to accomplish when he sent the message?

David knew all too well.

He had two directions ahead. He could have Miles report a follow-up that would tell Harold, in a round-about way, that the columnist had approached him and harassed him about the children's secret. Or he could keep it out of the news altogether, upset Harold a bit.

But did he really want to do that?

"Tell me, Jackson," David said, "are you out for a hot scoop, to make a fast name for yourself, or do you want to do some good?"

"I, uh, guess I want to do both," Miles said.

"Obviously, you can print the story of the cult, as much as you know, and expose the fact that we're on their tail and have received threats. That, in turn, would blow the whole pursuit wide open and I'd have every reporter from here to New Brunswick on my ass. Everything would be screwed up. The kid's would be in even greater danger than they are now." David rubbed his temples and prayed that his ad lib made more sense to the reporter than to himself. "Or," he said, "you can print an update, say that you've spoken to me and that I am progressing with the investigation at an acceptable rate under the circumstances. And that Harold James has helped a great deal." The last sentence nearly twisted David's tongue right off but he said it anyway.

And then he held his breath. He watched Jackson Miles think and study his notebook. Study David.

"May I quote you on that last statement, Sergeant?"

"Yes. Please." David nodded and released a slow steady breath, thankful that a few people in this world still had morals, grateful that one of them was Jackson Miles.

"I promise you the exclusive story," he said. "I promise."

When Miles slapped his book shut and walked away, David felt encouraged. Until Jessica brushed up against his arm.

Jessica. Her name hammered in his head. Her face loomed white in his eyes and in a rage, he swiveled around to grab Miles. "Damn him–"

"David." Screaming, she caught his shirt sleeve just barely enough to jerk him back to her as he darted away. "What are you doing?"

"I'm going to beat some brains into that bastard."

"Stop."

Her fingernails dug into his flesh so sharply that he halted, anger hot in his face.

"What is this all about?"

"You never should have seen, damn it. He should

246

have waited until I–"

"Stop it." She said it again. "Just stop. That's not what I'm talking about and you know it. Those letters are not from a cult."

"I was lying to him, Jess." David watched on as she stared at him, as her jaw dropped down to her chest.

"My God," she said, "I know it's a lie but how much, David? That note was real. Who is threatening you? Who is after our children?"

"Jessie...please–"

"Don't Jessie me." Gripping his arm harder still, she straightened her posture as if for combat. "Those are my children, too," she said. "I have every right to know, too."

"I can't tell you, Jessica." When he grasped her hand, her eyes burned with fire, her skin like ice and he knew she could see through any story that he dare dream up. "I just can't tell you."

"You can't," she said, "or you won't?"

"Both...damnit. I'm handling it. Let me handle it alone."

"No." Breaking free, her shoulders shuddered with a jerk. "I'll not accept that, David," she said. "I'll never accept it, ever, if we have a life together. If you're in trouble, the children, then I'm in trouble, and I have a right to know."

"Just trust me, Jessica. Please...trust me."

"How can I?" When David had no answer, her face collapsed. Twisting around, she ran toward the hospital steps.

"Jesus. Jessica. No." Dashing ahead, he planted himself in front of her. "Baby, don't go. God. Please, if I ever need your trust, your blind support, it's right now."

He gathered her into his arms to stop the earthquake in his chest. "I do need you but behind me," he said. "I need you behind where I can protect you, not beside me where you can get hurt. Sweet Jesus, please. Trust me." When her fingers warmed his spine, when he felt her body melt against him, David found that his lungs could work again. He could breathe. "It's not that I'm lying to you or trying to deceive you, baby," he said, "it's just that sometimes, if you honestly don't know anything...."

Jessica's nod stopped his words, her tears that soaked his shirt and he knew, whether she understood or not, that she would stand by him. "I'm sorry, Jess. Believe me, I've tried to keep you out of this." He whispered against her ear and her temple...her hair, so she could feel his need. His desperation. "Sweetheart, I know it's so hard to be in the dark. Jesus," he said, "I know it's so damn scary in the dark."

By the last week of August, six extortion letters hid between David's mattresses. He had no money for Harold. He had no plan. He had one week to go. As the situation stood now, he would walk into the next confrontation a blind man. But one thing was always clear in David's mind, he would gain control.

He kept good track of Harold. His money had foot the bill to San Diego, Las Vegas and Sacramento; the envelope today was postmarked Dareing. Harold was back in town to await another pay off.

David sank low into the sofa and tapped the letter. The house felt too quiet at noon; no children were around with cheerful noises to bring him up and Jessica worked odd hours at Brigham. Their relationship wasn't quite the same anymore. They were still in love, and David kept telling her, but all too often they just sat and looked at one another. Neither knew what to say. The plans for their marriage had all but ceased.

Pain shot through David's heart and he tried to rub it away after he'd tucked note number seven in with the others. He told himself the eighth one would arrive on Thursday and he planned the day. He'd come for lunch, alone, pick up the mail like today, before anyone else. Alone echoed in his head. He'd been by himself all his life and now that he had someone…damn it anyway.

By Wednesday evening, David felt more smothered than ever, even with Jessica at his side. She'd fixed dinner and helped him with Kurt and Sally at bedtime. They kissed the children goodnight together and walked arm in arm down the quiet hall.

"I could turn on the news," David said.

"How about some music, a CD or something. I rather like the peacefulness tonight."

"Peaceful?" David groaned. "I'm so damned…." Stopping at the sofa, Jessica tightened her arms around him and he looked down to see her face.

"You've lost weight," she said.

He nodded. Exhaling, his breath feathered through her hair in such a way that he stood to watch the shiny blonde shimmers along her skin. He didn't want to apologize. Damnit…he didn't want pity. He just wanted Harold James. Jessica hadn't asked specifics, thank God, but he knew the questions haunted her mind. He didn't want her asking now. He'd just tell her no.

"Where are your CD's?" she asked. "Anything instrumental?"

He pointed. "About all I have is instrumental,

249

none of that high-chord synthetic rap garbage they're trying to make us listen to."

Snickering, her reply filtered away and the air grew still, flutes and gentle strings bathed the room, the real thing. She pressed the volume so the music flowed just loud enough to where he had to focus to listen.

"Dance with me, David."

Jesus. He didn't feel like dancing and her mood confused him. Then she held her hands out to him so innocently, her smile so magnetic…he could not resist. "I'm only doing this so I can hold you," he said and pushed himself up from the sofa.

"I went shopping today," she said and they fell into step. He pulled her tight against his chest.

"Did you?" he said.

"I found a dress, David. A wedding dress."

He wanted to make her his wife so bad he could hardly stay in his skin but the timing fell all wrong. How could he marry her with Harold James still at his throat? Kissing her eyes so that they closed, she laid her head on his shoulder. He knew his silence hurt her.

"How much longer will it be?"

"I don't know, baby." He wanted to say tomorrow. "Not too long I hope."

"David," she said, "I know we've set our wedding plans to the back for now but September is almost here."

Gazing up again, the childlike expectancy truly radiated in her face. She looked so much like Sally to him sometimes, her excitement was so pure sometimes that….

"I still want us to get married," she said.

"Jesus, sweetheart, so do I."

"Then let's do it."

His feet stuck to the floor. His thoughts, like a pinball, darted from agreement to opposition and back again.

"David, I know nothing about this predicament," she said, "but I have promised to stand by you, and I will. Always. So please don't make it more difficult by setting me away."

"Setting you away...ah geeze." He rubbed her shoulders and her arms, her waist. "Are you feeling that? Honey, I don't mean to, and don't ever think it. I...what if something happens to me?"

"Are you thinking that way again?" Jessica clutched his arms. "I feel the same about it as Kurt and Sally," she said, "I want us to get married and adopt those kids."

The room spun about his head and he had to tell himself to calm down...to breathe. He wanted to adopt them too, but....

"David," she said, "please believe me with all your heart, I'd give anything to have one day of being your wife, behind you, than— It gets so lonely at night now."

"I know, kitten."

"I get so scared, sometimes."

"Baby, I know you do, I know you do." He kissed her hopeful blue eyes and her hot red cheeks; he kissed the blood that pounded at her temples and led her back to the sofa to gather her into his lap. He stroked her hair.

"I had the woman at the boutique hold that dress," she said. "I want you to see it first."

"I don't know a damn—"

"I knew you'd say that." She sat up. "I don't want to buy the dress unless you like it. What if you hated it?

251

Our wedding may not be–"

"Now Jessie, I haven't hated anything you've worn yet."

"This is for our wedding," she said. "I want to be beautiful for you." She pressed her mouth onto his forehead. "I'm assisting with surgery tomorrow but I'll be out by ten. I thought we could meet for your lunch hour and go see it."

"Tomorrow's Thursday." The words burned in his throat, the words like acid on silk and he watched her spirit disintegrate right before his eyes. He couldn't go because of the secret he kept from her and she damn well knew it. But just as surely, he felt compelled to get the mail as soon as he could. "Jess," he said, "how long will this take? Where is the store?"

"It's off the Meridian, that second ramp going east."

Her voice sounded muffled as she spoke to his chest, while he calculated time, distances. "Maybe we can meet there after work, sweetheart. I could get the kids–"

"No," she said. "I have a late schedule."

"How about Friday?"

"No David." Sitting up, she smoothed the front of his shirt with both her hands. Her fingers trembled at his chest. "It's okay."

And he might have believed her, if it weren't for her watered-up sapphire eyes. "Damn it," he said, "it's not okay."

"I told her to hold it for only one day."

"We'll call her."

"No." Jessica straightened up, taller still. "There are other dresses," she said, "and they may not sell that

252

one."

"Shit." David cursed the ringing phone. The timing. This damn situation had upset Jessica again. "Don't answer it." Dashing over, David slapped his hand down on the receiver and she halted, as if paralyzed, in the middle of the room. The phone rang twice more, echoing as the sound and the oxygen petrified while they searched each other's face.

David picked up the phone and pressed it tight against his ear. "Straus."

"This is Otis."

Thank God. David released the breath that had pulled his shoulders rigid and his throat drum tight. He would have bet money it was somebody else. "What's up, Otis?"

"Nothing really."

David frowned. He glanced at Jessica. "You're working kind of late, aren't you?"

Otis chuckled, or perhaps his words shook. "I just called to see how you were, how things were going."

"Things are fine," David said. Otis's tone had changed from the last time they'd talked. That guilt-ridden fear that had vibrated his every sentence had vanished. Yet David heard something different, something new. Nothing could have happened that he wouldn't already know. Could it? All the while, David studied Jessica, too; she hadn't moved, her ear tipped heavily toward the conversation. He weighed-out all his options. "Are you going to be at the mortuary in the morning, Otis?"

"I have a funeral at ten," Otis said. "I…uh…I just wanted to see how you were. I haven't seen or heard–"

"I'll make it over by eight." David rubbed the

back of his neck and held firm to the time. Otis was no poker player.

"Sure David, but I'm going to be busy and like I said...."

"See ya tomorrow, Otis." David hung up the phone. He swallowed.   But the more he stared at the receiver the faster his pulse beat at his ears.

"That was Otis Clark from the funeral home, wasn't it, David?

He nodded. Christ, how much should he say?

"My God." Jessica gasped. "Otis is threatening you."

"No." David grabbed her hands. "No, he isn't. I swear."

"But I know by your face that call had something to do with...with you know what. What does Otis Clark have to do with it?"

"Jessica. Nothing."   David tightened the grip around her fingers but he had squeezed her just a little too tight. Her eyes shot wide open.

"Harold James."

"Jessica drop it."

"You were right all along. Oh my Lord."

"Stop, this instant." He grasped her shoulders. "The subject is closed right now." He shook her, just a fraction, to control her attention. "And I mean it," he said and watched a huge hard swallow move down her throat as she stepped toward him. Her clutch at his waist came with a power he didn't think possible.

"We have got to get married." Her voice declared her own mark of control, her own resolve, her hands rock steady. "Next week, David, like we planned. We have got to protect those kids."

David drove up to Clark and Talbot's at eight sharp and proceeded to follow Otis around for fifteen minutes.

"Can't you park it for just a sec?" David had the distinct feeling that Otis kept himself busy to avoid conversation and eye contact. They'd gone to the lab, on to storage, and then down to the large chapel where the deceased lay for the coming service.

"No, David, I can't stop, have to get things lined up here."

Perching on the edge of the mahogany pew, David watched Otis arrange the woman's hands across her chest. He worked as if setting a dinner table −a table with linen napkins and seven forks, shrimp tines and soup spoons, for Christ sakes. "Otis, have you hired anyone to replace Harold yet?"

Stiffening, Otis flinched just enough to be noticed. Then he straightened the ruffled satin on the pillow. "I've interviewed a few," he said. "Harold never did this anyway, David. This is something I always do, get the loved one just so." Otis turned around, and for the first time during their visit, he looked into David's eyes. "Little things mean a lot to people when they walk by here, even if no one consciously recognizes that it's been done."

David agreed, just because he felt a little uncomfortable from Otis's behavior. He chuckled then to pass off the sensation. "I think I'll have you stick my finger up my ass Otis, that's what I think of this world, sometimes, and some of the bastards in it. Have you seen Harold?"

"No." Otis turned to shut the casket. "I thought he left."

"He's back."

"Is that so." Otis stood still a moment. "You know David, sometimes you get panicky about things and it comes to no good, only to worry yourself."

"Sometimes. Sometimes not," David said. "What are you trying to say, Otis?"

Shaking his head and with a deep inhale, Otis stepped up to squeeze David's bicep and David stood there, staring, reminded instantly of the man's strength.

"What I'm trying to say is that things very often have a way of working out on their own."

David nodded. He frowned. Was Otis trying to tell him something yet say nothing at all? David fell in the same pot. He certainly couldn't come out and ask Otis about any details, he'd been too damned closed-mouth and noncommittal himself during their last visit. "Sure Otis." Just words for David to say. He didn't agree. This extortion of Harold's just wasn't going to up and disappear, that is, unless Harold did. All at once David wondered if Otis thought Harold had left for good on the little vacation. "Did I tell you Harold is back?"

"You said that just a minute ago." Otis looked him straight in the eyes and squeezed him one more second before he let go.

David rubbed his arm. "Oh yeah." He put his hands in his pockets. "You seem a lot calmer, Otis, than when I saw you last."

"I'm going down here, David."

He accepted the off-hand invitation and followed Otis into a small, cubbyhole room curtained at the side with opaque panels for privacy.

"I always hated funerals. No offense, Otis." As David stood in the partitioned section for the immediate family, he remembered his time there when each of his parents had died. "Especially these rooms," he said. "More tears here, I guess."

Otis adjusted the small white Bibles and brushed off the velveteen-covered benches.

David talked to himself. "Maybe I'll get cremated instead," he said. "You do have a crematorium, don't you?"

Otis straightened from his dusting and nodded. He stared at the wall before him.

David gazed over. "I'm sorry Otis, didn't mean to come and bother you today while you're…so busy. I just, I don't know, wondered about your call."

"I told you, I just wanted to see how you were?"

"No better," David said and received that same odd expression. He said goodbye and walked away.

Had he misjudged Otis? Sure, the man was still concerned about what Harold may do, but maybe as the weeks had passed, the fear had too. Otis could wipe his hands of it. For all Otis knew, Harold had just grown tired of being a mortician and nothing more. Otis still had no clues of the blackmail, just the way it would stay.

When David arrived at his cluster box at noon to pick up the final extortion letter, he found an ad for auto insurance and a uniform catalog.

Nothing from Harold James.

"Son-of-a-bitch. Always something to screw me up." Now he'd have to worry one more day.

He grumbled all the way to meet Jessica for a bite to eat and a few minutes to look for another dress. She ran up to him through the parking lot.

"Dr. Morrison has found something about the children. He has a little more research to do but he's definitely on to the answer. He's asked me to call everyone together for this Saturday afternoon."

Jessica kept David more than busy until then, buying rings, suits, and dresses for the wedding. Everyday at lunchtime he'd drive home, yet everyday, he found no letter from Harold James in the mail. The fact disturbed him.

Driving with Kurt and Sally to meet the family at Brigham, he tried to work out the puzzle, again. David found it very odd that Harold failed to send one last letter, the one reminder that would impact him the most. Why did he stop?

"What in the hell are you up to, Harold?" David said, but when he walked into the conference room of the hospital, the discomfort vanished. Sheila Adams greeted him with a giant hug. He embraced her in return and shook her husband's hand at the same time. "Steve… things going well in Anaheim?"

"Wonderful."

"We heard the good news, David."

"Good news?" He glanced around. "Am I late?"

"No." Sheila groaned. "About Friday. Jessica said you've got all your plans ready for the wedding."

"Yes. Yes we have, but you know, there wasn't a heck of a lot to do."

"Are you kidding?" Steve said. "It took Sheila eight months to plan ours."

David laughed full out. "But this is a hurry up marriage," he said, "you know how it is with kids on the way?"

"Jessica's pregnant?"

"No. Good God no, I meant Kurt and Sally."

Sheila slapped his arm.

"I saw Steven," he said, "with Kristy." Twisting in a half-circle, David looked around to see all the parents now present for the meeting, Tammy Alexander the only little one, snuggling in her mother's arms. "That was great for Kristy to come along, help us all out with a babysitter. Thank you. How is Steven adjusting to all the family?"

Husband and wife looked at one another. "He has turned into the most spoiled child imaginable, David. He's every bit as independent as before."

"Only now," Steve said, "he wants to hang around the older kids. And they love it. The twins took him and spent the entire afternoon at the laser arcade."

David moaned. "I bet he's going nuts over that fusion jazz."

"I'm adding to our PC, we need to funnel his energies into the right direction. He's got a lot of catching up to do."

David nodded –sixteen years. The conversation shifted while they waited; John Alexander relayed his experience with the new home system he'd purchased. David walked over to speak with the usually quiet Marie, now chatting with Lynor.

"How are you and Tony getting along?" he asked.

"We are just fine. My Tony is going to start kindergarten in a few weeks."

"Already?" David took her hand to squeeze her fingers.

"You know," she said, "the judge, Mr. Bailey, and Dr. Bishop are helping me."

"Yes, Vin told me, Marie. I think it's great. You

settled into the new place, yet?"

"I am getting there. Stop in, David, please. I am so close now, to the hospital and Tony's school. I plan to pay them back," she said, and her smile grew with pride. "I am keeping track of every penny."

"They don't mean for you to, Marie."

"I know but I am most certainly going to try."

David had to hug her, he just had to. Marie was a good woman, she wouldn't squander the extra money nor grow lazy expecting help.

"I'll pop in next week," he said, "and bring the kids." He knelt down to put his finger near Tammy so she would grab hold. "And how is this littlest pumpkin?"

"Stronger and prettier everyday," Lynor said. "I heard you and Jessica are positively going to adopt Kurt and Sally."

"Positively."

"It must be the right decision, because I've not seen you or Jessica happier."

"Yes," Marie said, "your good mood is showing all over."

Good mood? Good God. The comment hit David like a jolt from a cattle prod and he stepped backwards. Marie was right. He did feel good today. Harold screwed up by not sending that final letter. He had actually forgotten about him for ten minutes.

A short ten minutes. As David looked around at the others, the shadow crept over him once again. A lot of happiness depended on what happened Tuesday night at the cemetery.

8:30. Happy hour.

When Jessica walked in, Gordon Bishop and Nevil Morrison followed behind her. Morrison motioned the family over, eager to begin.

"As you know, I have called you here because I believe I have come across the answer, and I stress those words," he said, "come across. That is just how it happened. I did every experiment, every test that I could dream up using the LS_5 and the children's blood. But LS_5 is toxic. To put it simply," he said with fingers entwined, "when this base solution interacts with blood, it unites with the red and white corpuscles. As the blood passes through the circulatory system, it absorbs other fluids of the body, in turn, thinning the blood to the consistency of water. The veins and arteries swell, unable to hold the added liquid, heart rate quickens to an immeasurable degree and one dies of heart failure, if their veins don't explode first. And this happens within an hour.

"To get to the next plateau of findings," he said, "I went through this chain of analysis using dead rats. I injected a mass dosage of LS_5 into the rats, just as Harold James saturated the five children. The chemical and blood readily combined because of the amount used. But since the heart had ceased its circulation, the LS_5-blood solution was very slow in absorbing the body fluids. In fact, not until two days ago, did the process begin. As yet, the rats are still full of poisonous LS_5. I keep them at cooler temperatures." Morrison raised his palms as if stopping any questions. "I realize that this process the children went through took sixteen years, but there has to be another element involved, a factor to alter the basic structure of LS_5, something to annihilate the toxic nature of the emulsion."

The family looked at Morrison. His expression brightened. "I told you before that the children all had something in common. The factor —they all died from lung failure of some sort. There lies the key." He wrote the letters R-CELLOXYN on the blackboard and turned back around. "R-Celloxyn," he said, "a natural chemical existing in each and every animal that has died from lack of oxygen. We've known about R-Celloxyn for many years," Morrison said, "and after we learned where, why, and when it appeared, we merely accept it as a part of certain deaths."

"You have to die," David said, "to have this R-Celloxyn?"

"Yes, Mr. Straus, you have to die, from lack of oxygen. R-Celloxyn is the chemical excrement of red cells after their last ditch effort to supply the body its needed life giving oxygen. Unless these cells are put to the test, you see, R-Celloxyn does not formulate. Any more questions before I go on?" He looked around.

"I have no R-Celloxyn," Morrison said, "so I can't prove that this small amount of chemical can alter LS_5 in the blood. But I am certain that it happened, with years of dormancy and the constant temperature and oxygen that the geothermal area supplied." Morrison pressed his hands down on the table. "I believe that the LS_5-blood solution is what kept the children from drying up in their time underground, and that a new, let's say, temporary circulatory system evolved through the liquid absorbing interactions of chemicals. LS_5 attracted the body fluids, in turn, supplying fluids through the years, slowly but surely, a perfect movement of blood came to pass. The R-Celloxyn, after a time, worked its miracle."

"So how did Tony come back to life, Dr. Morrison?"

262

"I would not be too outrageous in saying it happened along the lines of Frankenstein."

"Morrison–" No one escaped seeing Marie's whitened face. Morrison smiled.

"Disregard the deplorable laboratory, dear Ms. Rey, and of course the barbarous antics of the evil mad scientist. What happened to your son was natural, Mother Nature bearing herself new life in a most extraordinary way. She shook them until they awakened. The earthquake jolted their hearts and other vital organs into operation."

His near poetic explanation brought a settling image to the family. They remained quiet for a very long time.

But David couldn't stand the silence.

"Morrison," he said. "What are your plans for the future? I am assuming that you'll continue to abide by our agreement of secrecy even though you've figured it all out."

"You needn't worry, Sergeant." Morrison erased the blackboard in wide deliberate strokes. "I intend to keep my research under wraps. I've only theories now anyway, no hard documentation to prove what I've speculated here today. The future, as you say, could hold sixteen years of experiments and study, maybe more. I am in the midst of recreating the phenomenon, but my first challenge shall be gathering a significant supply of R-Celloxyn."

"R-Celloxyn." John Alexander shook his head. "I'd never heard of such a thing."

"It's a rarity," Dr. Morrison said, "and difficult to accumulate and collect, let alone keep in storage. The rats that I use shall supply their own but I must have a substantial amount to study in the depth it will require to fully comprehend."

"Rats do have R-Celloxyn then," Sheila said.

"Yes, but only if they have died from suffocation." Morrison frowned and turned toward Jessica. "I was hoping Harold James would be here. Didn't you call him?"

When Jessica looked at David, he felt his eyes burn, his whole body burn with his instant anger, and an uneasy moment passed before she answered.

"I've tried, unsuccessfully, several times, Dr. Morrison, from Thursday morning through early this morning."

Morrison shrugged. "He told me he was very interested and wanted to know everything I found. I thought, once, of asking him to assist in my research."

"I'll warn you not to, Morrison." David shot up from his chair. "I'm warning all of you, say nothing, do nothing with Harold James."

Jessica gasped and David felt her fingers grip his leg. He didn't know why he'd said it out loud.

Yes. Damnit. Yes, he did know why and he stared down at Jessica's startled blue eyes. Morrison had her call Harold, news that rocked his insides, and he vowed to make certain that it never happened again. Damn certain.

"What are you saying?" Dr. Bishop asked.

"Nothing," David said. "I'm warning. We can't keep Harold from knowing what he knows, but we sure as hell can make sure he learns no more about us."

"He has every right to know." Morrison stood as tall at the opposite end of the table. "We should be grateful. If it weren't for him–"

"That's bullshit, Morrison."

"You never liked the man, Straus. Why don't you admit it?"

Jessica grabbed David's hand this time and squeezed his fingers, hard, to come from behind with her blind support and he found that he could breathe; he found his next words with control. "I will admit it," he said. "It is no secret. I don't like him." David stopped to stare at each person in turn. "I've been a cop a long time and you learn people, you get to know what lies behind their eyes before they speak."

"Don't tell me you've never been fooled," Morrison said.

"Oh yes," David said. "I've been fooled. Many times. That's how the hell I learned."

"As we all learn, everyday."

"Alright, Morrison…" David tightened his grip around Jessica's hand. "You've made your point." Again he looked at the others. "But I hope to Christ that I've made mine."

"Are you finished then, Sgt. Straus?"

"Yes. Thank you, Dr. Morrison." Neither man sat down.

"Straus…would it be presumptuous for me to ask you to have Harold contact me if you see him?"

"Yes," David said. "It would. Besides, Harold has been out of town on a vacation." He didn't let on that Harold was back, just watched Morrison's mouth drop open.

"Is that so?" Morrison said. "Don't tell me you've put a sensor on the poor man. I don't know where you get your bluecoat intuitions, but I have Harold James's word that he would keep in confidence any scientific findings I shared.   In fact..." Morrison chuckled. "Harold James told me he'd be as quiet as a corpse."

As if he'd leaped off a cliff, David's stomach dived downward with a mile-long bungee cinched to it and he had no way to go but follow along, head first, while he waited out the sick sensation, waited for the heat to ease from his face. "And we all know, Dr. Morrison... how quiet Harold James's corpses really are."

Nineteen

As quiet as a corpse.

The words still bounced off the walls of David's mind, even now, days later, as he sat on the fender of his car at Oakwood Cemetery to await his dear friend, Mr. James.

"Corpse," David said through a chuckle, "too bad he isn't one." David could think of just one way to keep the man from talking. Oh, he'd considered arresting Harold again, considered exposing him to everyone. But Harold could still talk. The little man could extort money from all of them and get away with it.

David needed to turn this threat around, hold his gun to Harold's temple and David thought he might enjoy doing it. For a while. The intimidation would have to be continual and brutal to work. And Harold could still go to the media. The degenerate would, too, and Morrison, being an indecisive, intellectual bastard, would stand behind Harold. The truth would be out and Morrison would take advantage for his own scientific gain.

David looked at his watch for the fifth time. Christ. He'd arrived for the pay-off ten minutes early and the time was just now 8:30. Harold was nowhere in sight. The cemetery stood silent like last month; the evening summer birds held their private conversations and the soft Pacific breeze carried it along. He inhaled.

Jake Morgan's old tool shed caught his attention. The windows of the small building still lay in chunks on the grass and David wondered how the old man spent his time now. Morgan had discovered the first child and in the blink of an eye, in what felt like a lifetime, look at all that had happened. "Tammy…" David spoke to the birds. "The littlest pumpkin." If it hadn't been for her hungry cry. No, he didn't want to think about that.

But he did think about Jake. With Oakwood closed down and all the caskets moved and reburied, the retired man would have to keep busy some other way. He should call him sometime. They could reminisce.

After checking his watch again, David jumped off the fender and shoved his hands deep into his faded jeans pockets. The time, still 8:30, or so very near that it was ridiculous. Numbers had changed all right –the seconds, and for a moment he thought his timepiece had stopped. Unfortunately, only time had.

"Damn you anyway, Harold." David walked along the pavement, still lumped and torn from the quakes. This wasn't a tactic he'd planned on, Harold not showing up at all. What could it mean? What could the conniving parasite be up to?

David peered down the hill. The shadow of a vehicle shown through a grove of Oak and Maple trees along the drive. Did Harold buy a brand new Vet? Holy good God. The sleek sports car slowed as it neared the cemetery entrance gate but drove on past. "Kids," he said and looked over the graveyard, once again. He couldn't quite picture the setting as a place to have sex. He chuckled. God no. Every time he came near this place a flood of morbid memories tumbled out. Luckily, Kurt and Sally always tumbled back in to erase the gruesome picture.

8:39 p.m. David felt angrier now than if Harold had shown up. What was he suppose to do? Wait all night? He'd rather do that than go back to the apartment and have Harold pop up while Kurt and Sally were home. Jessica would be with him.

"Shit. Harold, you've screwed with my life enough. Every little thing I do hinges on what you do. Even now, when you're not here, you're being a son-of-a-bitch."

Jessica's eyes, as they'd been tonight, appeared before him. He'd told her he may be late and damn if it didn't look like he would. He'd hoped for a quick confrontation.

His personal Bernardelli waited in the front seat of his car.

Jerking, the sound of another car came to his ears and he stiffened. A rattletrap, he decided, from the drum and clatter, but not Harold's. Rattletrap. Jackson Miles, the reporter, drove an old heap. David spotted the sedan on the road and just as the color came to his mind, the familiar maroon shade flashed between the trees.

"I'll be damned, this make no sense at all." Harold James did plan to be here, he'd invited the press again.

David's watch said 8:45 and he walked to his car to wait for Miles.

"I didn't know you'd be here Sgt. Straus."

"You didn't?" David acted surprised –felt the same way. After all, Miles had witnessed his reckless exit from the hill last month, why shouldn't he be here for this shin-dig? "I didn't know you'd be here."

"Mr. James told me you'd appointed him as your spokesman for the newspaper, that the investigation had snowballed, and you didn't have time to speak to me. Have you received more threatening letters, sir?"

"When did Harold tell you all this?"

"Late Tuesday afternoon. Right after my daily deadline. He came down to the office and said you'd be meeting him up here for a quick consultation but that I should come later so as not to disturb you. Mr. James promised an important update for me. Are you prepared to tell me now?"

"Am I prepared? No."

"Then why are you here? Where is Mr. James?"

"Two, very good questions, Jackson." David climbed on his fender again and rested his elbows on his knees. "I haven't an answer for either one of them."

"When did Mr. James call you, Sergeant?"

"He didn't call me. It was…prearranged that I be here."

"Then this is a regular meeting."

"You can say that."

The young man hopped on the opposite fender to stare down the lane, like David. "Sergeant," Miles said, "if Mr. James were here, what would he tell me?"

270

"He would tell you that...." David picked at the hangnail on his thumb to think his answer through. He wanted to put an end to Miles's so called follow-up. He wanted to fabricate some kind of story to the case and finish things once and for all, like he planned to do with Harold. But the bastard didn't show up. "Did Harold say what to do if he was late?"

"Late." Miles gasped. "Are you kidding? When I told him I might be late he blew a circuit. The man wanted punctuality." Miles thumped his finger on the car hood. "He said eight-forty-five exactly, or no story, that he'd give it to someone else." The young man jumped to his feet. "I've had many compliments on my work, Sergeant. I've done a good job working with you. Remember? You asked me to keep the cult and the threats out of the news and I—"

"Yes." David hopped off the fender, too. "I remember, and I'd still like to kick your ass around this park for coming up to me while Jessica was there."

"Jessica? Your wife?" Miles backed away.

"Damn it man, if you're going to win friends and influence people it's a hell of a way to go."

"I'm sorry, Sergeant."

"I want you to know she knew nothing about it until you—" Catching his breath, David's clenched fists told him that his anger had surfaced. The torn, botched earth behind Miles reminded him, for no good reason. No use digging up old bones that made no difference anymore. "Jesus Christ."

"I am very sorry."

David dashed past Miles. "You can dig up old bones." He stared down the hill.

"What Sergeant?"

Swiveling around, David's stared a hole through Jackson Miles and straight to the Oakwood Cemetery sign. CLARK AND TALBOT MORTUARY. Otis. The name blasted in his mind. "Last Wednesday."

"Are you on to something?"

Grabbing Miles's shoulders in a powerful grip, David tried to fill his lungs. He frowned and stared still at Miles's face but he saw Otis's instead, that composed expression the man wore Thursday morning at the parlor. Thursday morning. David had labeled Otis's activities as busy work, disquiet energy.

A bombardment of echoes struck David's head– Things have a way of working themselves out... Panic comes to no good but to worry yourself... As quiet as a corpse.

His lips shook against his teeth –Little things mean a lot to people even if they don't consciously recognize that it's been done.

"Holy goddamn."

Otis. Otis. I can't believe it. David's mind raced. His thoughts jammed up so all he could see was a huge red arrow that pointed at his benevolent friend, Otis Clark.

Otis Clark, the man with a brawny frame and strong thick hands that could muscle the dead weight of any unfortunate six foot hulk.

Or smaller.

"I gotta go, kid." Releasing the clutch on Miles's arms, David spun around. Otis…this is not a little thing you have done.

"Sergeant. Sergeant, what about my story?"

David halted. "I…." He shook his head as if Miles had appeared from nowhere. "I'll give you the story," he said. "We'll wrap it all up. I promise. You see it just dawned on me; Harold's absence tonight has answered a question of mine." He turned toward his car. "The case is about closed, Jackson. Call me in a few days."

Exiting, David left the reporter in a cloud of dust and when he arrived at the mortuary, a tranquil display of garden lights escorted him under the porte-cochere. The time, 9:30. Dusk. No Otis Clark.

Parking by the front steps, David rubbed the hammer of his gun. His fingers and his heart still shuddered from the tremors inside him. He pressed the gun against the side of his leg, the metal warm, his car and his face hot to where the effects of his speculation encircled him in the darkness. He rolled down the window. He opened the door and stumbled out, desperate for air, for understanding and then stood there, bent at the waist, his head down to his knees.

At home, in bed and with Jessica snuggled tight to his side, scenario after scenario played out in his mind but not until dawn did all the clues and calculations settle into just one picture. Every angle and every premise boiled down to one vivid scene.

Otis Clark killed Harold James.

David squirmed inside, once again, from his thoughts of Harold's arrogance, hubris that Harold could not have been able to contain Tuesday afternoon after stopping by to see Miles. Harold so desperately wanted to be the alpha in this story that Miles could not have been the only stop along Harold's trail to re-establish himself after the little vacation. No...Harold would have had to go see Otis, as well, indeed to bask in the light of his own halo.

And then what happened there? David had played all night with the idea that Otis, weighted down by his own deep remorse —his outright fear, set out to extract the information from Harold but something didn't quite mesh with that picture. An extraction would not have been necessary; Harold's need to brag simmered too near the top. All Otis had to do was mention David's angst and Harold would have easily claimed to be the source…and with great pride.

Nodding his head against the pillow, David made sure to control his exhale, his still-at-the-surface astonishment, so as not to awaken Jessica. She slept so peacefully now and he wanted her to stay that way, serene…forever. God….

The strangest thought of all filtered back to David's mind, that Harold actually tried to involve Otis in the mess, as well. Indeed, once Otis knew of the blackmail, Harold would have to do something. He would either have to extort from Otis, too, or draw him in as a partner with the allure of riches and fame. Or both. David smiled. Christ. He wiggled. That felt so off-the-wall to him and yet the acceptance of it actually allowed him to finally settle down. Nothing Harold had ever done said that he yearned to be in the spotlight; he wanted to be wealthy and powerful, but out in front? No. And so that is where Otis would come in. Otis would be the man in the camera, the employee; Harold would be the boss. The puppeteer. David groaned from deep inside.

The partnership, the switch in roles didn't even get to the first act.

Harold's arrogance, again, took control. Indeed, could Harold even fathom the fact that Otis wanted the secret of the graveyard kept as badly as David? Perhaps more. Otis had deep family roots. Otis had a grandchild on the way. If the secret were exposed, all hell would break loose in the world and Otis would be the only one to hold the rope. If his family were to have any kind of a life, they would have to leave. But where could they possibly go to escape something of this magnitude? David shivered.

Murder would be easy for Otis, considering his size and Harold's, but more importantly, Otis's outlook on death. Seeing a dead man, no matter how one became that way, did little to Otis Clark. He'd seen too many corpses in his lifetime. David was wrong when he thought Otis didn't care and had wiped his hands of the situation. Otis took on full responsibility for Harold. Otis was ashamed about the hand shake. Otis guarded his loyalties deep within his soul.

And so David closed his eyes, once more; he worked to calm his heart and his breath, once more. Last night, he'd taken his gun. Last night, he planned to do the same thing to Harold.

This morning, questions still plagued his mind and he knew he would have to have another chat with Otis.

After having a rather surreal breakfast with his family, David kept his bearing enough to check in at work but as he drove his squad car to Clark and Talbot's, he still wondered if he should tell Otis about his suspicions.

Suspicions? Guesses? Speculations? He held no evidence. No one even missed Harold. David sure as hell didn't miss him and had no intentions to even go look. For all he knew, Harold had left on another of his little vacations.

Stepping through the glass door entrance, David

walked into the familiar mortuary. At first, everything seemed the same, until his ears adjusted. A wave of music greeted him, not the usual organ one would anticipate, but an instrumental blend of violins and woodwinds. The kind David liked. When he walked up to the reception desk, he didn't know what to say to Otis. He didn't know what to ask. But he wore a smile.

"Mr. Clark's in his office," the secretary said. Either Otis expected him, or David had become a regular fixture and needed no introduction. He preferred the latter.

"I like the music." David watched Otis look up from his laptop; he truly did appreciate the wide grin. "Makes the place seem less like a morgue."

"Is that so?" Otis said. "How are you, David?"

"Fine." When he shut the door, they looked one another over to size up the room's vibrations...to size up each another. "Any funerals today?"

"At two. Did you need something or just come by to gab? I have time this morning." Otis closed the computer, making the time.

David sat in the deep leather chair. "I needed to gab," he said. Otis appeared calm, like he had on their other visits. Except the last one. Last Thursday morning. "Have you hired anyone to replace Harold yet?"

"Just yesterday," Otis said. "Guy named Zandwich. You heard of him?"

"No. Should I?"

"God, I hope not." Otis chuckled. "This fellow's pretty up front, holds a good conversation."

"Not like Harold then." David's comment quavered in the air. "Have you seen Harold?" he asked. "Talked to him?"

276

"I haven't." Otis's eyes narrowed some and his shoulders tipped somewhat to the side. "He hasn't given you any more trouble, has he?"

David shook his head and when he pressed his lips together, they felt like a steady fine line. He'd caught the words– more trouble. Yes indeed, Otis found out about the blackmail. David hadn't mentioned any association at all on his other visits, had only said that he was leery of Harold, not that Harold had given him trouble. "Haven't seen hide nor hair of the bastard," he said, using his favorite description of Harold. "Maybe he's skipped out again. Hell, for all I know, someone did the son-of-a-bitch in before I got to."

Otis laughed out loud but his sudden rise upward seemed awkward to David, like the diligent walk to the window. Otis folded his muscular arms across his chest as he took a deep breath.

"That sounds to me like wishful thinking, David. Sounds like you wouldn't be a damn bit upset."

"Not a bit." More trouble. Yes. Otis knew of the extortion and he'd said the words on purpose. One more clue for David to digest –one more small detail yet to figure. "Tell me about cremation, Otis," he said. "I mentioned it the other day."

Turning to stare, Otis's lips parted. "I thought you were kidding me."

David shrugged. "I've been wondering about it this past week or so. Mostly," he said, "about what happens to the body afterwards."

There emerged a smile from within Otis's eyes and David knew he'd guessed right.

Otis straightened his shoulders. "The bones," he said, "remains that don't completely burn, are crushed into a finer substance and gathered with the rest of the residue. We put the ash into a mausoleum, or an urn for the family to take home, dispose of how they want to. In some states, though, it's illegal to scatter ashes."

"But damn hard to catch anyone doing it," David said.

"I suppose, if they made no big to-do about it, yeah, it'd be hard to catch someone."

"Hell," David said, "you could shake somebody out under your hydrangea bush, add a little iron to the soil, and no one would be the wiser."

"No." Otis grew solemn. "The ashes wouldn't work into the earth for weeks."

"The bay," David said, "dump them out in the middle."

"Too many people around. They'd spot ya in a minute. Jesus, for a guy who's supposed to be one step ahead of the nation's criminals, you're in poor shape."

"But I've only had a few minutes here," David said, "after all, our game has just begun." The two men stared so that their eyes penetrated one another, burned one another with an all-seeing fire. The seconds that passed could have been an age.

"But some games," Otis said, "are for keeps, David. You choose up sides and play till evil falls. Only the good are left standing, standing together, stronger."

David wanted to grab the big man. He wanted to squeeze Otis with all his strength and assure him that the deed would go no further. Ever. David was a deputy, yes, but he'd done things before that didn't quite go with the mold, like paying off Harold a month ago. David would sacrifice his morals again. He could live with the knowledge. Happily.

Harold was not a likable person, his final earthly act self-seeking and greedy. Cold. The little man's death would be mourned by no one and David would be grateful that the history of his children burned along with Harold. He would be insane to bring Harold's death out in the open, it would expose the very secret that he and Otis had fought so hard to keep hidden.

The secret was his universe, the murder a speck of sand.

"You know, Otis," David said, "it's funny sometimes how things happen and bring people together who might never have met through any other circumstances. And sometimes..." David drew in a deep breath, he wanted to chose the perfect words. "Sometimes," he said, "these people can have a bond with each other, a hidden tie that no outsider will ever see, never even guess that it's there. But it is there, just for them to hold on to."

Was that a smile on Otis's face? That minute change of expression was the only movement within the vibrant piqued energy that consumed them. Music filtered back into his senses to sooth the room even more, and the two men within.

"I have to be on my way." David drew in another deep breath. "Remember, Jess and I are getting married Friday. You'll be there won't you Otis, you and your wife?"

"Won't miss it." Otis took a deliberate step forward, the handshake between them potent. "Good luck to you."

"Thanks, Otis, I can't honestly see anything but good luck ahead."

When David turned to leave he knew that Otis had

taken Harold's life. The maze of nearly transparent clues were now spread out and solid before him –those certain sparks in Otis's eyes, words that completed a puzzle for only David to see.

He knew the truth but still, in the recesses of his mind, lingered skepticism. He needed a dead body to look upon for reality, the finality he'd had when he must accept each of his parent's deaths.

But did he really? Last night, two or three times, the play in David's mind had progressed to the point where Otis had twisted Harold into a choke-hold, his neck ready to snap but with a flinch –a jerk, David stopped the scene every time.

Just like every time David had thought about doing the murder himself, he had stopped it.

God…he pressed his palm on his chest to ease the palpitations. Maybe he couldn't have done it.

Maybe Harold knew that all along.

Shifting in the seat of the squad car, David told himself to breathe. To have a murder, there would have to be a body and he knew there would never be one of those. There might be an investigation for a missing person, but not a murder. Holy shit.

David smiled, he couldn't help himself, and he stopped at the signal, his foot light on the brake. Two directions stood before him. Right now, he could go one of two ways. Williamson was at the office. Today. Right now. He could go tell Williamson.

With a punch on the accelerator, he sped away in the opposite direction, away from the foreboding fork in the road.

The red and blue postal van pulled up to the curb just as he drove to his apartment. He stared at the strobe while the mail carrier filled the sectional cluster box. If he found no letter from Harold today, he'd erase the entire month's ordeal from his memory.

Forever.

"Goddamnit." His breath lodged in his throat. "Son-of-a-bitch." He shut the tiny mailbox door with white hot fingers on the small silver key. A long, white envelope had been bundled up with everything else. "You rotten, stinkin–" His guts felt like they hit the pavement and he could only stand there and curse, stand there while the river of sweat inched down his spine.

Stumbling to his house, he tossed the letter on the coffee table. He stared and gripped his hair at the roots near his temples. Had all last night been wishful thinking? Did he want this secret dead so bad that he'd imagined it? If that were the case, Harold had tunneled a lot further under his skin than he realized, and for a wild moment, he couldn't decide what was real and what was fake. David had nothing solid anymore, nothing to hold on to.

Except the envelope. "Goddamnit…."

He sat down and he touched it. He moved his fingers across the black, typed address. Like the rest, there was no return residence, but somehow this looked different, rare in thickness compared to the others. The envelope held more that a thin, single-page threat.

Grabbing up the letter, his confusion and his curiosity –his anger finally overwhelmed him enough so that he could release the seal and again, he stared.

Money.

Shaking, he pulled out the bills, crisp and new. They opened before him like a palm leaf. "Five thousand," he said and counted out the cash so that the currency splayed through his fingers in divisions of five-hundreds, one-hundreds, and one twenty dollar bill.

David wiped the river from around his nose with his wrist. He'd sat this way just a month ago, stacking a pile of money to stuff *into* the white wrapper. All he had then were five hundreds. Five hundreds, identical to the ones returned.

It is true, David, and you by God better believe it now. A rush of blood burned his face. His legs and arms felt weak and cold and heavy. His brain and chest flooded over from emotions of sublime relief and delight along with a definite affliction of guilt and he would accept it all, damnit, with no questions. When he'd paid Harold, he'd written off the money to protect the children he'd carried up from the stinking gut of the earth. He still must protect them. He always would, just as he always would keep this thing with Otis hidden, for their preservation.

Re-stacking the money, David tucked the wad into the front pocket of his pants. He took the envelope to his bedroom and gathered Harold's letters and wrappers from in-between his mattresses, all evidence that he no longer needed.

Or wanted.

The old blue ashtray that David used when he smoked an occasional cigar sat in the back of his clutter drawer. He placed it in the kitchen sink and reached for the matches he'd set high in the cupboard from Kurt and Sally.

The papers turned to flames and as they burned to black char, David grabbed a fork to feed the long letters into the fire and he watched them curl until the remains all formed into chunks of stiff dark matter. He pressed on them to break the pieces into to small wavy bits.

The scorched odor of the blaze followed him into the bathroom where he shut the door and dumped the cinder-pile into the toilet. He pushed down the lever.

"Ashes to ashes…" David stood to witness the remains swirl around the bowl, collect in a whirlpool, and funnel into the sewer, gone forever.

He smiled.

"So this is how you did it, Otis," he said out loud and flushed the toilet again to rid the water of left over pieces of char…to finish his own private funeral as the bowl emptied out.

When he grabbed his keys to leave, he couldn't say he felt good. Nor could he say be felt bad. His emotions just kind of hovered above him, suspended out of reach. He stared at the sofa and Sally's baby came into focus. The doll lay on Kurt's flannel pillow and had been carefully tucked in with Jessica's blue sweater −the one that matched her eyes.

"I'm coming, Jess," he said, and pushed the wad of bills a little deeper into his pocket. He ran to his car.

David's stride grew light as he walked up the hospital steps. He felt the tension around his temples and eyes relax so that the creases regained their former array. The ache along his spine disappeared, his shoulders straightened, and he knew that Jessica would see all the troubles of the long month were behind them.

When he shifted the money in his pocket again, a deep inner smile shone onto his face.

"I'll be damned . . . .

www.ingramcontent.com/pod-product-compliance
Lightning Source LLC
Chambersburg PA
CBHW071307170626
46809CB00001B/365